Driving through Shaker Heights

A Novel

S C O T T J A M E S O N S A N D E R S

PAGE PUBLISHING
Conneaut Lake, PA

First originally published by Page Publishing 2022

ISBN 978-1-6624-6307-5 (pbk)
ISBN 978-1-6624-6308-2 (digital)

Printed in the United States of America

PROLOGUE

Stop Signs

I saw him in my rearview mirror, and I knew immediately that he was coming after me. I slowed down considerably and kept looking back, but the red-and-blue lights didn't come on. The police car followed me down Shelbourne Road, which twists and turns like most of the streets in this tree-lined suburban neighborhood. I looked for a speed-limit sign to try to ascertain how much trouble I would be in when he inevitably pulled me over. I took a turn onto Fairmont Circle and passed the Campus Drugstore and pulled down the entrance to John Carrol University and started to look for a safe place to pull over, but as I turned into a parking lot behind the Our Gang Restaurant, the cop still did not hit the siren or lights. I stopped in the nearest parking lot just in case.

I was driving my father's old Ford, and I knew that he would have the proper insurance and registration up to date, so I pulled them out of the glove compartment and waited. The officer did pull in behind me and put his car into Park. I took my license out of my wallet and then realized that I was holding the fake Iowa State driver's license that showed my age as twenty-two. With the drinking age in Ohio for hard alcohol at twenty one, I needed this to get into the good bars around town. In truth, I was not even eighteen yet. I quickly pulled out my real Ohio driver's license and rolled my window all the way down, but the officer just sat in his car doing... something. It was a balmy summer day in northeastern Ohio, and my father's car did not have air-conditioning. With greyish cloth interior, it could get really hot in that car at this time of year.

"Why pay for something you only use two months of the year?" my father said when he brought the new bare-bones Ford Custom model home to show the family. It didn't even have a radio, so I would always bring my transistor radio with me when I drove his car. I was pretty sure having the single-radio earpiece in my ear when driving was illegal, but I had not been listening to it on this afternoon. With no air-conditioning and the fan vents blowing hot air in my face, I began to feel warm and then a drop of sweat trickled down my face.

The officer finally got out of his patrol car and walked slowly toward me, carefully looking my car over as he approached the driver's side window.

"Son, I need to see your driver's license and registration," he said.

"It's all right here...um...sir," I said nervously while handing the papers and license out the window.

The officer looked at my driver's license for what seemed like an incredibly long time and then handed it back to me. I could hardly believe it as I assumed he would take the license and go back to his squad car to write me out a ticket.

"You live around here, Sean?"

"Yes, sir! I live right around the corner. Just over there actually," I said, pointing in the general direction of my street, Colby Road, which ran between Belvoir and Warrensville Center Road in Shaker Heights.

"You go to the high school?" he asked.

I knew he meant Shaker Heights High School, and he probably knew I wasn't a private-school kid based on the bare-bones Ford that I was driving.

"Yes, sir. I'm a senior."

"You play football?"

"No...no, sir," I said and then saw a hint of disappointment on his face. "But my brother Danny does."

"Danny Stevens? Is that your brother?"

"Yes. He's my younger brother. He's pretty good."

"He is incredible. Best running back in the state if you ask me," the middle-aged cop said with a smile.

"Yeah. He's the athlete in the family. He got all the talent and muscles, not me."

"So you must be the smart one then?"

"Actually, no. I didn't really get any brains either. Um…wait. I do okay in school, I guess. I don't know why I said that."

"Okay. Listen. I have been following you for a while now, and you coasted through at least three stop signs and didn't use your turn signal when you turned into this lot."

"Yeah. It doesn't work. Only the left turn one does," I said, immediately regretting my confession.

"You will need to get that fixed right away," he said while handing me back the registration.

"Yes, sir. I will get my dad to do it. He works at the Ford dealer."

"And, son, you need to slow down. This is a community with lots of children and students walking the streets. You don't want to be one of those people that ruin their lives by hitting someone or getting into legal trouble. You understand?"

"Yes, I do. I will start stopping completely at stop signs and keep it slow. I'm very sorry, Officer."

"All right. Tell your brother we will all be rooting for him against Heights on Saturday."

"I will. Thank you."

He was referring to the neighboring Cleveland Heights High School, which was Shaker's biggest rival. I am not sure why I thanked the cop, except that he didn't give me a ticket for doing what every other person does at stop signs. My friend and I used to joke that red stop signs that were outlined in white trim were *optional*. In this part of Ohio, they were all red with white trim. But as the officer drove off, I did consider that I needed to pay more attention while driving. I loved to drive, and I still do, but we are, in fact, moving at high speeds in a machine that is more than capable of killing another person or yourself if you are not paying attention. And I was a daydreamer for sure and rarely thought about the consequences of doing stupid things that might have a lifelong effect on my well-being.

As I drove toward my home, I wondered how I could tell my father that we needed to get the right-turn blinker on the car fixed without telling him that I got pulled over by the police. Wait. I would just tell him that I noticed that the turn signal wasn't working, and I wanted to do the responsible thing and fix it. The problem was, he would never believe that.

CHAPTER 1

"Go All the Way" (Raspberries, 1972)

There was an incredible song by the Raspberries that came out when I was about thirteen years old called "Go All the Way." The songwriter was a very talented musician from Cleveland, Ohio, named Eric Carmen, and he lived not too far away from my hometown of Shaker Heights, Ohio. The first time I heard this tune on the radio, I was practically mesmerized by it. It was nothing like anything I had ever heard before, and I simply loved it. The music reminded me a little bit of the Beatles, but Eric Carmen's vocal range was expansive and unlike anyone I had ever heard. Plus, the song starts out like a huge rocker but transforms into a soft ballad with a cascade of amazing backing vocals from his group of Cleveland buddies. It was their first hit song, and the Raspberries were on their way.

At thirteen, I was a little bit naive, and I thought the song lyrics to this tune were about him wanting his girlfriend to marry him. But the title "Go All the Way" was clearly about the girl wanting him to keep going sexually. That's right. She was the one saying the words to him to keep going all the way. But back then, I was happy to believe my more innocent beliefs about what the song meant.

In the summer of 1973, there was a girl that I had a huge crush on named Sherry White. She was a year older than me and went to another school across town. I was not very comfortable with girls in those days, but I met her at one of the community pools, and we used to hang out a lot on those long summer days. My parents used to drop me and my brother off at the pool in the morning and pick us back up near dinnertime. It was mostly a way to get us out of their hair, and it worked. Nine hours is an eternity to hang out anywhere for a couple of teenagers, but the fact that there were girls there too really helped pass the time.

It was on one of these summer days when Sherry and I had our first meaningful conversation.

"So you go to Byron Middle School?" Sherry asked as we strolled around the track surrounding a football field adjacent to the pool area.

"Yeah," I replied as I kicked a stone down the track. "It's okay. I hate chemistry. It doesn't make any sense. How do they know those atoms look like tinker toys anyway?"

"You mean elements, don't you?" she asked.

"Oh, I don't know. Yeah. Maybe I do. I forget. What is a molecule again?"

"I took chemistry last year, but I already have forgotten all that," Sherry said. "I agree it seems like pretty useless information unless you are going to be a scientist or some kind of doctor. And I am. I'm going to be a veterinarian. I love animals."

"You do?" I asked as we wandered off the track toward a willow tree.

"My family has horses, but I like all animals—dogs, cats. I just love them. Do you have any pets?"

"Nah. My father won't let us. We had a dog once, but he got run over."

"That's awful. How did it happen?"

"My dad ran over him."

"He did?"

"Yeah. The dog's name was Abner. We found him in a field and adopted him. We weren't supposed to let him off the leash, but Danny forgot to put the chain on him, and my dad hit him while backing down the driveway."

"Oh my gosh, when did this happen?"

"It was when I was seven and my brother Danny was only five. It messed him up pretty good to see that. I was inside watching television. My mother wrapped the poor dog up in a sheet and took him to the vet, but he didn't make it."

"Your poor brother. To see something like that must have been horrible for him. Was it?"

"Yeah. He still won't even talk about it. And because of that, he never wants to have a pet again. I think he loved that dog more than anything."

"I'm so sorry."

"Yeah. But that's great you want to be a vet. I have no idea what I want to do. I don't think I am much good at anything. At least in school I am not."

"Don't you have any hobbies? Anything you really like to do?" she asked.

"I like to draw. I draw all kinds of things."

"Oh yeah? Like what? Scenery? Flowers? Portraits?"

"No. I…uh…I mostly like to draw…cars."

"Cars? What kind of cars?"

"It doesn't matter that much. I draw regular cars like…uh… Chevrolets, Plymouths, Pontiacs. Cars like that."

"That's interesting. My father and brother are obsessed with car racing."

"Huh. Well, I don't really care about auto racing. I draw mostly family cars, coupés, sedans, and sometimes station wagons."

"Station wagons?"

"Yeah. I like station wagons for some reason. Makes a lot more sense to have all that extra room in the back of the car instead of putting in a stupid trunk. It's just wasted space. You see what I mean?"

"I see, I think," Sherry said as we sat down underneath the shade of the willow tree.

Sherry and I were both wearing our bathing suits under oversized T-shirts. Mine was a red with a picture of a 1970 Firebird on the front and the words *just try to catch me* on the back. I was barefoot, but Sherry had on a cute pair of pink flip-flops. She had very fair skin, but mine was practically dark brown from all the sun I was exposed to on those long summer days. In my opinion, Sherry was very pretty. And for a girl going into the tenth grade the next fall,

Sherry was also, for lack of a better term, *built*. She had the largest chest of any girl I had ever seen in my life to that point. But remarkably, I was more fascinated with her face and hair. She had long platinum blond locks and the sweetest smile I had ever seen. No matter what she said or did, she always seemed like she was happy and in a great mood.

This was the summer before entering the ninth grade for me, but I can tell you that what I felt for this girl seemed a lot like love to me. I know now it was just a huge crush, but I was definitely enamored with this girl and hardly knew what to do with these intense feelings. I was a geeky thirteen-year-old boy that had little to brag about and barely knew what to say to such a pretty girl. Fortunately, Sherry asked questions. Lots of questions.

"Do you play any sports at Byron?" she asked as we reclined against the trunk of the large billowing tree.

"I suck at sports. My brother, Danny, is the real athlete. He is only eleven and already has the attention of the high school football coaches."

"He does? Why?"

"Well, he literally could not be tackled in his seventh-grade games, and he outweighs even the fatter guys on the team. But Danny is not fat. He is solid as a rock."

"And only in the seventh grade. Wow!"

"Well, he is lucky they haven't left him back. He isn't the best student. But neither am I."

"Don't you study? Don't you care about getting into a good college?"

"I will be lucky to go to any college. Plus, my father isn't a rich man, so it will have to be a state school."

"Well, there are plenty of good public schools right here in Ohio. What's wrong with them?"

"I don't know. I just don't see myself enjoying the college life— fraternities and stupid drinking games. It just isn't for me."

"So then you'll get a job after high school? Right? What will you do to make money?"

"No. My father will make me go to college whether I want to or not. I just have to get good-enough grades to get in someplace."

"You seem plenty smart to me. Don't you study?"

"Not really," I replied.

"You do your homework, though, right?"

"If I can't get all my work done in study hall, I don't do it. Once I am out of school, school is out of mind."

"Well, you better start learning to take books home. High school is a big step up from junior high, and Shaker Heights High is a good school, but it is really hard."

"I like to write, but I hardly know how to read."

"You are kidding, right," Sherry asked. "Please tell me you can read."

"Yeah, but I get really sleepy after only a couple of minutes."

"Maybe you need glasses. Have your eyes been tested?"

The truth was that I had never seen an eye doctor to that point, and it turns out I did need glasses, but I didn't know that then.

"I did read a book this summer," I offered up to regain some credibility.

"You did? What book?"

"My English teacher told me to read *Great Expectations* by Charles Dickens. He said he thought it kind of applied to me."

"I wonder why he said that?" Sherry asked.

"Beats me. But I loved the story."

"Maybe he was motivating you. Pip is from nothing, but he becomes an English gentleman."

"Yeah. But when reading it, I just fell in love with that Estella girl. I don't know why. I didn't want the book to end without her and Pip getting together."

"But she used and abused him throughout the story."

"That's okay with me. I don't mind," I said with a smile.

"I see," Sherry said as she started to stand. "I'm ready for a dip. Let's go back to the pool. Okay?"

I don't know why, but I instinctively started to brush some dirt off the back of Sherry's T-shirt when she turned around abruptly and slapped my arm.

"You better be careful there, Sean. I'm not that kind of girl."

"I uh…I…"

I had no idea what to say. I didn't mean to touch her derriere, but it was covered in dirt, and I just did it. I don't know why.

"I'm sorry. It's just that there was some dirt there. I didn't mean to touch your…your…I didn't mean to do that."

"To do what? Feel up my butt?"

"Well, yeah. That's just where the dirt was. I'm sorry."

I stood and playfully dusted the dirt and grass off my behind, and Sherry laughed.

"If you play your cards right, Mister, I may let you touch something else. Come on. You want to go get a Coke or something?" she asked.

I actually wanted to start singing the lyrics to the song, "Go All the Way," but I resisted that temptation. Still, whenever I hear that song, I think of Sherry.

"Sure," I replied as we walked back toward the pool. "I'll even pay."

"Why? So you can touch my butt again?"

"Would you let me if I did?" I said with a smile.

"I might consider it. You might have to buy me some candy too."

"No problem," I said as I reached over to hold her hand.

It was a bold move to be sure, but I knew I had to do something. I knew she liked me for some reason, but for the life of me, I had no idea why. I wasn't trying to be humble about my grades or aspirations. I just didn't have any sense of what I wanted to do with my life. As we walked hand in hand across the field, I could only think of how much I liked this girl. I wanted her to know it, but I was still way too nervous to try to kiss her. I had, after all, never kissed a girl before that summer, but as we entered the pool area, she leaned over and kissed me on the cheek. I am certain I turned red all over as for sure the blood ran out of my brain, but I didn't care. I was euphoric.

I saw Sherry just a couple more times before summer ended, and in the fall, we both went back to our respective schools. But every time I hear "Go All the Way," the intense feeling I had for her comes rushing back into my mind.

During the first week of school, I was surprised how fast word had gotten around my school that Sherry and I had been a *thing*. She was in high school, and I was still in middle school, and I guess this was a big deal for a boy to have kissed an older girl. But I had only just turned fourteen right before the ninth grade began, and I couldn't drive, so I really couldn't ask her out. I called her once, and we had a nice but awkward conversation, and that was about it. But I knew that feeling was something I wanted to feel again. Maybe that was what I was meant to do—to be the best boyfriend a girl could ever want. And as far I was concerned, we did go all the way. We went all the way for me, anyway, as I thought I truly loved the girl. That day, walking the track and getting that kiss was the best day of my short life so far.

CHAPTER 2

Where the Heck Is My Car?

I was only seventeen years old in June of 1977, and in that era, I had a head of long and rarely combed light brown hair. I wore the same ensemble almost every day: faded and usually ripped blue jeans, wrinkled oxford-cloth shirt, and Adidas sneakers that I never laced up. In my mother's words, I looked *dang ridiculous*, but I didn't care. I wasn't really trying to impress anyone, and long hair on teenage boys was still somewhat fashionable in those days. I was also able to grow long sideburns for the first time that year, and I copied the style John Lennon had on his *Imagine* album cover (from 1971). I am a huge John Lennon fan. I thought the sideburns looked cool, but nothing else about my physical appearance would have been considered impressive.

My name is Sean Stevens, and I am from a relatively large suburb on the east side of Cleveland called Shaker Heights. I had just graduated from Shaker Heights High School in 1979 where I made a lot of good friends but didn't learn very much. The entire Shaker school system had a great reputation back then and was nationally recognized for producing exceptionally bright students and some incredibly talented artists. I was neither of those things. I was an okay athlete, and I liked to draw and write, but only as a hobby. I was planning on attending college that fall, but that was because my parents insisted that I go. My father had some clear and very firm expectations regarding academics.

"You are going to college, my son, and don't worry, I will pay for it. College is an essential part of your growth as a man, and it will help develop you into the person you are meant to be," my father began in his most solemn of tones.

My father was pretty much a serious person all the time and could lecture me and my brother endlessly on topics such as this. He would pace while he talked, and usually my mother would nod in approval at whatever he was saying.

"But if you go one semester or even a single credit hour over four years, the tuition and everything else you spend on beer and pizza is on you, not me!" my father said sternly when I told him of my decision to attend Southern Ohio University.

My dad thought my going to college was going to be a challenge for a guy like me who had below-average grades and unimpressive standard admission test scores. He was probably right about that, but I knew exactly why my scores were so low, and it was obvious to most everyone who knew and interacted with me. I had an absolutely horrible memory.

"Don't worry. I'll make it, Dad," I responded, but I wasn't really sure I would.

When I contemplated my future, I wanted to be a success at something, but I simply didn't have a clue on what that something would be. In many ways, I was a typical high school senior. I lacked direction and purpose and figured college might help steer me to something that made sense for my life. I admired many of my peers at Shaker, who somehow did know what they wanted to do when they grew up. Somehow, even at the young age of seventeen, they knew. From doctors to lawyers to inventers to writers to musicians, there was no lack of smart, talented people in my school. I just wasn't one of them.

To illustrate this point, here is an example of my brain problems. It was a beautiful summer day in Cleveland, Ohio, and the city's professional baseball team was playing a doubleheader down at the old (awful, smelly, and cavernous) Municipal Stadium. The first game was scheduled for 1:00 p.m., and the next game would follow thirty minutes after the first one finished. No one really cared about the outcomes as the Indians were terrible in those days, and so the games were mostly just a poor excuse to drink beer. My good friend, Ben Goldman, was offered the luxury loge for this event, and he invited me to come along. He also allowed me to bring a date. I asked a sixteen-year-old girl named Mandy from my school, and she agreed to go. I'm pretty sure she still regrets that decision.

Ben's father owned a large plastics company, and they often entertained clients in the luxurious enclosures, which were new for that stadium and very nice. The loge was fully stocked with liquor and deli foods, and that made for a very nice afternoon of baseball, conversation, and, of course, drinking. I was a fairly seasoned drinker for a recent high school graduate, but drinking during the day was something I had rarely done, if ever. We started early that day and so did the girls that we brought with us. I can't tell you which inning it was, but the four of us had moved into the inside section of the loge, and Ben had subtly turned the lights off before returning with another round of drinks. Ben had his date on the couch, and I had mine on my lap in one of the two large cushioned chairs. While we were both busy making out with our dates, it seemed like I was far more intoxicated than normal.

"What did your friend put in those drinks?" Mandy asked me during a brief break in our French-kissing.

"I don't know. Gunpowder?" I responded.

I have no idea who won either of the games that day. Honestly, I really didn't care that much what had happened until I walked through the front door of my Shaker Heights home. It was probably eight o'clock in the evening, and my parents were sitting together in the den that was adjacent to the front hallway.

"Uh...son. Did you forget something?" my father asked as he scooted up slightly on the couch to face me.

"I don't think so," I mumbled. "Why?"

"Your car. Our car. You came in the front door. Where did you park your father's car?" my mother asked while adjusting the reading glasses on her face.

"The car. Oh yeah," I said, trying desperately to think where the car actually was.

My mom was right. I had entered through the front door instead of the garage like I normally did when returning home in one of our two family vehicles. My mother's car was a large navy blue 1966 Ford Country Sedan station wagon that was almost eleven years old. I tried never to take that one out unless my father was using his car, a green 1969 Ford custom coupé. His car was a little bit sporty and had some pinstriping down the sides, but it was still a traditional Ford sedan. And like my mother's station wagon, my father's car was also getting on in years, but it was the better of our two-family autos.

"Did you leave your car at Ben's?" my father asked while placing his book on the coffee table. "If you did, you need to walk right back down to his house immediately. I need my car first thing in the morning to get to work."

My father was the finance director for a string of car dealerships in the greater Cleveland area. He was an accountant by trade, but he managed to work his way up to be the finance director where he handled all the auto loans and applications. He had been in that same job for as long as I could remember. The largest of all the dealerships was called Bud Larson Ford in Shaker Heights. And so for that reason, I think, my father always drove a Ford. And it was almost always a big stripped-down Ford sedan.

I'm not sure why exactly, but I hated the Ford cars my father purchased and lamented that we always had to drive them until they were ready to completely fall apart. My father cared for his cars meticulously, and he savored great pride in how long he held on to them. For me, once you have owned a car for a few years, the thrill would wear off, but not for my dad. He washed, waxed, and buffed them almost every weekend and had this little bristle brush that he used to clean the carpet inside. He would fix any exterior blemish or dent almost immediately and kept a meticulous log of his mileage and recorded all the maintenance in a little spiral booklet that he kept in the glove compartment. My dad did everything he could to keep his cars as long as humanly possible.

As a high-level employee at the dealership, it also puzzled me why my father wouldn't at least get to drive a nice new demo (demonstrator model for those that wanted to test out the car beyond a test-drive). And amazingly, my father didn't even seem to care. He saw cars as a travel necessity and nothing more. Not me. I loved cars, and I vowed that when I got older, I was going to own at least a dozen of them. I loved all types of cars, especially sporty ones. The only Ford that ever drew my attention was the first-generation Mustang. In fact, one of my goals after high school was to work enough in the summer to buy a 1964 1/2 to 1966 Ford Mustang. I didn't care if it was a coupé, convertible, or fastback; I just wanted one.

"You'd better call Ben's house before you head over there. It is getting late. You have the keys to the car, I presume?" my mother asked.

"Uh…I think so," I blurted out as I shoved my hands deeply into both front and back pockets. But to my chagrin, there were no keys there to be found.

"You don't have the keys?" my father asked sternly.

"I must have…uh…left them in the car," I said, hoping that was true.

"I'll just call Ben's mother and ask her to check if the keys are in the car. We don't want Sean going all the way over there if he doesn't have the keys," my mother said to my father. "Dear, why don't you go get the spare set, and I'll call the Goldmans?"

"No, Mom. Don't do that please. I'll just take Dad's keys and ride my bike over there."

"You are not riding your bike at this time of night," my mother responded. "That is just too dangerous. I will just run you over there in my car. It's less than a mile."

"I'll go get my keys. But you are paying for replacements if you lost them," my father said.

"No, wait. Mom, don't…"

My mother picked up the phone in the den and quickly dialed a number.

"Hello, Delores. This is Vicky Stevens. I'm so sorry to bother you, but Sean just showed up here without his car, and we need to head over to your house to…"

It was at that precise moment that I knew the car wasn't at Ben's house. I don't know exactly how I knew that, but I did. The problem was that was the only thing I was sure of.

"Oh, so it's not in your driveway?" my mother continued. "This is so embarrassing. I am so sorry to trouble you. Good night, Delores. And no, I don't blame Ben at all. Just my son. Thank you."

My father had already left the den to retrieve the spare set of keys, which left only one set of disbelieving eyes staring intensely back at me.

"What?" I asked sheepishly.

"You are something. You know that?" my mother said.

"I have a bad memory. That's all," I replied.

"So, Sean, if the car is not at the Goldmans, where is it?"

I wanted to respond, but I couldn't. The truth was the last time I remember being in the car was pulling into the parking lot at the old baseball stadium.

"Did you leave it somewhere downtown? I sure hope not," my mother asked.

"I…uh…I guess I could have. You see, I did drink a little and I didn't want to…uh, drive drunk."

"How much is a little?" my mother asked.

"Uh…just a few beers maybe, I don't know. Maybe three?"

Truth was, I had no idea how many drinks I had consumed, and they were not beers. We were drinking whiskey and Cokes, and I lost count after the third. It could have been many more than three. I was 180 pounds, and I could drink a lot back in those days. But most of the time, I was able to handle it. And I hate to admit now, but I drank and drove a *lot* back then. We all did. It was the 1970s, and DWIs were not yet that common. It would be years before the police started to really crack down on this offense.

"You father is going to throw a conniption, you know?" my mother said while shaking her head in disgust.

"I'll just get Ben to drive me down there in the morning, and I will get the car. Guess I still need Dad's set of spare keys as I don't know for sure if I left them in the car or at the stadium."

"What stadium? What are you talking about?" my father said as he entered the den.

"Your son left his car downtown. He and his friends got drunk at the stadium, and he couldn't drive."

"I see," my father responded. "So Ben took you home, but the car isn't at Ben's. So where is it?"

"It has to be down there," I said. "I'll find it. Don't worry, but at least I didn't drive drunk. Right?"

"How much did you drink?" my father asked.

"I'm sure it was plenty!" my mother said. "You call Ben now and see if he can run you down there."

"I will call him first thing tomorrow. Dad can use your car tomorrow morning. Right, Mom?"

I was stalling as I wasn't sure at all if the car was down there.

"Call him right now," my father demanded.

I walked slowly over to the phone, and both of them followed me. They stood on either side of me when I dialed the number. Fortunately, Ben was the one who picked up the phone this time.

"Hey, what's up?" Ben said. That "what's up?" thing is what we said whenever we called or saw or talked to each other back then. We still do it to this day.

"Uh, yeah. What's up? Just a quick question," I uttered nervously.

"What's up?" he repeated.

"You know my car. The green one. My father's car?" I said nervously, trying not to feel the intensity of the evil stares bearing down on me on both sides.

"My mom just asked me about it. I was going to call you. Mandy has it," Ben said bluntly.

"What did he just say?" my mother questioned directly in my ear.

"I think he said Danny has it, but Danny is upstairs," my father responded.

"No. Mandy, my date. She has the car," I said defensively.

"Oh fuck," Ben said on the line. "You are up the creek, aren't you?"

"Oh, I think that would be the case. For sure," I replied.

"Good luck, Sean," Ben said before hanging up.

We also never said *goodbye* on our calls back then. It just was much cooler to hang up when we were finished with whatever it was we were talking about. Ben was a good friend, and we understood that this was not only not rude but also the coolest part of our phone conversations.

"So who is this Mandy, and where does she live?" my father asked.

Mandy O'Brien was a year younger than me at my school. She was really pretty and had just broken up with her boyfriend who was, quite frankly, a raging lunatic. His name was Russell Weiss, and we played baseball together on the JV team my junior year. He was a pitcher and was always yelling at other players on the team. He was a good pitcher, but we had a horrible team, and he hated to lose. I didn't care that much about baseball and often lost track of the game while playing in the outfield. One time I was daydreaming, and an easy fly ball plopped down right in front of me. He went ballistic and asked the coach to pull me out of the game. I was actually one of the better hitters on that crappy team, so the coach left me in the lineup, and Russell was livid. He stared me down when the inning was over.

"Nice fucking play, you asshole," Russell said as I laid my glove down on the bench.

"Sorry, dipwad. Don't walk so many guys and maybe we can all stay awake out there."

It was a witty retort, and I was proud of it, but that just made Russell that much madder.

"Fuck you, Sean!" Russell yelled.

"That's it, Russell. Get your stuff and go home!" the coach screamed as Russell stormed past the rest of the team, who stared fearfully at him.

Russell was an idiot, and none of us liked him. I knew he and Mandy had dated for over a year, which was very rare for any couples back in those days. They had only been broken up for a week or two at that point, but I thought I would take a shot and ask her for a date. I was happy she said yes. I didn't get a lot of dates back in those days or, for that matter, ever.

"You are calling this Mandy person right now," my mother demanded.

"All right. Let me get her number," I said as I looked inside my wallet for the wadded-up scrap of paper where I kept a variety of important numbers and addresses.

"Hello, Mandy? It's Sean."

"What's up?" she said very coolly.

"Do you…uh…by any chance…do you have my car?"

My parents inched even closer to me to try to hear her response. I twisted around, hoping and praying they wouldn't say anything to embarrass me.

"I have it. I was driving you home, and you jumped out when you saw the party."

"What party?" I asked.

"Heck if I know. We were driving around Shaker looking for this party Ben told us about. You saw lots of people standing outside one of the houses near your street, and you told me to slow down. I couldn't find a parking spot, so you jumped out."

"He jumped out of a moving car," my mother said in disgust.

"Son, just tell her that we are on our way to pick it up," my father said, shaking his head.

"Um…can we—" I tried to ask, but Mandy interrupted.

"I think it was an adult cocktail party, but you thought it was some friends of yours."

"Huh!" I blurted out.

"Get her address," my mother said.

"I circled back around the block a few times. I called your house, but no one answered so I called Ben." Mandy added.

"I'm going to go start the station wagon. Get off that phone and meet me out on the driveway," my father said as he turned to leave the den.

"I'm really sorry, Mandy," I said.

"I know. I think maybe Ben was spiking those drinks," Mandy said.

"If he did, I will murder him. But I'm glad you are all right."

"I'm fine. You were the one that jumped out of the car."

"You better go with your father, young man. You are in deep trouble. I hope you know that," my mother said.

"Is that your mom?" Mandy asked.

"Yeah."

"Tell them I will meet you in the driveway of my house, 324 Greenlawn, off South Woodland Road."

"I know how to get there. I do remember that much. See you in ten minutes."

"Bye, Sean. Good luck with your…situation."

"Thanks," I said before hanging up. Even when I was in deep, deep trouble, I could still be very cool in my hanging-up routine.

"Don't think you are going to be going to any parties anytime soon," my mother said as she walked into the hallway. "How does a person lose a car? I mean, how does someone do that?"

"Beats me, Mom," I said as I went outside to get in the car with my fuming father.

My friends still tease me about that night, and the story just seems to grow in legend from year to year. Mandy didn't seem interested in me after that night either, but I was okay with that. I was about to go to college anyway, so it didn't really matter. The entire event embarrasses me to this day, but back then, it also gave me good cause for concern for the way my brain worked. My mother was right. How does a person forget where they left his car?

CHAPTER 3

The Big Dance

It would be an understatement to say that Shaker Heights is a diversified community. I haven't lived or learned of any other large city with the differences in incomes, religions, and races that Shaker has. In fact, in my group of friends, I, the white Christian guy, was the minority. I'm not sure exactly why, but my friends were either Jewish or Black. Yes, there were plenty of white Christians in Shaker, but I didn't seem to know many. It seemed to me that if you were white skinned and lived in Shaker, there was a good chance you were Jewish. If you were something besides Jewish, you were probably black. And if you worked in downtown Cleveland, you were probably a doctor, lawyer, or executive at one of the many Fortune 500 companies that were headquartered there in the 1970s. During that decade, Cleveland was thriving, and I was proud of the city and rooted like crazy for their professional football team, the Browns, even though they have maybe the ugliest uniforms in the history of sports.

Some of my friends from high school were rich, and some were not. And the most amazing thing was that it really didn't matter, and most of the time, we didn't even know who had money and who didn't until you saw their house. We all went to the same parties. We all did the same types of things after school. And even if you had a mansion or a home on one of the scenic Shaker lakes, we all lived in Shaker Heights, and that was a bond that held us together no matter which section you came from or what you believed in. And I loved it.

One of the events that summer was an annual school charity dance (for cancer research) that was held at the Canterbury Country Club. It was an event that no one wanted to miss, and it usually meant asking a date several weeks in advance to make sure you had someone to go with. You could go stag, and some people did, but I wanted to have a date for this, and I started thinking about who to ask in late July. The dance was in early August.

I thought about asking Mandy, my date from the baseball game, but I had the feeling that she wasn't really that into me. And she was younger, and this seemed like an event to which I should take a girl my own age. We would be dressing up in tuxes and nice dresses (like a prom), and it would be the last big event of the summer before many of us headed off to college. Then the thought hit me. I would ask a girl that I barely knew but had always wanted to get to know. Her name was Kathy Sheer, and she was in the same grade as me at Shaker and would be heading to the University of Michigan in the fall. I thought about applying to UM as I really liked their football uniforms, but I was assured by my guidance counselor at school that I had literally no chance of being accepted.

I talked to a few of my high school buddies, and they tried to discourage me from asking Kathy.

"She is out of your league, man. Don't do it," Ben cautioned me one evening on the phone. "She goes out with college guys, and she wouldn't even think to look at any of us. Have you seen her since she got back from Mexico?"

"No, why?" I asked.

"She is a delicious golden brown now, and that hair looks even softer and more beautiful than ever."

"Sounds like you want to ask her," I said.

"Nah. Shit. She would say no to me in a heartbeat, and no offense, Sean, I got it going pretty good compared to you."

"You got what going?"

"I got it, man. I got the look."

"What are you saying? That I am ugly?"

"Shit, Sean. You always go there. You gotta get more confidence, or you are never gonna get laid."

"But you just called me ugly," I said.

"The key, Sean, is to get laid, right?"

"I'm not trying to get laid, Ben. I just want a date to the cancer thing."

"I know. But listen to me. If you are going to ask a girl like Kathy Speer out on a date, you gotta have some game."

"I know. I got no game. Whatever that means. But I thought I would try asking her. What do I have to lose?"

"Well, your dignity to start," Ben added.

"I don't have any dignity."

"You go ahead and ask her then. But don't say I didn't warn you. Why don't you ask Mandy?"

"I would, but every time I see her, she looks like she is trying to get away from me."

"Where did you see her?"

"I saw her a couple of times at the mall. Danny likes to go there on weekends, and she works at some store there. I drive him there so he can shop for his shit."

"What is Danny doing shopping?"

"They have a GNC Nutrition store, and he is starting to get into that healthy stuff. You know, vitamins and supplements."

"I think he needs a good shrink."

"Me too," I said, laughing.

"Okay. Listen, I gotta go, but do what I told you. Ask somebody else. Someone safe. I mean it."

"I will think about it," I said while hanging up the phone.

Again, we never said goodbye before handing up, but Ben was still talking when I put down the receiver. I wanted to call Kathy right away and get it over with. He was right. She probably would say no to me, but I didn't care. I picked back up the receiver to the phone and started dialing. I had her number in my wallet, and I could hardly breathe as the phone rang and rang. Eventually, someone picked up, but it was a man's voice.

"Hello? Sheer residence."

"Um…yeah. I was calling for Kathy. Is she there?"

"Who is calling?"

Oh god. I was suddenly so nervous that I couldn't immediately remember my name. My heart was beating so hard I literally thought about just hanging up, but instead I said nothing.

"Excuse me. Your name, son?"

"Uh…it's—"

"It's not a difficult question. This isn't Barry, is it? I thought I told you not to call here anymore."

"No, it's…it is…"

I thought for a second about whether to make up a fake name and just get off the phone. This guy, who was probably her father, sounded like a person you didn't want to get in the wrong way with.

"I'm Sean. Sean Stevens…sir."

"Sean Stevens. I know you. Isn't your father Don Stevens?"

"It's Dennis Stevens. My father is Dennis…Stevens."

"I know your father. He sold me my last car. Kathy's car, actually."

"He doesn't sell cars. He does the financing."

"Nice guy. Made buying a car not a horrible experience like it normally is."

"You bought her a Maverick. I know."

"You do?"

"Sure. I know the kind of car she drives. I'm kind of a car guy. I like them, I mean."

"Okay then. If you are a Maverick man, okay. Let me get Kathy on the phone. Hold on."

At that moment, I could only think how right Ben was and how wrong I was about doing this. What was I thinking? This girl was way out of my league. She would surely say no, and I would be humiliated.

"Hello?" Kathy said softly.

"Hello. Uh…hi, Kathy. This is Sean. Sean Stevens."

"Who?"

Uh-oh. This was not a good start. I cleared my throat and blinked my eyes a few times and silently hoped for some kind of atom bomb to drop from the sky and kill us both.

"I go to your school. I mean, I went to your school. You know me through Ken Newfield. We all took geometry together. You know, Mr. Higgins."

"He had all that hair growing up his neck. Disgusting!" Kathy said.

"I know. It was like he was wearing a hair shirt inside his sweater vest."

"Why would a man not shave that? He looked ridiculous."

I was still pretty sure Kathy had no idea who I was, but this was no time to try to find any other common ground. And I was pretty sure there weren't any anyway.

"Look, Kathy. I called to see if you would want to go with me to the Cancer Classic dance. It's two weeks from Saturday at Canterbury."

"I went to that last year."

"You did? Was it fun?" I asked while pacing with the long corded phone in the kitchen.

"It's a bit cliché, but I guess I had fun."

I had no idea what *cliché* meant, but I persisted.

"Well, I can't dance very good, but I think it could be a good time. You know, I will be polite and everything."

"I guess that sounds okay. You will pick me up, I assume?"

"Yes. Of course, I will."

"And you won't drink too much and lose your car?"

Yep. She knew who I was, unfortunately.

"Listen, Kathy. I think Ben put something in those drinks. Probably nitro glycerin, but I don't drink like that. I won't even drink that night if you want."

"Oh no. We will drink. I won't dance unless I have had a few gin and tonics in me. You get the alcohol and bring it with you, and we will fire up in the car before we go in."

Holy cow! This girl was saying yes to me.

"Okay. I will pick you up Saturday night at eight o'clock. Sharp."

"Don't forget the corsage."

"The what?"

I knew that I was supposed to bring a flower to pin on her or put on her wrist, but I hadn't heard that term before.

"So you will go? With me?"

"I will see you Saturday, Sean. Goodbye."

"I can't wait to tell Ben. He is going to shit."

"What did you just say?"

Oh shit. I thought she had hung up. I was so used to the quick hanging up thing, that she must have heard my comments before I could walk back and hang up the phone myself.

"Oh, nothing. I was just thinking out loud."

"All right. Goodbye," she said before hanging up the phone.

"Shit!" I said out loud and then feared that she might have heard that too.

I would need to remember that people outside my friend group didn't do the quick hanging up routine. But it didn't matter that much to me. A super pretty and popular girl had just said yes to going to the dance with me. I was certainly excited that I didn't get humiliated the way Ben had predicted, but I wasn't as happy as I thought I might be. She sounded almost ordinary on the phone. I guess ordinary with great looks was a big deal to most people, but it wasn't to me. I wanted extraordinary, and I knew I was meant to have it. Or at least, I hoped. We all should have that, I think.

CHAPTER 4

The First Time

I had no idea how hot I would feel in a rented polyester tuxedo. Between the shirt collar being too tight, the bow tie choking me, and the cummerbund cinching in my waistline, I have never felt more uncomfortable in my life. My mother had suggested that I cut my hair, but I refused and regretted that decision as I saw the lack of congruence between my appearance in a formal tuxedo and a head of sloppy long hair. As I rambled downstairs to leave, my father saw me from the den and called out to me.

"Sean, come here!"

"Yeah, Dad?"

"Well, don't you look dapper," he said.

"What? What does dapper mean?" I asked.

"It means you look good, other than that hair."

"I know. I should have gotten it cut. But it's too late now."

"I have some hair cream upstairs. You should rub it in, and it will at least look a little better and not so sloppy."

"Good idea. I will do that, Dad."

"Oh, and, Sean, please be careful. Don't drink, and drive safely. And please keep track of where our car is at all times."

"Sure, Dad," I said as I turned around to head upstairs to apply the hair gel. The stuff he was talking about was called Brylcreem, and it came in what looked like a toothpaste tube. They claimed that this would control your hair without making it look greasy. ("A little dab will do ya" was their motto.) But as soon as I rubbed it in, it looked like an oil tanker had just crashed into my scalp. I hated how it looked and tried to comb it out, but it was no use. I felt even more foolish as the greasy look only made me look more like a down-and-out street bum who hadn't washed his hair in weeks.

When I stopped in Kathy's driveway to pick her up, I tried once again to fluff out my hair, but it only seemed to make things worse. I grabbed the wrist flower or corsage and walked slowly toward the front door of her home, taking in deep breaths to relax my jittery nerves. Somehow, I knew that her father would be the one to open the door.

"Well, well, well. Look at you," he said while looking me over up and down.

Mr. Sheer was a tall man with jet-black hair, but he had a look about him that somehow made me feel relatively comfortable.

"Hello, Mr. Sheer. I'm sorry if I am five minutes late, but my father told me to put this cream in my hair, and I think it made it look worse."

"I see," he said while holding the door open for me to enter the large entryway.

The house was a bit odd as it was modern and very square on the outside with lots of large windows. But the inside was all rounded angles. The stairs circled their way to the upper floor, and the walls and the rooms did not have corners. I liked it, but it was really different than what I thought it would be. My home was nothing if not traditional on the outside, inside, and everything in it.

"If I were you, I would go to the bathroom and run some water through your hair. That will get some of the grease out."

"It will?"

"It should, but I don't know. You got a lot of hair and a lot of… cream in it."

"Okay. I will try it," I said.

Mr. Sheer showed me to the bathroom which was around the curved hallway, and I went in and locked the door behind me.

"I will go see if Kathy is ready," he said from outside the door.

I ran water into my hands and then tried pouring it on top of my head to let the water trickle down. Unfortunately, it trickled straight down over my hair and onto the front of my shirt. I tried toweling it off with one of the dainty hand towels in the bathroom, but it didn't work. And then I realized that the water had collected some of the Brylcreem before heading down onto my fluffy tuxedo shirt, and all I was doing was rubbing that cream into it, creating a huge round stain on the front of me.

"Kathy said she would be down in a minute."

"Okay," I said.

"Is it working?" he asked.

"It is…But, uh…well, my hair looks a little better, but now I have grease all over my shirt."

"What size shirt are you, Sean?"

"I'm, uh…I don't know. I am a medium or large, I think. Large would be better."

"I will get you a white shirt. Wait in there."

Mr. Sheer came back a few minutes later and knocked on the bathroom door. He handed me a crisply folded white shirt that was, quite frankly, a *lot* nicer than the rental shirt with the puffy lace on front. I took it and put it on and attached the tie (which was a clip-on) and came out trembling.

"Much better!" he said as he again looked me over.

"I can't thank you enough, Mr. Sheer."

"Don't worry about it. Just have Kathy and my shirt back here safely before one o'clock. You got that, young man?"

"Yes, sir, 1:00 p.m."

"No, Sean, that's 1:00 a.m."

"Oh yeah. Of course."

"Don't disappoint me. You got that?"

As I stepped back out into the hallway, Kathy was coming down the spiral staircase. She looked like a queen, and her expression indicated that she knew darn well how good she looked.

"Wow!" I said.

"Thank you," Kathy replied as her father kissed her on the cheek.

"You two have fun, but not too much fun," he said.

"Don't worry, Dad. We will be fine."

I handed Kathy the flower and noticed that my hand was trembling. She noticed it too.

"For Christ's sake, relax, Sean. It's going to be a long evening."

"Okay," I said as we approached the front door.

"Goodbye, Dad," Kathy said as we started toward my car.

"Yes. Goodbye, Mr. Sheer," I added.

I opened the passenger door for Kathy, and she got in. I made sure her long chiffon dress was completely inside the car before shutting the door. She immediately pulled down the mirror to adjust something on her face. As I got into my seat, Kathy was rooting into her purse.

"What are you looking for?" I asked as I shut my door behind me.

"I have some vodka in here, and it looks like you need it."

"I'm fine. I brought some vodka, too, but it is in a jar in the trunk. I don't want to be pulled over with it inside the car. You know?"

"Just take a sip of this, and let's get rolling," Kathy said while handing me a leather-covered flask.

"Thanks," I said as I carefully sipped the high-proof vodka. "I am just a little nervous wearing this stupid penguin suit. Plus, I spilled hair grease all over my shirt, and your father had to loan me one of his. It is a little big on me but looks better than the frilly one with a huge grease stain. Wait! I think I left the tuxedo shirt in your bathroom."

I'm not sure Kathy heard a word I said as she gulped down a large sip from her flask.

"You want to take another turn?" she asked me as I backed down the driveway.

"Maybe when we get to the dance. I don't want to drive…you know…with liquor in me."

"Suit yourself," she said as she took another long sip from the leather-wrapped flask.

As we drove along, I couldn't think of anything to talk about. I looked around at the street signs and hoped desperately that she would start asking me questions, but she just kept drinking. Finally, a thought hit me, and I knew what to ask, but it turned out to be the wrong thing.

"So, uh…where was your mother tonight? Didn't she want to see you in your dress before the big dance?"

"My mother? Are you serious?"

"Uh…I…well, yes. Was she there?"

"My mother died of cancer almost four years ago."

"Oh shit. I'm sorry."

"Yeah, well, I thought everyone knew about that. I guess you didn't."

"No, I didn't at all. I am so sorry. What…I mean…how did she…What did she die of?"

"It was breast cancer. This was her second bout with it, and it came back so strong. She was a great and strong lady, and she fought hard, but the cancer finally took her."

"Oh man. That must have been really tough."

"It was, but let's not talk about that. What about your parents? Are they both still around?"

"Yeah. They are together, I mean. My father doesn't say much to me, but my mother is pretty cool. But they are parents, you know. They don't know much about anything."

"What about your brother?"

"Danny?"

"You have a brother, right?"

"Yeah. I have one brother. He's pretty cool. I mean, we fight a lot, but he is all right. He is a little less than two years younger than me. Girls really like him. He is pretty good-looking, not like me."

"You look fine, Sean. You should cut your hair, but I think you are handsome."

My gosh. No one—and I mean no one, not even my parents—had ever called me handsome. I once heard that a girl from a lower grade thought I was kind of cute. But the guy that told me emphasized the *kind of* part.

"Come on and have some more of this. I don't want to drink it all," Kathy said as she handed me the flask.

I took a few more sips and almost threw up in my mouth. It was awful, and she could tell that I hated the taste. Up until that time, I drank mostly beer, except for the night when Ben was serving those toxic drinks at the Indians game. I knew not to drink too much that night as I would have to be on my best behavior with a girl like Kathy.

"I assume this is your father's car?" she asked as she looked out her window at the houses passing by.

"Yeah. My father likes Fords. I don't, but this one is okay. It has a shit-slow engine, but it looks all right."

"My father bought me a Ford. Piece of shit."

"I like your car. It's a blue Maverick, and you have the six-cylinder engine. Plenty of power for a compact car. And it gets good mileage too."

"How do you know what kind of engine it has?" she asked.

"By the sound, Kathy. Fours rev at a much higher speed. Sounds like a blender. Six cylinders rev at a slower rate, and they sound more like a Humm."

"That is sick that you know that," Kathy said with a smile.

"I know," I replied.

"I'm saving up for my own. What I really want is a vintage Mustang or Camaro."

"I see."

"Yeah. I like cars a lot. But my father isn't ready to shell out the cash just yet. Maybe next year if I do well in college."

"Where are you going again? Miami University?"

"No. I wish. I only got into two schools—Southern Ohio and Ohio State."

"Why didn't you choose to go to Ohio State? At least I have heard of that one."

"Believe it or not, I don't like their football uniforms. I like Michigan's flying wedge helmets, but I couldn't get in there, so it was SOU or a trade school. And SOU's uniforms were a cool design."

"You chose your school because of the football uniforms?"

"Pretty much."

"That's…interesting."

I could tell that this line of conversation wasn't impressing Kathy at all, but fortunately, we were just about to pull into the Canterbury Country Club on South Woodland Boulevard in Shaker Heights.

"Well, here we are!" I said gleefully as we pulled into an open space.

There were kids in their formal attire scattered all around the parking lot. Kathy took one more giant slug from her vodka flask and put it in her purse. I rushed around to open her door, but she had already gotten out.

"Sorry. I would have gotten that for you," I said.

"No need, Sean. I'm fine. Let's go."

When we entered the club ballroom, Kathy saw some of her friends over in the corner, and she rushed over toward them. I followed a few steps behind and tried to look as cool as I could. I wanted people to see me with Kathy as I knew they would be impressed, but a strange thought came over me. As I watched Kathy interacting with her friends, I couldn't help but think that while she was pretty to be sure, she was also fairly ordinary. She wasn't super friendly, and she wasn't all that interesting to talk to. I know I wasn't either, but the more I looked at her, the less pretty I perceived her to be.

I stood next to Kathy as she rambled on with her friends and glanced casually around the room. I looked at the kids looking idiotic on the dance floor and then at those who were obviously drinking some type of alcohol. Near the stage at the back of the room were the parents who were supervising the entire event. But then something else caught my eye. There was a girl on the dance floor who was dancing so confidently she looked like she was on *American Bandstand*. She whirled and twirled as if she were the only one out there, and I simply couldn't take my eyes off her. I didn't know her from my school, so I assumed she either went to a private school or one of the other middle schools in Shaker.

When the song ended, I kept my eyes on this girl, and she was soon walking my way. She was alone and appeared to be heading over to the refreshments table. As she passed me, I looked directly into her eyes and couldn't help but smile broadly.

"What's your problem, moron?" she asked as she looked back at me.

What do they say about first impressions? Well, in my case, they were incredible. I asked around and found out her name was Deborah Robbins. I wandered close to her on purpose several times that night, and I would smile back at her whenever she caught me staring at her. I can only say at that moment I felt transfixed, the same way I did with Sherry White. It was an almost magical feeling and I had to find out more about this girl, not the one who I took to the dance (that most would surmise was way out of my league) but this Deborah person whom I had never spoken to in my life. Kathy would glance over at me occasionally, but she did not seem concerned that I wasn't talking to her.

"Let's go dance," Kathy finally said toward the end of the evening.

She grabbed my arm to head toward the dance floor, and we danced to about six songs in a row. I think I did okay. My main goal was not to step on her feet or look into her eyes. I just pretended that I was home alone and no one was watching me. When they started to play a slow song, I pulled Kathy close to me, and she reciprocated and put her head on my shoulder. It was then that I knew that Kathy had drank a lot of vodka as the smell was almost overwhelming.

After a few more dances, Kathy stumbled back toward the stage, and I grabbed her arm to steady her.

"Whew! I think I am dizzy from all that dancing."

"Yeah. We should go find a seat or something."

"No. I have a better idea," Kathy said as she took my hand and headed to one of the corner exits in the room.

"What…Where are we going?" I asked.

"You'll see," she said as we entered s stairwell and started climbing the steps.

When we reached the top floor, Kathy literally flung herself at me and started to kiss me. I had obviously kissed a few girls before this night, but it was never like this. She was, for all intents and purposes, mauling me. I tried to reciprocate and keep up with her, but I couldn't. Before I had even approached her breasts, she was stoking my groin vigorously. Quite frankly, it hurt more than it felt good. As we continued to make out, Kathy reached under her dress and pulled off her panties and wadded them up and threw them to the floor.

"Are you ready for this?" she said as she smiled and proceeded to lick my neck.

"I don't think I am, actually," I replied, but she ignored me.

Kathy leaned on the railing and then flopped to the floor. She unzipped my pants and proceeded to pleasure me orally, which was a first for me. It was all I could do to not orgasm right there, but I did what I was told to do by peers and thought about baseball and my fat gym teacher. Thinking this could be over all too soon, I bent down and tried to reciprocate the act on Kathy, but I had no earthly idea what to do. So mostly I just licked things down there that seemed to be in the right vicinity, and it wasn't long before Kathy pulled on my hair and straightened me up.

"Put it in me, Sean. Do it."

I didn't need any further encouragement than that, and a minute later, for the first time in my life, I was penetrating a female vagina. And it felt great. Even as inexperienced as I was, I knew what to do here—in and out and in and out and we both get pleasure. But Kathy had other ideas, and she wasn't doing the simple in-and-out thing. She was moving side to side and all around like a maniac, and the pleasure was simply too much for me. And just like that, it was over. If I had to guess, I had lasted all of two minutes.

"What the hell? You came in me? You already came inside of me?"

"I guess I did. Sorry."

"What the fuck. We were just getting started. Dang it, Sean. Haven't you done this before?"

I wanted to say yes, but I didn't.

"No. This was my first time."

"Just my luck. I get all liquored up, and what do I get? A stinking virgin. Come on. Let's go back to the dance."

I can't describe how awful I felt at that moment, but it wasn't because Kathy was unhappy with my performance. No, I felt badly that this would be my memory of my first time. I didn't love this girl, and I certainly didn't think that this night would end up with the two of us having intercourse. As we walked back through the ballroom, I saw a lot of faces looking back at me. Somehow, they all seemed to know. They knew what we had done, and I felt so ashamed. And then I saw Deborah Rollins. She gave me a steely glare as if she, too, knew that I had just been deflowered. And it was with a girl that pretty much didn't give a heck about me. With the exception of sort of meeting this Debbie girl, I tried to forget the rest of that night, but I couldn't. I have tried since then to forget about it, but I never have. And that was the last time I ever saw Kathy Sheer. I think she moved or something.

CHAPTER 5

What a Way to Go!

I believe that human beings can be mostly defined by habits and fears. If we have good habits (like painting, volunteering, reading, working out), then things usually turn out pretty good for us. A life well lived is mostly judged by how much we gave back to others. Paul McCartney said it best in his last words on the last Beatles album recorded, which were "The love you take is equal to the love you make." If, however, you are a person who develops bad habits (drugs, carousing, burglary, etc.), then it is likely that you will have suffered pretty poor consequences for your actions.

Fears are similar, but while we can usually choose our habits, fears seem to choose us. For example, I did not want to grow up being horribly afraid of snakes, but I was. I had horrifying snake nightmares when I was little and would often run crying into my parents' room for comfort. For example, there was one dream where the snakes came pouring out of the waterspout in the bathtub one after another. I hate snake dreams, and I still have them from time to time.

Another time, I had a neighborhood friend bring his boa constrictor over to our house mostly to prove to me what an idiot he was for owning a snake as a pet. Worst of all, he was allowing the stupid thing to slither all over the place, and for a moment, it disappeared under the living room couch. He eventually coaxed it out of there, but I could only imagine that his slimy serpent (named Belinda) had just laid about a thousand eggs under there. The dreams that night were of me being completely covered with baby snakes while lying on that couch. Awful!

I know boas and other constrictors aren't poisonous, but to me, all snakes have the potential to kill a human. From the smallest garden snake to the man-eating anaconda, in my opinion, all snakes are dangerous and deadly. Yes, I know that there is no proof that an anaconda has ever eaten a full-sized person, but I sure as heck don't want to be the first one consumed. Why God invented a reptile so enormously creepy (no arms, no legs, and, well, nothing but a man-eating mouth that can open wide enough to swallow a Volkswagen Beetle) is beyond me. Did Noah have these creepy, crawling things on the ark? I doubt it or most of the animals would have been fatally bitten or strangled to death.

It is not just me that is afraid of snakes. I think most people are actually, and in in some ways, it can be a good fear. I am not going to risk handling a snake in the wild, and that will likely increase the odds that I will live a long life. But there are other fears, like the fear of public speaking or of certain social interactions that can dramatically impact a person's day-to-day life. The fear of heights, for example, or flying could keep you from getting that good job that requires travel. Then there is the fear that I think might be the most debilitating of all, and that is the fear of *death*.

When I was growing up in the 1970s, I hardly knew anyone that had died. My dog was euthanized when I was only thirteen, but he was an old dog and had lived a good, long life. My parents and most of my relatives lived long lives, and I had only somewhat experienced what human death and grieving was like from watching shows like *Marcus Welby, M.D.* and horror/slasher films. During my childhood, some of the greatest horror films ever were released such as *The Shining, The Exorcist, Poltergeist*, and the one that I considered to be the scariest of them all, *Jaws*.

Most people now have seen *Jaws* so many times that they have forgotten the impact this movie had on them the first time they saw it. I believe it is one of the best and scariest movies ever made, and the acting, screenplay, and directing were good enough to overcome the extremely poor and now horribly outdated special effects. But when Ben Gardner's head popped out of that hole in the hull of his boat,

I hit the roof along with everyone else in that theater. I have never and probably will never enter the ocean again without thinking that sharks are just a few feet away, trying to decide which one of the body surfers they are going to eat first.

While being eaten is a terrible way to die, there are others that may be worse. My brother and I used to play a game where we tried to come up with the most horrifying and ghastly way to die. Being burned alive at the stake has to rank up there pretty high for most of us. Having our head chopped off by guillotine may actually be fairly quick and humane, but the idea of my body being headless is not something I want to think about. During one of our conversations, I came up with the idea of being placed into a giant frying pan where the sides were such that you couldn't climb out. Yes, you would be fried or sauteed to death, but it would take awhile. I told my brother that I would try everything I could to run headfirst into the side of the pan and knock myself out so I would not suffer too badly.

Cancer and heart attacks and other illnesses (flu, pneumonia) are some of the most common ways that people die, but the one that seems to be the cruelest to me today is dementia. This is a slow, agonizing death where you not only lose your memories but you also lose yourself. People with senility or whatever you call it today (Alzheimer's) eventually forget who they are. And then their brain is no longer capable of regulating normal bodily functions, and they are alive but also gone. The person inside is not there, and in many cases, they simply starve themselves to death. Honestly, I think I would rather drive my car off a cliff than go out this way.

This fear of dementia so overwhelmed me when I was a kid that I decided I would write down everything I did each day so I would always have a record of who I was and what I did with my life. I know I would probably not be able to read my journals toward the end of my life, but I could always have someone read my daily summaries back to me so I would know who I was. For example, here is a page from when I was eleven:

March 18. 1968. Went to play with Danny and some other kids who lived down the street. We started a club called the Apollos (after the moon rocket), and I was named the president. I got to be president mostly because I was not only the oldest but also because I was the one making up all the rules for the club. To gain membership, you had to go into the sewer system (by way of a small creek) and crawl through a long cement tunnel until you got to the manhole cover next to the curb on Brainard Boulevard. You could crawl out of the manhole cover, but first we poked sticks up through the holes in the round metal cover to freak out any cars that might be driving down the road. Everyone crawled down the tunnel, except for this one eight-year-old boy named Monty. I don't know his last name, but he froze at the entrance to the tunnel and then started to cry. His older brother yelled something incredibly mean at him, and he must have run home. So that left only five members of the club, and we meet here every day after school to think of other ways to initiate and scare our new members.

The habit of writing or drawing in a daily journal or notebook was my only true passion, and I wrote in them constantly. I jotted down little stories that I hoped I would someday put into a book. I thought I might end up being a good writer someday as I really enjoyed good love stories and sappy movies. I admitted to myself in my writings that I tended to cry way too easily at sad movies and happy movies, too, but only at the part where people cry because they are happy.

I would also use my notebooks to sketch things and record ideas—from stupid inventions (none of them ever made any sense like a toothbrush that had a handle full of toothpaste that you squeezed into the bristles as you brushed) to trivia games that required no knowledge (only common sense) to toys and just about anything else that popped into my mind. I also liked to draw sports uniforms.

That's right—baseball, hockey, football, and basketball uniforms. Those who knew I designed these uniforms thought I was nuts. Maybe I was a little, but I loved it.

My mother once came in my room and noticed that I had started tracing the outline of a football player from a magazine. I would use this as the template for adding the colors and stripes and team logos. I especially believed there needed to be symmetry in the uniform. The helmet stripes should match the stripes on the sleeves and socks. (LSU uniforms did a great job of this, and I liked their football team more because of their uniforms than who they were as a school.) I drew hundreds of uniform designs and kept them all in my spiral notebooks. Sometimes, I just drew the uniforms of existing teams like the Dallas Cowboys and Oakland Raiders over and over. These two teams, in my opinion, had the best uniforms in all of professional sports, and for that reason, I rooted for them.

Finally, after the Cancer Dance, I wrote about Deborah Rollins. I tried to learn as much about her as I could. She went to The Hawken School (a prestigious private school near Shaker Heights) and was a cheerleader. She lived over in a part of town that had huge old homes that looked like mansions to me. The only odd thing (and this is an odd thing about Shaker Heights neighborhoods in general) was that the palatial homes were all very close together. The only area separating them on either side was a driveway. The lots may have been half an acre, but it was all front to back. There were no side yards, except for a small patch of grass. It looked kind of like the way you lined up houses on the Monopoly board.

I even drew pictures of Deborah, which were badly done, but I looked at them at night when I thought of her. That night at the dance had made quite an impression on me. I did write about the first time with Kathy, but I also wrote that I felt, in some way, like I had cheated on Deborah. I know that sounds crazy as I hadn't even formally met this Deborah Robbins yet, but I was determined to.

For safekeeping, I kept my notebooks on a bookshelf in my room, and I warned everyone in the family that if they ever looked in any of them, I would get back at them in some evil way that they would regret the rest of their lives (e.g., like being placed into a giant frying pan).

"Oh, Sean. Don't be so dramatic," my mother replied once over dinner. "No one cares about your stupid, crazy drawings."

"I'm serious, Mom. Those are my own personal ideas and thoughts, and they are not to be shared with anyone."

"He's probably got pictures of naked girls tucked in those notebooks," my brother said.

"Danny!" my mother said loudly.

"Just leave his crap alone," my father added. "It's his room and his stuff."

"Thanks, Dad," I said.

"No problem," he replied. "But get rid of those smutty magazines, the both of you."

"I bet he draws pictures of girls' boobies," Danny said through a mouthful of food while trying not to laugh.

"That's enough from you, young man," my mother said to Danny.

He was right about the pictures of breasts, but I wasn't going to admit it. It was, after all, my own business. I don't think I was the only boy out there that was fascinated with girls' boobs. And I would bet anyone a beer that Danny's room contained similar contraband materials, probably under his mattress. I will admit it. Boys, especially teenage boys, are disgusting.

"You two finish up your dinners. Your father and I are going to go to the parent-teacher conferences at your school tonight."

"Uh-oh," Danny said.

I thought exactly the same thing.

"You know, Mom, some of those teachers are out to get me," I said, "especially Mrs. Applegate. She hates me and for no reason."

"You called her a bitch," Danny said.

"Sean!" my mother blurted out.

"She gave us an assignment and told us to write about something relevant to today's world," I began. "Something about current events. Almost everyone wrote on Nixon, Vietnam, or Watergate. And the best essays would be published in the school newspaper."

"I am against the Vietnam War," my mother said. "Seems like we had no business over there, but that's just me."

"I agree," my father added. "Seems like killing of any kind should only happen if we have been provoked. And I don't think anyone provoked us in this case."

"Why didn't you write on that, son?" my mother asked.

"He doesn't know anything about any of those things," Danny said.

"I do too. I just wrote a bit too much."

"What did you write about?" my father asked.

"I wrote about dying," I replied.

"Dying? Why dying?" my mother asked.

"The story was about a guy that dies but comes back to life and is able to tell everyone what death is like. Everyone thought the guy was crazy, but he saw both heaven and hell and sure didn't want to go to hell. But he wants to go to heaven, so he decides to volunteer to go on a super dangerous mission for the government where he was sure to be killed. That way, he got to go back to heaven, but he didn't have to, you know, off himself."

"How is that about current events?" my father asked.

"How is it not?" I said incredulously. "People are dying all the time."

"Tell them what you got on it."

"Shut up, Danny," I yelled.

"What grade did you get, son?" my father asked.

"I got a D minus."

"I told you!" Danny said with a huge smile.

"A D minus. Oh my," my mother said while shaking her head.

"She only liked the title of it," I said. "Nothing else."

"What did you call it?" my mother asked as she stood and began clearing the table.

"'Back from Eternity,'" I said proudly.

"And she liked that title? Why?" Danny asked as my mother pulled the plate he was leaning on out from under his elbows.

"And so you called her…that word?" my father asked.

"No, I wrote it. I wrote it right under the grade."

"Okay. That's not so bad," my mother said.

"Yeah, but I forgot that we had to hand them back in to her so she could pick the best ones for the newspaper. Mine didn't make the cut, obviously."

"Did you use a crayon?" Danny asked, laughing.

"I'm going to murder you, shit for brains!" I blurted out.

"Now, boys!"

"Why didn't you just scratch it out?" my father asked.

"I tried. But she could still see it under the scratches, so she gave me detention."

"So that's why you have been coming home late from school."

"When he goes," Danny interjected.

"I wonder why the school didn't tell us about this?" my mother questioned.

"I'm sure you will hear about it tonight."

"All right, dear," my father said to my mother while standing. "Let's go face the music."

"Danny, do you have anything we should be prepared to hear for from your teachers?" my mother asked.

"Nothing as stupid as that."

"Boys, just finish up here. Sean, you do the dishes. Danny, you clean the table and vacuum under it. I think half of your food ended up on the floor."

"Come on, dear. Let's go get this over with," my father said as he threw his jacket over his shoulder.

"Don't kill each other please!" my mother said as she grabbed her purse off a hook near the back door.

"We won't. Sean is afraid of dying. Remember?" Danny blurted out.

"Yeah, well, at least I'm not afraid of the dark, wimp."

It was true. Danny slept with the light on. So just about every night before I went to bed, I made sure to turn off his light as I passed his room.

"Turn it back on, motherfucker!"

It is nice to have a brother as a best friend.

CHAPTER 6

The Unbelievable Buick Century...Regal

Another thing about the community of Shaker Heights that was unique was that none of us really knew a lot about what other students' parents did for a living. Turned out that some kids in my class were from superrich families who owned multimillion-dollar corporations. Remarkably, there were also some kids from what many might consider to be near-poverty level. But how much money a student's family had didn't matter. If they were a friend, they were a friend. But I did learn later that some of my friends were from incredibly rich families. Ted Steinberg's father, for example, was a many people knew around town. He and his partner owned a large steel company that employed a lot of people in Shaker Heights, and he was known to be a very tough manager. I also learned that Deborah's father was also a big shot at some insurance company in downtown Cleveland. I didn't know what his job was exactly, but I knew he was a boss. Unlike my father who had a boss, these guys were at the top of their companies.

Turns out, my father was just about to trade in my mother's pathetically old station wagon the summer before my freshman year of college, and he allowed me to go car shopping with him. This for me would be so much fun. I would be an impulsive buyer, but my father was the type that had to look at just about everything and read all the reviews before he would decide which model to purchase. And the truth was, he had no idea what he wanted to purchase this go-around. It just had to be rated well, and he had to get a great deal. My father was so cheap, in fact, that he once had the dealer take out the radio on the Ford Fairlane that he was currently driving. That's right. He deleted the radio on a car he would probably be driving for ten years. Thousands of hours behind the wheel and no radio. Imagine that. *No* radio for ten years and all for a twenty-five-dollar credit.

But this time, my father seemed to be enjoying the car-shopping experience a little more than usual. And for once, he wasn't just interested in buying a Ford. I didn't know if he had gotten a raise at his job, but we even test-drove a base Mercedes Benz sedan. Ironically, that same day, we test-drove a Ford Fairmont. You wouldn't need to delete any options on a Fairmont as they didn't have any. This was the most boring car I have ever seen in my life. And Ford sold millions of them. It made no sense to me, and this wasn't the first awful car that Ford had great success with over the years. They also sold millions of the smaller, but very similar, Mavericks, and they may have sold billions of the dreadful Pinto, which probably is the worst car ever built. *What is wrong with people?* I thought as we took a test drive around the block in a metallic blue four-cylinder Fairmont. I think 90 percent of them were this color, and they had the absolute worst-looking interior ever. The seats were covered with some kind of houndstooth-patterned fabric that looked like the cover of a spiral notebook I once had in sixth grade.

We didn't buy a car that first weekend, and that was okay with me. There were simply so many cars to choose from, especially now that my father wasn't doggedly determined to buy a large Ford sedan. One of the better models, in my opinion, was the Oldsmobile Cutlass Supreme, which I loved. It was the best-selling midsize car of that era. Then there was also the Ford Gran Torino Elite. Great design and close enough to the *Starsky & Hutch* Torino from the television show to be supercool. Then there was the elegant Buick Regal. All were great coupés and very fashionable at the time. And to my amazement, my father walked by my room that December and proudly announce to me that we were going down to the Buick dealership that afternoon to bring home our new car. I was so excited that I tripped going down the stairs to where my father was now standing, holding a glossy brochure in his hand.

"Is that it, Dad? Is that the car we are going to buy?" I asked, pointing at the brochure.

My father smiled and winked at me as I pulled the pamphlet out of his hands. I looked it over on both sides and then flipped it over again.

"What the hell is this?" I asked as I looked down at the colorful pages of the trifold brochure.

"Sean! Watch your mouth!" my mother yelled out from the kitchen.

"Dad, please, not this car. There are so many better ones than this. Please."

"I already talked to the sales manager, and they have just the model I want. Amazingly, it was right there on the lot the entire time. I don't know how we missed it."

I did. It was so ugly and cheap that the dealership probably stuck it way in the back, knowing that no one in their right mind would buy it. Here is a brief description of the car:

- Buick Century custom sedan (which means four doors)
- Dark brown metallic exterior with a cream-colored vinyl roof
- Carmel-colored vinyl interior with bench front seat
- Standard dog-dish hubcaps (not even full-wheel covers)
- Three-speed transmission with the stick shift on the steering column

That's right. A three-on-the-tree as they called it. Only the cheapest, and I mean the cheapest, of patrons would ever order a medium-sized sedan with a small six-cylinder engine and a stick shift on the steering column. Pathetic.

When we arrived at the dealership, it was right there in front. They had obviously cleaned it up and shined it, but it didn't help.

They must have been so relieved that someone was willing to buy it, and I sensed that there were salespeople hiding in their cubicles, snickering. I am positive that the person who originally ordered the car from the factory, saw it, and refused to take it home. And it was a year-old model with 137 miles on it, so someone had ordered and driven it. They just didn't buy it.

As we returned home, I played with the manual window crank on my side of the front seat. Of course, all the other vehicles that he had previously considered had electronic windows. The round plastic knob on the end of the window crank broke off in my hand, and my father immediately noticed.

"What did you do, Sean?"

"I rolled up the window, Dad. That was it."

"Don't fool around with those things. They are not toys."

"It's a window crank, and it broke off the first time I touched it."

My father spent two hours after dinner figuring out how to put that window crank knob back on, and I watched him through the den window during television commercials. But one time, when I looked out, I noticed something very odd. I was staring at the back of the car, and I had to rub my eyes a few times before I could believe what I was seeing. The back taillights on either side were not the same. They were not symmetrical. I rushed out to the driveway to take a closer look, and sure enough, it was true. The taillights did not match. I could remember enough about the more upscale Buick Regal to know that the right taillight on my father's Century was from that car, and the other was the correct one for the Century.

Yep. The idiots at the GM factory had put the wrong taillight on the right side.

I considered immediately calling *Ripley's Believe It or Not!* to report the incident as this was truly a "believe it or not" story. It is true that the Regal and the Century were built in the same factory and on the same basic platform, but that is hardly an excuse for a mistake of this magnitude. This was GM's esteemed A-body, which also included the Pontiac Grand Prix and the Oldsmobile Cutlass. The Chevrolet Monte Carlo and Malibu were also made on this platform back in those days. But the Century was a four-door model, and it had completely different styling. Unlike the almost vertical and more elegant roofline of the Regal, the Century had a sloping back window and completely different side trim. The only similarity between the two models from a styling standpoint was that the openings for the backlights were similar. And similar enough that the line worker at the assembly plant was able to shove a Regal back taillight into the slightly smaller Century housing. Unreal.

The question now was whether to or how to tell my father. He was a bit of a stickler for quality issues, and I knew it would concern him greatly if he noticed it. When he finally reattached the window knob, with some duct tape no doubt, he climbed out of the passenger-side seat and smiled broadly.

"There you go, son. Good as new. No harm done," he said while wiping his hands off on his beige corduroy slacks.

"Um…Dad. You may want to come take a look at this," I said nervously.

"What is it, Sean? Did you smudge something on the back of the car? I saw you poking around back there."

"No, Dad. Come look and see."

My father walked slowly around to the back and joined me there to stare at the tail end of the car.

"What?" my father asked.

"Keep looking," I said.

My father looked up and down and back and forth and then over at me. He saw it. I knew he saw it, and I immediately regretted telling him about it so soon. He would have found out eventually, but it would have been a lot better if he had seen it himself first. He was livid, but he didn't want me to know it.

"What are you going to do about it?" I asked.

"What can I do? I already paid for the stinking thing. If I try to get them to replace it, they will probably tell me that I got a free Regal upgrade on that side."

My poor father shook his head and walked slowly inside while I continued to stare at the dark chocolate metallic exterior of this hideous beast of a car with mismatched taillights.

"Shit" was all I could say.

And that term was a perfect description of this car. It looked like shit, and it drove like shit. And it broke down so much that our neighbors thought the rental car in our driveway was our new family car. The Century was a perfect lemon. Turns out that era of poorly manufactured automobiles actually led to the legal term *lemon law* and the associated buyer protections this law provided. From that time on, if you got a sucker of a car like this, you could take it back, and they had to return your money. My father was furious at the dealer, and he went back to hopelessly argue his case. He even bought back my mother's old station wagon (the Ford Country Sedan), which also had no options on it except for a V-8 engine as my father wanted to use it to tow things. I don't think he ever actually towed anything, but there was a trailer hitch on the back just in case.

My father is twenty-six years older than me, but for the first time in my life, I actually felt sorry for him. He only kept that brown piece of junk for a year and then sold it to an unsuspecting sucker who came to our house for a test-drive. He must have been amazed at how little money my father was asking for it. But if the guy thought he got a deal, he knew within days why the cost was so low. I bet he cursed every day he drove that piece of shit until he, too, sold it to some other sucker. I picture it now at the bottom of a large pile of Pintos and Fairmonts in some awful junkyard.

There were cars I hated and cars that I loved, but overall, I was and I am still fascinated with motor vehicles. GM, Ford, Chrysler, and others did sell millions of awful cars in the 1970s and 1980s. And somebody actually bought a Yugo at some point. [Yugos were the paper-thin cars made in communist Yugoslavia back in the late 1980s. That car is a punchline now as they had problems with just about everything including the slowest motor ever installed in any car ever sold in America.] I saw cars as an extension of our personalities like the college you attended or your religion. To this day, I can tell you almost everything I need to know about a person based on the car they drive. That may sound a bit crazy, but it is the best way I know how to judge a person before I even meet them.

CHAPTER 7

Driving Defensively

Even though it was a fairly small school, SOU had quite a lot of pretty girls. And as pretty as many of them were, I really only had my sights set on one girl. It was Deborah Robbins.

Deborah Robbins was average height, but she was not average in any other way. She had a beautiful face and a very attractive figure, but the most impressive thing about her could be summed up in one word: *attitude*. She didn't seem to give a damn about what anyone thought about her, and I loved that. In high school, she was a cheerleader, but you would often see her badly missing a step or just throwing down her pom-poms in disgust, spitting at the ground, and walking off. She chewed gum while doing the routines, which I am sure was against the cheering etiquette of the day (or any day), but she didn't care. She was also a really good tennis player in high school, and I thought maybe that was why she decided to attend such a middle-of-the-road school like SOU. We did have a fairly renowned tennis program at SOU, and we competed with some of the best schools in the Midwest. Other than that, her decision to attend the same school I did was like having our valedictorian skip college to go to Hamburger University (a.k.a. McDonald's employee training school).

Deborah also didn't fit the stereotypical image of a rich girl. She drove a cool car (an orange 1967 Karmann Ghia), but it wasn't that expensive. Karmann Ghias were built on the pathetically slow

VW frame, but they were shaped more like a 1960s Porsche 911. She wore bell-bottom jeans to class and almost always had some sort of cute ribbon in her hardly combed mane of curly reddish brown hair. I saw her once in the school cafeteria, and she had loaded up her tray with what most of us would have considered *guy* food—things like cheeseburgers, fries, pudding, and chocolate milk. She cursed a lot and had just as many guy friends as girlfriends. But as far as I knew, she didn't date anyone seriously at college. I assumed that she was just too independent to be tied down to anyone. Yet I wanted to go out with her in the worst way. And whenever I would see her on campus, my heart would almost stop beating.

"Hi, Debbie," I said once when passing her.

"Uh. Sure. Hi there, Steve," she responded.

I learned from asking around that Deborah's father was an executive at one of the largest insurance companies in Ohio. Apparently, he and some of his attorney friends must have seen that the real money was being made by the insurance companies that sued just about anyone and everyone and made money whether the case was won or lost. My father used to complain a lot about how high insurance costs have gotten, but clearly part of the reason was that the attorneys took advantage of suing anyone who got into a fender bender. I know for sure my father cringed at his car insurance rates with two driving teenagers. It was on Danny's sixteenth birthday that he got into his first wreck. And it was a doozy.

In Danny's mind, he was not the cause of the accident even though the police cited him as the one at fault. It happened in a mall parking lot, and I was along for the ride. We were driving our family station wagon, and Danny was actually being quite careful. Once we were done buying whatever it was we needed, we went back to our car, and Danny proceeded to back out of his space. But when he did, there was a large pickup truck on the left side of us, and it was almost impossible to see around it. As Danny inched back into the flow of traffic, he saw a Pontiac Astre (a rebadged Chevrolet Vega) coming toward us. Danny stopped immediately, but that didn't prevent the lady in the piece of shit Astre from laying on her horn.

"Get the fuck out of the way!" the woman shouted from her open window as the car rolled by us.

Danny took a deep breath, and I honestly thought he was going to pop. His face turned beet red and his hands, which were both on the wheel, were shaking.

"What the heck?" I said as I turned to watch the woman turn the corner at the end of the aisle. And as she did, she gave us the middle finger.

"Fuck that. Let's get her!" Danny said as he quickly pulled back and shifted gears to follow the woman.

As Danny rounded the corner, he could see that the woman in the Astre had driven two lanes over in the parking lot. He quickly surmised that if he cleverly snuck across the parking lines, he would be able to cut off the woman just as she turned down the lane heading to the exit. He reached the exit lane just in time to stop and wait for the woman. His plan was to accelerate and jump out right in front of her. If there was to be an accident, it would be her fault as she would be the one to hit him from behind.

But Danny forgot one very important thing. He didn't look to see if there were any cars coming from the other direction, and when he did hit the gas, he ran right into the front of a Dodge Omni coming from the other direction. Our station wagon was a four-thousand-pound car, and the Omni was barely half that weight, so the crash was very one-sided. We had a large dent in the right fender, but the Omni was effectively totaled. Fortunately, the man driving the Omni had his seat belt on and was not hurt. Unfortunately, the woman driving the Pontiac had witnessed the entire event.

"Serves you right, you moron!" she said while, again, raising her middle finger in our direction.

After filling out the police report, we were asked if we thought our car was drivable. Danny looked down at the fender, and it appeared to be pressed up against the front tire, so he pulled the entire fender off the car in one mighty and impressive yank. We put the fender in the back of the station wagon and headed home. There was only one thought in our minds at that point: what the heck would my father say when he saw the car?

Turns out my father was remarkably cool about the entire thing. Someone had once told him that you almost had to hope that your children would experience a minor fender bender with no injuries, so they would be more cautious in the future, and that would help keep them out of a potentially deadly accident. It was sound advice, and it turned out that Danny became a very safe driver after that. My father didn't say much to me as he knew Danny had a bad temper, but he did advise me to heed the same advice he gave Danny.

"Driving a car is probably the greatest responsibility a person can have. You are literally driving a weapon that can do permanent damage or even end the life of an innocent victim. But you also have to drive defensively as you never know if some other idiot may be out there trying to get back at a lady just like the two of you. Be careful is what I am saying."

I have always remembered that, and I hope it made me a safer driver too. Our punishment, if you can call it that, was that my father never fixed the fender on the station wagon. Danny was forced to drive it to school like that, which would have been incredibly embarrassing and humiliating for me. Danny seemed to think it was cool.

CHAPTER 8

Giving It the Good Old College Try

Another reason I was a below-average student was that I rarely saw the point in what I was learning. Physics? Chemistry? Biology? In my mind, these subjects were pointless when it came to preparation for life (unless you were going to be a doctor or an engineer or something important, which I was not). I also never understood the need to diagram a sentence, and I certainly had no need for learning about the inside guts of a frog. One practical subject I did see was a need to learn about cars. We all have them, and we all drive them, and we all need them. They are also an extension of our identity. For example, if you were the handsome captain of the football team, but you drove a rusted-out Chevrolet Vega, something just didn't add up.

"He must not be very good," I once heard a cheerleader say about our quarterback at Shaker, who drove a rusted-out Opel. That was a GM car that could have been advertised as actually "worse than a Vega." Well, he also wasn't that good-looking, and he was a horrible quarterback. If he had been good-looking and talented, he would have insisted on driving something like a Pontiac Firebird. Right? That would be image appropriate for a starting quarterback, not an Opel. I know none of this is complementary to the way our society perceives people and cars, but that rusted out Opel would be suited for an environmentalist living in Portland, Oregon. That's where our former high school quarterback lives now, by the way. I wonder if he still has that Opel.

Like it or not, cars are important to us and our society, and you can ascertain a lot about a family, too, from their car choices. My aunt in Victoria, Texas, drove a Lincoln Continental. That meant they were rich and sophisticated, and thus, we were rarely invited to their home. Some of my buddies (with rich parents) had supercool sports cars like the Datsun 240-Z or Chevrolet Corvette. No one in their right mind would give a sixteen-year-old a Corvette unless they had so much money; it didn't really matter. One of my friends, Barry Slavic, from a nearby private school had a Firebird Trans Am, and man, was that car sweet. His dad owned the Pontiac dealership downtown. So while they were certainly rich, they also gave their kids fast cars since they were simply...not thinking!

It was on a rainy Friday night in early November when my friend and I were cruising in his Firebird down Shaker Boulevard in the area of town known as Pepper Pike. I always thought it was funny that Pepper Pike bordered Shaker Heights. All we needed now was a nearby community named Salt City. There was a neighboring township called Orange, which was a cool name but didn't really fit the condiment concept. All of these neighborhoods were nice, but not as racially diverse as Shaker Heights. I liked being the one Gentile in our friend group, and my Jewish friends never let me forget that I was not one of them.

"You are lucky," my friend Doug Switzer once said to me. "I had to memorize like the entire Bible in a foreign language, and I had to sing it in front of hundreds of people."

"Did you get a ton of money for that?" I asked.

"What? You think because I am Jewish, I am all about the money?"

"How much did you get?"

"A ton. It was awesome!"

On this rainy night, Barry and I were testing the traction of his new Firebird by going seventy-five miles per hour down a stretch of road that ran right past a number of schools and residences. I think the posted speed limit was twenty-five miles per hour in most places, thirty-five in the others. The street was lined with Caution! Slow Children signs. I used to think that meant the children in that neighborhood were not very smart. Based on that assumption, I could have been one of them.

Barry was speeding along happily when the first sound of trouble occurred. It was a siren, but neither of us could tell where it was coming from. Instead of slowing down, Barry hit the gas pedal, and I think we were up to over one hundred miles per hour within seconds. In this part of town, instead of stop signs or stoplights, they have these roundabouts that allow many streets to converge into one intersection. Very few, if any, residents understood the roundabout rules of who was supposed to yield to who (incoming, exiting, or those in the circle), but Barry didn't have time to think about any of that. He quickly rounded the circle and turned abruptly down Gates Mills Parkway and, in the process, lost control of the car. We hit the curb hard, and my head was jacked sideways against the window. The car frame was certainly impacted by the collision, but Barry just kept going.

As he sped along, I looked over and saw that his steering wheel was no longer positioned correctly. The impact with the curb must have done something to the turning mechanism as the wheel was cocked badly to one side. Barry kept speeding down the parkway, but now it felt like we were driving over railroad ties. We had probably bent the frame or at least one or two of the steel wheels. Continuing to drive the car like this was undoubtedly doing unimaginable damage to the underside of the car, so Barry eventually slowed down and pulled into a random driveway to assess the damage. While we were looking underneath the Firebird, I could see two sets of black boots walking toward us. It was the police, of course, and they immediately handcuffed Barry and threw him into the patrol car. I stood up to face the two men and smiled nervously.

"Uh...I didn't do anything. I was like...uh...slow down. That's what I said."

"Is this your house?" one of the officers asked.

"No, sir," I replied. "We had to pull off the road. I think he hit something back there."

"You hit a lot of things back there. Do you realize you were going 107 miles per hour?" the other officer asked.

"Wow," I blurted out. "That's really fast."

Barry rolled down his window partway so he could be close enough to hear our conversation.

"I am just glad you guys didn't kill yourselves driving like that," the officer added.

"Excuse me, Sergeant. I wasn't watching the speedometer, but I thought I was going at least 110," Barry offered sincerely.

"We will get to you in a second, Barry. You just sit there and imagine what a lifetime in prison will be like," one of the officers said with a crooked smile.

"You know him?" I asked innocently.

"We know him. The last time was a Formula convertible, and he almost ran into one of the Rapid Transit trains."

"Oh no," I muttered.

"I didn't even come close to hitting that train. If I had wanted to hit it, I would have!"

"Jerry, roll his window back up and lock it please," the officer said to the other cop who was trying to push Barry's head back into the patrol car.

"All right. I am going to need to see your identification, too, son," the officer said as he approached me.

"But I wasn't driving. Can't you just…you know…throw the book at him?" I pleaded. "I would never have been going that fast. I was scared half to death."

The officer took my driver's license and looked at the front and the back and then handed it back to me. I hated myself for blaming this all on Barry, but it was, after all, completely his fault.

"Please, sir. My parents will kill me if they find out about this. I think there is something seriously wrong with him," I said as Barry pounded on the back seat window, making faces and sticking his tongue out at me.

"Looks that way," the officer said. "All right, you can go, but we are impounding the car. Do you need a ride home?"

I was at least five miles from my house, but I had no problem walking. Being dropped off at home in a squad car was not a good idea under any circumstance. If my parents saw it, I would have to explain, and the less my parents knew about my friendship with one Barry Silvic, the better.

I felt badly for Barry, but he was the idiot who wanted to race his rear-wheel-drive sports car on wet pavement. We were both lucky to be alive, but I am not sure Barry thought that. His father almost killed him when he found out about his second arrest. In addition to taking away his car (which was fine with Barry since his license was suspended for a full year anyway), his father put him to work washing cars at the dealership to pay off the substantial damage done to the Firebird. The story of the car chase was spreading throughout my school the next day, and I enjoyed being a bit of a cult hero for a while. But my friends knew instantly that Barry was the driver and the car was his, not mine. My father's car, fortunately, had a small six-cylinder engine and it could barely make it up steep hills, so no one would ever suspect me of driving that car too fast.

Even though I knew Barry had a giant screw loose, we remained friends and decided to be roommates our freshman year at Southern Ohio University. SOU is a so-so school situated in the southeastern corner of Ohio. It has no relation to a good school an hour away called Ohio University, but most people think they are related. Unlike Ohio University, SOU is not very large (about three thousand students), and there is literally nothing within thirty miles of SOU in any direction except cornfields, cows, and dirt roads. I simply hated this school, but there were a lot of us average students who found our way there because it was relatively cheap and obviously easy to gain acceptance.

When it came time to head to college, Barry had a new car. But there would be no eight-cylinder sports cars for Barry anymore. His parents had learned their lesson. Instead, they offered him a 1979 Jeep CJ-5 to get to school and back during our freshman year. The reason for them choosing a Jeep was clear. First, it was slow, and second, it would be able to navigate the often-snow-covered back roads that were the only way to get to the secluded SOU campus. What his parents didn't realize, however, was that a Jeep was just as cool as a Firebird, but in a completely different way. Barry and I took that Jeep everywhere, and I mean everywhere. One great thing about Jeeps back then was that they were truly off-road vehicles and were capable of riding through and over the roughest of terrains.

One evening during our freshman year, Barry and I went to a local tavern, and we both got quite intoxicated. When we got in the car to go home, Barry decided it was okay to drive. And by okay, that meant that he would rather drive on the uneven slate sidewalks criss-crossing the college campus than the smooth asphalt streets. It wasn't long before the campus police spotted the Jeep cutting through one of the residential quads, and they were after us. Unfortunately, the large rear-drive Chevrolet Impala police sedans of the day had no way of chasing us down, and we eventually eluded them and made our way back to the dorms. Unfortunately, for me, Barry liked partying a little too much and his grades dropped below a 2.0, which was his father's minimum requirement for keeping the car. During the Christmas break of that year, Barry called me to deliver the bad news.

"Hey, Sean. What's up?"

"Nothing. What's up with you?" I asked.

"Nothing but the sky, brother."

"Got my grades today, and my father already saw them," I confided.

"How'd you do, brother?"

"I got a 2.2," I responded.

"That's good, right? Or good enough?" Barry said.

"Not for my father. "… He told me that I had to get a 2.5 or better goring forward or I would have to go to summer school. And I would have to pay for it myself."

"Shit, man. That's brutal."

"So how did you do?" I asked.

"Well, let's just say that I was just a few ticks off from a 2.0."

"How many ticks off?" I inquired.

"I got three Ds, a C, and an incomplete."

"No way. That's too many ticks, isn't it?" I asked.

"Looks like it."

What did you get the C in?"

"Italian."

"Well, that's pretty good, at least," I said.

"It was beginner Italian, Sean. I-TAL 101."

"So what?"

"So, I took Italian all through high school. I thought it would be an easy A," Barry reasoned.

"Did you even go to class?" I asked.

"I only took the exams. I looked at the chapter reviews and figured I would get by."

"Fuck," I replied.

"So my father took the Jeep away."

"No way. What are we going to do? How are we going to get around?"

"We'll have to do some hoofing, my brother."

What Barry meant by that was that we would actually have to walk to the bars. That was probably a very good thing for the safety of ourselves and the other students at SOU.

"How are we going to get down there when school starts back up?" I asked.

"You think your parents could take us down? I know mine won't. My mother told me to take the Greyhound bus. I'm not doing that unless I get a pound of pot in me."

Back in those days, I had no idea where to get marijuana, but strangely, everyone I knew seemed to have it. I didn't smoke it as I didn't like to smoke, and I wasn't into sitting around all night playing backgammon and listening to jazz records.

"The eighties are going to be the worst, man," one of our dormmates said after sucking in a huge amount of hashish smoke from his bong. "The country is going to the dogs."

"That's for sure. Washington is the pits, man," another pot-smoking dormmate replied.

"Who is this Ronald Reagan anyway?" another one asked.

"Fuck if I know."

And that pretty much summed up most of the political conversations of my pot-smoking friends at SOU.

"I'll ask my parents if they can take us to school," I said to Barry. "I'll call you after I talk to them."

"Cool. I'll go see if I can round up some weed," Barry said before hanging up—without saying goodbye, of course.

CHAPTER 9

Oh (No), Danny Boy!

When it came time to head back to college for sophomore year, my father reluctantly let me take his Ford Fairlane to school. He would continue to drive the brown bomber as I called it (Century/Regal) for a few more months, and my mother would drive her old Ford station wagon. All was well in the world at our house. My mother worked as a volunteer at the prenatal hospital downtown, and my younger brother, Daniel, or Danny, was still in high school for one more year. Danny had a love for drinking and womanizing that was becoming legendary at Shaker Heights High School.

Danny was not just good-looking; he was male-model good-looking. Girls loved him, but he also had muscles on top of muscles and simply excelled at every sport he tried. He could literally play any position in football, but he performed best playing defensive positions where tackling was involved. Danny did some major damage on the gridiron, and teams were actually scared of him. He was fast and heavy (190 pounds, which, back in those days, was *huge*). He was also the most competitive person I have ever met. And he competed with me on everything. He wanted to win no matter what it was and was always trying to get me to do push-ups, pull-ups, or squat thrusts with him. But it was really just a way for him to show off how much stronger he was than me.

Just to get him off my back and to let him see just how weak I was in comparison, I would (once in a while) try to compete with him on how many sit-ups we could do. I was okay at sit-ups and did them just about every morning to make my weak stomach muscles look a little less...flabby. Danny would stare at me in disgust as I struggled to get past ten or eleven.

"Give it up, Sean-O. You are going to pull a muscle."

But I was not the one that pulled muscles. Danny was so tight, in fact, that he once tore a pectoral muscle from throwing a ball and was projected to be out of action for at least four months. That meant he would miss the end of football season and the beginning of basketball season. But remarkably, in only two months, Danny was back lifting weights and running. It turned out that he only missed one game of the basketball season. Danny was not a shooter and was horrible at free throws, but he was a rebounding and defensive machine. He was only six feet tall, but he could jump through the roof. In his first game back, he had fifteen rebounds, and he only played about half of the game. He had four points on put backs, but he also had five personal fouls. (That was the max in high school, and he fouled out in almost every game he played.) At times on the basketball court, Danny seemed like he would forget that he wasn't playing football.

Given all this, you would think Danny had it all, but he didn't. Danny really struggled in academics of almost every subject. At Shaker Heights High School, they had an alternative program for students like Danny, and most of their classes were in the basement. Danny wasn't ashamed of being in the special-help part of the school as it allowed him to continue to play sports despite not being able to keep up with the majority of his classmates. On top of all that, Danny often lacked common sense, and I feared he would end up in prison for simply not knowing any better. You could talk him into anything, and if you were coy about it, Danny would walk away happy just having traded his dollar for a dime. I was scared of what would happen to him down the road, but in the meantime, he was enjoying his immense popularity in high school. I had to wonder why the girls didn't seem to mind that he could not do simple math, but they didn't.

When I returned home from college after my freshman year, I was shocked at how Danny looked. He was more muscular than ever, and he acted differently. He seemed like he was hyped up on caffeine, and you could see the strain in his physique.

"What's going on with you, Danny Boy?" I asked sincerely. "You look like you just got beat up."

"I'll beat your ass up any day, Sean-O."

"Are you taking pills? Is that how you got so…big?" I asked Danny sincerely.

"Fuck no. I would never do that to my body," he responded angrily. "I only take vitamins and supplements. You can get 'em anywhere. They aren't drugs."

"Are you sure?" I asked.

"Well, I did get some 'roids from a friend, but that was only when I was healing up from my pec injury."

"Well, they must be messing with your…biology or something. I don't know. You just don't look…right."

Danny looked down at his impressive, but jittery, frame and then back at me.

"I think maybe I'm fucking too much with…myself."

"It's not a big deal, Danny. Stop taking the drugs and just eat healthy. You don't have to be all muscle, you know. Look at me."

I immediately regretted suggesting that as Danny looked me up down and around the sides. I knew he was disgusted with my pathetically unathletic physique. I had nothing except bones and blubber, and I didn't care. To spend the kind of time in the weight room that other kids did to get buff seemed crazy to me. I liked sports all right, but what I really loved was cars. And Danny knew it. He liked them, too, but not as much as me. I would sit in my room at night and draw out new car designs. I studied how cars had evolved over the years and found some interesting changes and fads in the shape of cars. Some were a little hard to explain like:

- Fins (late fifties, early sixties)
- Rocket-shaped chrome (mostly fifties)
- Convertible hardtops (1957 Ford Fairlane Sunliner)

- Hood emblems (throughout most of the century but on everything in the seventies)
- Mercury's inward slanting rear window—so it could roll down (mid-sixties)

Some of the most fascinating design elements occurred in the late fifties and early sixties as there seemed to be no end to where the designers would go. For example:

- The backlights on the 1959 Chevrolet looked like cat's eyes. They called the back-end design *bat wings*, and they looked like that.
- Vertical quad lights (mid-sixties to seventies).
- Rectangular lights (instead of round) in the mid-seventies.
- Slanted quad lights (1959 Lincoln Continental, 1959 Buick, and various Chrysler cars in the early sixties).
- Hidden headlights (sixties and seventies, plus the 1936 Cord 810, an amazing car).
- Even the Tucker (one of my favorite designs of all time) had a third headlight in front that turned with the steering wheel. Amazing invention and, as far as I know, the only car that ever had this extra light that could shine brightly around corners.

I took shop in high school, and I planned to take it again in college once I was done with the mandatory but, quite frankly, useless classes. My freshman-year schedule was full of basic liberal arts classes like English and biology, but my sophomore year allowed me to take an elective class, and I chose auto mechanics. I didn't want to be a mechanic necessarily (although there was certainly merit in that occupation). In my mind, I wanted to either design cars or build them. And I wasn't a car snob either. I liked cheap cars like the Chevrolet Corvair just as much as I did the expensive ones like the Buick Riviera and Cadillac Eldorado. It was clear that I was enamored with automobiles of almost any type, and I wanted to be a part of that business in some way.

The best thing about this particular auto-mechanics class is that we would be restoring a 1966 Mustang coupé (meaning, not a convertible or fastback). The 1966 version of the Mustang was virtually identical on the outside to the 1964 1/2 and 1965 version, with the exception of the front grille and some side trim. The interior dash was different as this one was made specifically for the Mustang. The previous years were the same as the Falcon dash and not nearly as sporty looking. It was strange how that car was cobbled together. It was basically a Falcon underneath and a newly designed *pony car* on the outside.

Lee Iacocca of Chrysler Minivan fame (or infamy, depending which side you were on) was supposedly the brainchild behind the Mustang although I see him more as the guy that simply pushed through a good idea. The concept of the Mustang was to offer teenagers and young couples an economically priced sporty car with good lines and lots of options. In fact, you could option that car so heavily that it would almost double the price. The stripped-down version, however, was so cheap that it didn't even come with reverse lights. Those were actually an *option* in 1965. The car turned out to be an enormous success with people of all ages. Women loved the lines. Men loved the large engine versions, which were very fast, and kids and teenagers loved the hip new image. Nothing like it had come before, and people rushed to buy it in astronomical numbers. It was Ford's biggest success since the Model T, the car that made Henry Ford one of the richest men in American history.

The Mustang we were working on in the auto-mechanics class was a metallic green with black vinyl interior. It was one of the stripped-down versions and even had a *radio delete* option. (My father would have approved as to him, the radio was not only too expensive, but it was also a distraction to safe driving.) No air-conditioning either, but it did have backup lights. Reverse lights remarkably did not became mandatory until 1966, but after that, you couldn't delete them even if you wanted to. The person that ordered this car must have had only one thing in mind, and that was *going fast*. Despite the lack of luxury items, the car was equipped with a dynamic 289cc V-8, which was probably the most popular of the Mustang engines.

It was a great engine for Ford and was used in other vehicles besides the Mustang. But what made this particular car so special is that it was a four-speed T-10 transmission with the stick on the floor. The four speed was a rare engine option for that model year, and it was phased out after 1966.

Mustangs have always sold well, and in the year 1979, Mustangs were still as popular as ever. The new Fox platform Mustang was a huge improvement over the Mustang II. Unfortunately, in 1974, Ford downsized the car and made it into a smaller economy car built on the same frame as the Pinto. That's right, some brainiac at Ford made the decision to build a car called a Mustang on top of one of the shittiest cars ever made. He had to have been fired shortly after that. The Mustang II (the Two as the executives at Ford called it) was small and underpowered and not that good-looking. I hated it at the time, but people still bought them. For me, the true Mustangs were gone after 1970 when they became huge, full-size muscle cars. They lost their way with both of those cars, and the still-good but much-lower sales figures reflected the waning public interest.

As we took the car apart and sanded and cleaned just about every inch of that 1966 Mustang, I knew that this was the car that I had to have in my life. I asked the shop teacher what they did with the cars after they were all fixed up.

"We auction them off, kid. Sometimes a student or faculty member buys them. Why? You think you might want it?" the shop teacher asked.

"Oh yeah. I want it. But how much? I mean, can I get it for a good deal? My father won't buy it for me unless it is a really good deal."

"We'll assess the value, but you'll get it for a fair price. These Mustangs are going to be collectibles someday. They will only go up and up in value."

Boy, was he right! And to my delight, I was able to talk my father into making an offer.

"I can see this being a good investment for you, Sean. You can pay me back over time, and we'll sell it before you graduate from college."

Heck, that was only a few years away. I knew I would want to keep this car way longer than that, but I didn't argue with my father. He offered the school two thousand dollars for the car, and they took it without even countering him. I assured him the car was in excellent shape after all the repairs. But the first thing I noticed when the car legally became mine was that it leaked oil badly. I took it in to have it looked at by the shop teacher, and he replaced the oil pan, but that didn't seem to help. The car still left a puddle of oil wherever I parked it. That could only mean that the oil was leaking from some other part of the engine. And it would be a much more complicated repair than just swapping out the oil pan.

After two more attempts to ascertain where the leak was coming from, I decided to take the car to the auto garage in New Vienna, a small city near SOU.

"Ya gotta cracked block, son," the mechanic mumbled through a wad of chewing tobacco.

"Shit. That's bad. That's really bad for a car. Right?" I asked.

"It ain't good, that's for sure."

"What do I do? Can you…can you fix it?"

"I can't fix the motor if that's what you mean. It's shot. But I can put a new one in."

"What does a new motor cost?"

"It ain't a new, new one. I can put an old one in there, but it will run."

"It'll run?" I asked.

"I'll get her running again. But it won't be cheap."

"How much will that…run me?"

"Well, first I gotta find another 289. You don't want to go putting a six in this baby. It was made for an eight, and you gotta get another eight."

"Eight cylinders you mean?"

"Fuck yeah! Too bad, though."

"Why do you say that?" I asked.

"The motor you had in there is street rocket 'cause you got the eight with the four speed."

"I know, but how much will a new old one be?"

"Let me get back to you on that. It might be I can do it for about two hundred bucks. But I have to find an engine and then the labor and all."

"Okay," I said disappointedly.

I didn't have two or three hundred bucks or anything close to that amount, and I knew my father would not be happy. But what could I do? I had to have a car, so I told the guy to go ahead and fix it. I planned to call my dad that evening, but it was my mother who answered.

"Hey, Mom. It's Sean."

We didn't do the cool "What's up?" greeting thing.

"Hello, dear. I've got some bad news for you."

Uh-oh. I don't think I had ever heard my mother say those words. This must be really bad. Maybe Danny was dead from all those steroids. Oh shit. Maybe Dad was dead. He seemed due to have a heart attack. I think he was fifty-something.

"Your grandfather passed away this morning. We have been trying to reach you down there, but those idiots at your dorm just leave me on hold and never come back."

"I'm sorry, Mom. That's what they do. I'm so sad about Granddaddy. That sucks."

"Well, listen. You'll need to come home in two days for the funeral. Your father is counting on you to be here. Just let your teachers know there was a death in the family and drive up here on Thursday. Okay?"

"Uh, Mom, I can't. The car is…well, the car is not running right now."

"I see. Did you do something to it?"

Strange that my mother just assumed that I had done the damage. She would have been right most of the time, but this time was, indeed, different.

"No. The car was leaking oil, and it turned out to be the block."

"What is a block, son? I don't know these car things."

"It's basically the entire engine. I need to get a new one, and it is going to cost like three hundred dollars."

"Oh, Sean. I do not want to tell your father this now. Can you just take the bus home?"

I think I would have rather had my eyeballs plucked out with a rusty pocketknife than take a Greyhound bus back then.

"I will see if I can borrow a car. Or maybe the Mustang will be ready by then. I will have to check."

"Wait. You are fixing it? How?"

"I have to fix it, Mom. The car is worth two thousand dollars."

"But where are you going to get money?"

"I wasn't sure. I just figured—"

"Sean, that is how people get into serious financial trouble."

"For three hundred bucks? Come on, Mom."

"Well, I'm just saying."

My mother said "I'm just saying" a lot whenever you disagreed with her.

"Can you loan me the money?"

"We will see. But one way or another, you need to get up here. Okay?"

"Okay, but what happened, Mom? What happened to Granddad?"

"It's very sad, son. He was only seventy-two, but he was so senile. So this is a blessing in a way."

A blessing to be dead? I guess I could see that. *Senility* was the term that most people used back then for individuals that had brain function or memory issues. The last time I saw my father's father, he didn't even know who I was. He offered me some hard candy, but I could tell he couldn't talk. My father was very gentle with him and simply talked to him like he could understand his words. He couldn't.

"Mom, I will ask the guy at the garage to let me have the car if it is ready, and I will be there. If it isn't, I will make it there somehow. Tell Dad I'm…uh…sorry."

Our family wasn't one for sentimental exchanges, except for me.

"I love you, Dad," I said eagerly one day as he went to pick me up at elementary school. I think I was six.

"Uh-huh! That's great. Now be a good boy and don't give your father any trouble at the hardware store, and I will let you steer the car on the way home."

Okay, steering the car was probably worth about a thousand "I love you too" statements, so I let it go. I knew my parents loved me. I didn't need to hear it. I didn't even hug my mother when I went off to college. My father practically pushed me out of the car. He meant well, but it was definitely time for me to leave the nest.

"Thank you, son," my mother said. "Let me know when you plan to arrive, and please tell your idiot friends to go get you when I call."

"It won't help, Mom, but I will tell them."

"Okay, dear. See you soon."

"Hey, Mom, can I ask you something?"

"Sure. What is it?"

"Did Granddaddy still have the 1959 Buick Skylark?"

"Good grief, Sean. He's not even in the ground yet."

"Sorry, Mom, but that car is so cool. The angled lights in front, the side designs."

"Oh my gosh. Who cares about a dumb car at a time like this?"

Ouch! Right in the gut!

Fortunately, it turned out that the Mustang was ready to drive the next day, but there was one huge change. The new engine was an automatic. The shifter was still on the floor, but the coolness of the four speed was gone. I promised the guy at the auto garage that I would return from home with the money. He was sympathetic about my grandfather dying, and that helped me get the car without paying him right then for the new motor. The 289-replacement seemed to be even faster than the previous one, but that might have been because this one actually had fluid running through the manifold to lubricate the moving parts. I didn't mean to do it, but I burned rubber pulling out of the mechanics parking lot after picking up the car.

I was a little sorry about asking my mother about the 1959 Skylark, but I loved that car too. In my opinion, it was one of the best designs of the fifties and sixties time period. Instead of vertical fins, it had body moldings that ran into V shapes over both the front and backlights. Plus, the car had symmetry. The front lights were also set at a diagonal, so the car looked just a little bit *mean*. I loved it. I knew it was a bad time to ask about it, but I didn't want the car to end up being sold off before we got a chance to have it. And I wanted it. Turns out, the maid living with my grandfather inherited it. I was not happy about that.

There were a few other cars over the years that I thought had good designs. But I was mostly moved by the expression on the face of the car. For example, Oldsmobiles of the fifties had headlights that were housed in a way that made the *eyes* of the car look droopy or sad. Then there was the 1950 Buick Special that had a front grille so menacing that it actually scared me. Lastly, there was the 1960 Austin Healy Sprite that had what they called bubble eyes. Add a round hood ornament for the nose and a grille that turned up on the ends and you had the happiest-looking car ever made. Kids loved it. They didn't make a lot of them as they were super small and didn't even have side windows, but I liked it. It was likely the happiest-looking car ever made.

CHAPTER 10

A Mind Is a Terrible Thing to Lose

On my way to the funeral, I was zipping along in my Mustang at just over seventy miles per hour. Crazy as it sounds, the maximum speed limit on the highways back then was only fifty-five. That's right. President Richard Nixon mandated that ridiculously slow speed (down from seventy miles per hour) to supposedly reduce fuel usage. It may have worked, but no one paid any attention to it, and I'm sure the government spent a fortune on all those new speed limit signs. Plus, if everyone drove that slow, there would probably be countless pileups on the interstates today. It was a horrible idea, and fortunately, they later changed it back. (More money wasted on signs.) I didn't know what I would say to my father when I got home. My dad's mother had passed away when he was only a teenager, so this was the last parent he had left. My mother's parents were both still around, but we didn't see them all that much. Quite honestly, I don't think they cared much for me and Danny. They seemed to stay for very short intervals when they visited, and they always stayed in a hotel. It made sense to me years later as we could be awful around them at times. My grandmother had zero sense of humor and didn't understand sarcasm. And if Danny and I were speaking back then, it was usually meant to be funny or sarcastic.

During my trip home, I thought a lot about this senility thing and how cruel it was for everyone impacted by the disease. I remember how talkative my grandfather was just a few years before, and he even used to be fairly musical. He always had instruments like maracas and tambourines at his house, and he allowed us to play them as noisily as we wanted. He would laugh and pretend to be playing along with us. My father would growl at us and give us the "stop that shit" slashing sign, but we kept going. Granddad, in his younger days, was clearly the one in charge at his house. He was funny, and he even told some relatively off-color jokes. They weren't dirty or racist or anything. Well, okay, they were a little racist at times, but I think he mostly meant well. He lived in a different era when (unintentional) racism was much more common and, sadly, accepted. My mother was especially disapproving of his jokes and would let us know after we left their house.

And then suddenly, it was like he wasn't there anymore. He was in his house, but he was gone. He had a maid that took care of his house, and she seemed to be there whenever we visited. Turns out, she was making her move on him or his finances, and it worked. She was able to change the entire will so that all my father inherited was a crummy old wheelbarrow. My father didn't care that much and even seemed to like the wheelbarrow. We still have it in our garage, but I think the bottom of it rusted out years ago. My father must not be able to throw it away for sentimental reasons. Either that or he asked me or Danny to do it and we never did. The latter is more likely.

The longer I ruminated on this mind/memory issue, the scarier it got for me. I had always assumed that we took our memories with us to heaven (or whatever comes after this life). If not, what would be the point of our existence? It simply made no sense to get up there to heaven and have no memories of what we did to make a difference (good or bad). I guess it must be like having a leg amputated here on earth because of an accident or illness. I sure hope we get that leg back when we get up there. They say that God is fair and loving, and it would seem ungodlike to not give you a new leg when you got to heaven. Right?

Memories, though, are more than an appendage. They are who we are or were. Our lives are simply seventy to ninety years (we hope) of gathering experiences and lessons. Our mind is like a computer with many parts, but the most important part is the storage of those experiences. The rest of the mind is like a processor that makes us say and think things (like why Deborah Robbins didn't like me more?). I was, after all, still holding on desperately to my crush.

I had not really met many girls since coming to college. I didn't join a fraternity, so that left me out of a lot of social (a.k.a. drinking) gatherings, but I didn't care. I liked my dorm friends, and we had a good enough time. I really just wanted to go out with Deborah Robbins, and I let my friends know it. Since SOU was a small school, I would see her hanging around campus from time to time, and I simply loved to hear her laugh. It was a confident laugh that indicated she knew what was funny and what was not. That scared me a bit, but I wasn't daunted. She was a really good tennis player too, and I would watch her home matches, and she really put on a show out there. Some of her more classic statements on the court included as follows:

"I'm calling everything out if you hit an overhead at me again."

"The police just called. Your serve is missing."

"Just so you know, if you come to the net like that again, I am aiming my return right at your face."

Deborah talked throughout the match and would imitate the opposing players' mannerisms. If they grunted when they hit the ball, she would grunt even louder. She usually won, but when she didn't, she wouldn't shake hands. She was a horrible sport and reminded me a lot of how Jimmy Connors played in the 1970s. I enjoyed watching Connors play, especially when he would yell at the umpire. It was good entertainment and so was Deborah. She even made rude and insulting comments in the classroom at times that made the teachers and other students dislike her immensely. It was very common to hear people talking about what a jerk she could be, but I never joined in. For whatever reason, I liked her occasionally abrasive style and wanted her to know it.

Deborah always dressed like she was going to a hockey game or a boxing match. Certainly nothing frilly, overly feminine, or fancy. She often wore vests, which I thought was really cool. To this day, I don't think I have ever seen a girl with more shapely legs (except for maybe every female ice-skater). I would see her around campus at times and would wave, but she either pretended not to know me or maybe, despite my efforts, she really didn't know who I was. It didn't matter to me. My goal was to find a way to get her to notice and like me. I asked around about her, and it turns out that she was rumored to have dated a guy her freshman year. He was a tall, geeky, redheaded guy, and I knew of him, but I didn't really know him. He was awfully average to be the boy of choice for a girl that I considered to be so cool. And it turned out that she hadn't dated him at all. They were just lab partners. I am sure he liked her, but Deborah was not going to be an easy catch for anyone.

My plan to get Deborah to notice me was to start taking some classes with her. She was a political science major, and I figured I knew enough about that subject that I could do all right in the class. As dumb as I could be about some things, I did pay attention to politics, and I loved reading histories of the world wars and biographies of famous generals and political figures. Turns out, political science was none of that stuff, and I was immediately in over my head. But not Deborah. She always raised her hand in class and wouldn't hesitate to disagree with the professor. She had an opinion about everything, and if I had to guess, I would say that she was a communist or, at the very least, a socialist, but I am still not totally sure what the difference is.

In one of our classes together, I made sure to sit where Deborah could see me. Then I timed my exit from the room so I could walk out either right beside her or behind her. That would give me my opportunity to say something to her very casually, and I did that one day my sophomore year.

"Hey there, Debbie. What's up?"

Yep. That was me being casually cool.

"Yeah. I'm in a hurry and got to get to my next class. Nice seeing you, Steve."

Okay, that didn't go as planned. And she called me Steve, again. One strange thing throughout my life has been whenever anyone calls me by the wrong name, it is always Steve. I figured I must look like a Steve, whatever that means. As mentioned before, I was not muscular or toned, but I think I was okay looking. I could get dates from time to time with pretty girls like Mandy O'Brien or Kathy Speer, but I was no ladies' man like Danny. It is sadly true that you could be ugly and get girls if you were exceptionally good at a sport or could play James Tayler songs on the guitar. I couldn't do either, so I was left hoping that someone might like me because I could tell the difference between a Datsun and a Toyota. No such luck there.

The funeral for my grandfather was the first funeral I had ever attended, and it was not what I expected. First, my grandfather's body was lying there in a coffin, but he, the person, was clearly not in it. It hardly even resembled him as the body looked much too thin, and he had chalky makeup all over his face. His lips were almost purple, and they looked like they had been sewn together (maybe they had). I could hardly remember the healthy version of my grandfather without a big smile on his face. As I looked down at the body, I had a terrible temptation to touch it. I looked around me, and I was the only person in this part of the funeral home, so I did reach down and touch the chest of the body just below the breastplate. I don't recommend doing this to a dead body as it felt like I had just touched the delicate remains of an Egyptian mummy. I'm not sure they even left his ribs inside this faint facsimile of my grandfather's human body. I immediately recoiled and turned to go search for my father.

"Hello, son," my dad said somberly as he wandered into the main part of the funeral viewing area.

"Hey, Dad. I'm...uh...well, it's too bad about—"

"I know, Sean. Why don't you go find Daniel and see if you can help your mother with anything?"

"Okay, sure," I responded.

There was no way my mother could have told my father about the three hundred dollars to fix the Mustang, or I would have heard about it right there. I glanced around and saw Danny talking with one of my dad's two sisters. Neither of my aunts lived in Cleveland, so we barely knew them. I could tell from the expression on Danny's face that he was miserable, so I went over to save him.

"Hi, Aunt Mary."

"Oh, hello there, Sean. How are things?"

In those days, I had absolutely no sense of social propriety but instead of asking how she was, I answered with far too much information about myself.

"Well, I think I'm passing most of my classes. It's sophomore year for me now, so they are a bit easier. I still haven't decided my major, but I am taking auto mechanics. I may want to work for a car company someday, but not like my dad. I want to design the cars there in Detroit and see how that goes. I don't have a girlfriend yet, but there is this one girl at school that I really like named Debbie, but she likes to be called Deborah."

Yes, I was well aware that I was rambling, and it gave Danny a chance to escape. He walked away with a huge smile on his face and gave me the circular "you are crazy" sign with his finger. My aunt looked like she was searching around the room to find a way to get away from me too. I have never been good with socializing at things like this. Even parties were difficult for me unless I had a few drinks. If I am the least bit nervous, I will talk and talk and then when I run out of things to talk about, I will start talking nonsense—unless I am drinking. Then I stay and ramble senselessly. I could tell when people were anxious to get away from me, and it happened a lot, especially when I was drinking.

"That all sounds good, Sean. I need to go find your aunt Estelle. Have you seen her?"

Aunt Estelle was my father's older sister. I had heard some rumors that she was not doing too well, but I had not yet seen her. Later that day, I asked my mother, and she told me that Aunt Estelle was also having some troubles with her memory and was not able to make the trip. She must have been really bad, I thought, to miss her own father's funeral. But the more I thought about my aunt, the more I realized that these two people (my grandfather and Aunt Estelle) were both genetically related to me. And both were losing their memory. (Note: I was now using the word *memory* instead of *mind* as they were still mostly sane but couldn't remember anything.) Would I be going down this same path someday? Someday soon?

"Danny, what do you think of this memory issue in our family?" I asked my younger brother when he approached me.

Danny was looking much better these days. He was not quite as muscular, but he looked very athletic and fit. He was even eating a doughnut, which he would have never done before. Yet I think the funeral home knows that people who are in mourning will eat anything, and they especially enjoy doughnuts. Dieting on the day you are burying your loved one just isn't going to be at the top of your mind. Danny was still a health freak, but I was happy that he was willing to eat something that didn't come from a nutrition store. It even had chocolate frosting on it.

"What do you mean memory thing?" Danny responded through a mouthful of sugar, butter, fried flour and frosting.

"Well, like Grandad. And now Aunt Estelle. They both got this senile thing. Right? What if it happens to us? What if we lose our memories too?"

"It'll never happen to me. I will just take memory supplements. They make 'em, you know."

Now there was the Danny I knew so well.

"But what if they don't work? What if you don't even know me in a few years? Or Mom? Or Dad?"

"You need to take a chill-out pill, Sean-O. Dad is already super old, and he doesn't have it. Maybe it skips a generation, like baldness."

"I have never ever heard that about baldness. I thought the gene came from the mother's side," I replied logically.

"Women don't go bald, you idiot. Only men."

It was clear now that Danny would have even more trouble in college than me.

"I just don't want to lose my memories. That's all. It seems like memories are the pictures that our mind stores, and over time, those pictures become us, and they tell our story. How can we still be who we are without the pictures? You know?"

"Jesus, Sean. I need some punch or something to drink. You want to come with me or stay here talking crazy shit?"

That was Danny. He was not deep.

"I'm going to go talk to the minister. Maybe he knows what happens to a person when the memories go."

"You go do that, Sean. Good idea," Danny said as he wiped the doughnut crumbs off his pants. He had chocolate frosting all over his face and shirt.

CHAPTER 11

Meet Father Dave

The minister at my grandfather's funeral was a guy our family had known for several years. We called him Father Dave. I didn't even know his last name or if Dave was really his first name, but as ministers go, he was very cool. He had been the assistant minister at our church for about four years, and he gave the best sermons. They were not only funny, but quite frankly, they weren't even that religious. You almost expected him to start singing at times as he talked a lot about being a musician and playing guitar. I bet he had no trouble getting girls when he was in college. Naturally, he had longish hair and a salty gray beard and was dressed like a hippie. He was smart and used really big words in his sermons that no one understood. At least I didn't, but despite that, I thought he was awesome.

Father Dave also drove a very cool white 1967 Chevrolet Corvair convertible. This is the car that Ralph Nader publicized as being "unsafe at any speed." But that comment was made about the first generation Corvair, which had plenty of issues besides rolling over when you made a right turn. One of the most remarkable things about that car was that reverse lights were not only an option, but if deleted, they also came with a cheap tin blank that covered up the place where the reverse lights would have been if you ordered them. Talk about cheap. This original iteration of the Corvair was designed with the engine in back and it was air-cooled, but the car suffered from being way too slow, and the boxy uneven design was indeed dangerous.

The second generation fixed most of the first-gen Corvair issues, but by then, sales had really taken a beating from the Ralph Nader comments. Plus, Chevrolet had introduced the more conventional Camaro (engine in front) pony car that same year, so the Corvair was doomed. So what was not necessarily cool in 1967 became ultracool in 1979, especially when people realized that there was an interesting story behind that car. Amazing how fickle the car-buying public could be. Evidence of this is that, today, people are still talking about the 1958 to 1960 Ford Edsel. The Edsel was introduced as the most *completely new car* in automotive history. It was that indeed. It was also the most completely hideous car ever made. The fabled horse-collar grille was comically large and out of proportion for an otherwise ordinary car. People hated it then for its bad looks. People love it today for its bad looks. Crazy.

When I found Father Dave in the corner of the funeral home, he was talking to a couple of old women who I did not recognize. Apparently, they were women who used to work with my grandfather at a now-defunct department store called the May Company. I think my grandfather was in the personnel department, and he retired from there after about forty years of service. My granddad was in business during an age when you took a job when you were nineteen or twenty and worked there until you died. And that is what he did. He was still employed there when it became obvious that he was no longer mentally competent. My father told me a story once of his dad showing up to work in his pajamas. Were it not for his dementia, showing up to work in sleep attire almost made losing my car seem not quite so bad.

"Well, hello there, Sean. How are you doing?" Father Dave began.

"I'm fine. As usual, I'm trying to figure out how to get through college with the minimal amount of effort."

"Sounds smart," Father Dave said, laughing.

"Yeah. My major is still undeclared, so I pretty much take all electives I can like horseback riding and tennis."

"That sounds like fun."

"Not as much as it sounds. I got a D in horseback riding. My horse didn't like me very much."

"I see."

"Yeah. His name was Homer, and he liked to roll in the mud with me on him."

"Horses do that," Father Dave said.

"So if you have a minute, Father Dave, I would like to ask you something."

"Shoot," he said eagerly as the two elderly women wandered off. They seemed somewhat irritated that Father Dave had turned his attention to me.

"Yeah. So my father is related to my grandfather, and I am related to him. Right?"

"I assume so. Unless they found you in a sewer somewhere."

"That might be the case, but I have been wondering about this memory thing. My grandfather didn't even know his name there at the end."

"I know. Very sad."

"So you are a minister and you understand God, right?"

"I guess so. I am a minister, but I am not so sure about understanding God."

"Yeah, well, if we live our lives here and do a pretty good job, but we lose our minds, what happens when we go to heaven? Are our minds in a different place than our bodies?"

"Wow. Good questions. I'm not sure I can help you there."

"You can't?"

"No. You see, Sean, God is a mystery and so is this ephemeral life. We just aren't going to know everything there is to know until we join him in heaven."

"Ephemeral?"

"Fleeting."

"Again?"

"It doesn't last very long."

"Okay. Well, that sucks!"

"Not really. I'm not sure we want to know everything while we have these human brains. It could be a bit too much for most of us."

"But that is what I mean. If we live the last years of our lives without being able to remember anything, what is the point?"

"You got me," Father Dave said with a smile.

"Sorry, Father Dave, but you aren't helping."

"Maybe I am not the person to ask."

"You did go to religious school for this God stuff. Right?"

"They call it *seminary*."

"What?"

"Sean. Why are you so concerned about this? You are a young man. By the time you get old, they may have a cure for senility."

"I doubt it. But that won't help people who are head injured or just have plain bad memories."

"Are you concerned that you have a bad memory?"

"Did you hear about me losing my car?"

"We all heard about that. But you were drinking. That's different."

"I wasn't drinking when I took that history test."

"What?"

"Yeah. I took the test on a Tuesday, and the teacher lost the tests and made us take the same test again on Thursday."

"So? People lose things all the time."

"Yeah, but by Thursday, I had forgotten everything I studied, and I did terrible. I couldn't even remember simple basic things about the civil war. I got an F."

"That's not good."

"No, but then the teacher found the tests from Tuesday, and I got a B plus on that first one."

"Hmmm."

"You see? I have no capacity to retain things even a day or two after I learn them. I can't even tell you what the class was about now. I think it was on the civil war, but maybe not."

"Look, Sean. That does sound bad. Maybe you should see a specialist?"

"That's why I am talking to you. Don't you guys have a super-secret ceremony to fix the brain? Like a séance or an exorcism. That Raven girl got her brain fixed, and she could turn her head all the way around and hang down from the ceiling. Scared the shit out of me."

"That was just a movie, Sean. And I don't do exorcisms."

"Dang. Do you know anyone who does?"

"I can call a friend of mine that has some experience with cognitive things like this."

"That would be great. Does *cognitive* mean the brain?" I asked.

"Yes, Sean."

"Thanks, Father Dave."

"Sure, but, Sean, I think you are making a big deal out of nothing. So you lost your car once and flunked a test. You seem pretty normal to me."

"Honestly, I don't even know where my car is right now."

"I will call my friend right away," Father Dave said, laughing as he shook my hand.

"Thanks, Father Dan."

"What?" he said in surprise.

"Just kidding," I replied.

"Good one," he said before turning to leave.

CHAPTER 12

Debbie Does...Me

My mother slipped me a three-hundred-dollar check to pay for the Mustang repairs before I drove back to school. My mom was super protective of my father and didn't want him bothered while he was dealing with the loss of his father. The car drove well on the way back to school, and I was happy that the oil leaks seemed to have ceased with the installation of a new motor. I was trying to resist the temptation to peel out from stoplights as someone told me that this was not good for the tire tread. Since a lot of that tread would be left on the pavement and not on the tire, it made sense to me that I shouldn't do that.

It was only a couple of weeks after I returned from the funeral when I ran into Deborah at the student union cafeteria. She was just finishing up her dinner when I passed by her on the way to put my tray away.

"Hey, Debbie. What's up?" I asked.

"The name is Deborah. I go by Deborah, not Debbie or Deb or Debs. Got it?"

No wonder she called me Steve the last time I saw her.

"Yeah. Okay. Sorry. Do you know my name? It's not Steve, you know?"

"Your name is Sean Stevens. You went to Shaker Heights High School. You lost your car when you were on a date with Mandy O'Brien. I think you sat behind me in my World War I history class last semester."

Okay, so that was what that class was about, *not* the civil war.

"Did you want something?" Deborah asked in a curt manner.

"No…well…uh…I was going to see if you…if we…no, if you would want to go get a beer or something…like that."

I was suddenly trembling with nervousness, and I knew it was obvious to Deborah.

"Are you okay?"

"I'm not sure yet," I said.

"Well, it was nice to see you, not-Steve," she said before chugging the remainder of her glass of milk.

"I…uh…I have something I want to say to you. It'll only take a minute. It's kind of an anecdote, actually."

I hoped desperately that I had used that word properly.

"An anecdote? Okay. This I gotta hear."

"You know John Lennon?" I asked while wiping my sweating hands off on my pants.

"The Beatle? Sure."

"Do you know how he and Yoko met? It's pretty cool."

"No, how did they meet?"

"John was in London in this art gallery, and one of the exhibits had this ladder."

"Okay. A ladder in an art museum. What is interesting about that?"

"No, you see the ladder had a magnifying glass on a string at the top of it, and you had to climb up there and look at what was painted on the ceiling."

"Okay, I'm game. What was written on the ceiling?"

"It was just one word," I said excitedly.

"What word was that?" Deborah asked.

"The word was *yes*," I said dramatically like I was pulling a rabbit out of a hat.

"Yes? That's it?"

"He knew right then that Yoko was the one for him. It's like they fell in love right there because of the ladder and everything. And that's how they met."

"I'm not sure I get it," she said as she picked up her food tray.

"You don't?"

"No. It sounds like of stupid, actually, but it doesn't matter. I will go out on a date with you."

"You will?" I asked.

"Sure. Meet me at my dorm tomorrow night. Six o'clock. Don't be late, or I won't ever go out with you again. Got it?"

"Got it!" I said as she turned to walk out of the room.

I was mentally exhausted from the conversation with her, but I could hardly wait to tell my friends. They knew I had been harboring a huge crush on Deborah for the longest time, and I could brag that patience had finally paid off. It wasn't like I was some kind of ladies' man. Clearly, I wasn't. But I did have some kind of odd inner confidence that I could, if given enough time, win over just about any girl my age. It had taken two years to even get a first date with Deborah, but we had one on the calendar, and I was not going to blow it. My plan for the date was as follows:

1. I would arrive right on time—not early, not late, but exactly at 6:00 p.m. as we planned.
2. I would let her do most of the talking at the beginning, and I had memorized a list of questions that included things like "How are your parents doing with you away at college?" or "What do you like most about being away at college?" and finally "Do you have any sexually transmittable diseases?" (Okay, I was kidding about the last one, but there were a lot of things going around in those days, and I had no idea if Deborah was sexually active or not. There was no question with me. I was clean as I hadn't had sex since that dance in eleventh grade. And even that was a fairly horrible experience where the girl actually told me that I was horrible at it when we were done. I probably was.)
3. I would walk slowly and hold the doors open for her when we entered the bar/restaurant.
4. I would try not to drink my beer too quickly. I would sip it casually and not any faster than she drank her drink.

5. I would wear a crisply ironed shirt. Actually, I didn't have an iron, so I would have to borrow one from someone in the dorm. Most likely, it would have to be from a girl as I didn't know any guy that ironed his shirts.
6. I would be polite and cordial and focus on her and not me.
7. I would *not* kiss her good night no matter how well the date went. I would give her a nice hug if it seemed appropriate, and that is it. That would keep her wondering what my feelings were for her.
8. I would not call her Debbie. Just Deborah.
9. I would not call her after the date for at least three days.

Needless to say, I broke every single one of these rules. I never did find an iron, and somehow, my watch stopped working the same day, so I arrived almost thirty minutes late. I was way more nervous than I expected, so I chugged down two beers before she had even taken a second sip of her wine. I was talking so much that I wasn't sure I was even making sense. I told her about my love of cars and the work I had done getting this Mustang into shape. I told her about my plans to design cars someday and how I wanted to have a dozen or more cars when I grew up and got superrich. It wasn't like I was a snob about it. I really didn't desire expensive cars or to have a lot of money, houses, boats, and other pretentious shit. I wanted the cars I loved growing up, like an AMC Javelin and the Plymouth Duster, or the Chevrolet Monza. These weren't fancy cars. I just liked their designs. They were all pretty much crappy cars in terms of performance and prestige.

By the end of our first date, Debbie or Deborah was not at all like I had imagined her. She joked around and laughed a lot, and she actually talked a little bit like fraternity guy. She mentioned a few boys I knew from my dorm and actually called them *pussies*. She told me that she liked masculine guys like me and my brother, Danny. I looked down at my pencil-thin arms and wondered if she needed glasses. And God forbid she finds out that I like sentimental movies and sometimes tear up at the mushy parts. But the one thing she must have concluded about me was that I was a car nut. And car nuts are not usually wimpy or particularly scholarly. And that just about summed me up completely.

Not only did I kiss Deborah when I dropped her off, but we also French-kissed, and I pretty much squeezed her butt the entire time. She didn't seem to mind. I even expected to get pushed away at some point, but she acted like she was just as into it as I was. I told her that I would call her the next day, and I did. We went to a fraternity party on campus where I had a friend that had once tried to talk me into joining his house. But I wanted absolutely nothing to do with Greek life. Few things seemed more stupid to me than learning some (probably satanic) ritual and living in pure filth. No, the dorm life suited me much better, but the best parties were always at the fraternities. There would always be kegs that never seemed to run out and plenty of liquor or pot if you wanted it.

Deborah and I were moving casually around the party and bumping into various friends when she nudged my arm and asked me if I wanted to see if we could find an empty room inside the frat house. It was early spring, and the weather was actually quite nice, so I didn't know how to respond. Still, I assumed she was cold, and I would lead her inside so we could warm up.

"Are you cold? You want my jacket?" I offered as I opened the door to the fraternity.

"No, you idiot. I want to have sex."

"Ha. Seriously. What's up? Do you want to go somewhere else?"

"Enough of the 'what's up' thing. I hate that," she said.

"Sorry. But what do you want to do?"

"I told you. Let's go somewhere and have sex."

Never in my entire life did I ever imagine a girl saying that to me in that way, much less my longtime crush. I could hardly respond, and when I did, my tongue was dry and not connected to my brain.

"Me...well...I...sure...I...inside...uh..."

"Come on, Sean. Get some balls!" she said as she grabbed my hand to lead us inside the Chi Delta Chi house.

As expected, the large rooms inside and the hallways were pathetically dirty. Carpets were stained and smelled like mildew. As much as I wanted to have sex, I wasn't sure if it was even safe unless we found an exceptionally clean room, and that wasn't likely to happen. Not only were most of the rooms filled with pot smokers and other couples *doing it*, but there were also no locks on any of the doors. So if we did find a room, the chances were very good that someone would walk in on us.

"I don't think this is the right place. Would you be willing to come back to my dorm room?" I asked sheepishly.

Deborah gave me an odd one-eyed squint, and we left the house and started toward the dorms. I reached over and held her hand, but she quickly let it go and put her arm around my waist. The entire walk, I was praying that my roommate would be out somewhere. We had devised a clever plan to leave a sock on the doorknob if either of us ever got a girl to go back there with us. I knew there was literally no chance that this would ever happen with my dorky roommate, Wayne, but it was also a long shot for me. Just not tonight.

In the late 1970s, the dorms at SOU were either male or female. It would be another six years before any dorm went coed, and even then, they were divided by floor, so there would only be one sex using the bathrooms on each floor. But in my day, the dorms were strictly policed, and girls were absolutely not allowed in any of the boys' dorm rooms past 10:00 p.m. Given that it was past eleven, I would have to sneak Deborah in through the back entrance and up a side stairwell to my third-floor room.

As I opened the door, I could already smell the tobacco smoke from Wayne's stupid pipe. He had gotten addicted to smoking a dumb, old-fashioned-looking pipe to the point where he simply could not study without it. Smoking was also forbidden in the dorms, so Wayne had to sit next to the window to keep the room from smelling of smoke. It didn't work, of course, and our room smelled like the bottom of an ashtray. I had never cared about that awful smoky smell until this moment, but I sure did now. Wayne looked pleasantly surprised when we entered the room.

"Well, hello, young people. How has your evening been so far?" Wayne asked politely.

Wayne always talked like he was older, and this made him seem even dorkier to those of us that knew him. Wayne was from a small town in central Ohio called Washington Courthouse. He wore tur-tleneck sweaters all the time even when it was warm out. He drove a white two-door 1961 Ford Falcon that he called Mr. Magoo. Man, Wayne was a dork.

"Do you folks need the domicile this pleasant night?"

"Well…I don't want to put you out," I replied.

"Just for an hour," Deborah blurted out. "If he can last that long."

"No problem-o," Wayne said as he gathered some books together and stood. "I'll just go down to the tube room and see what is shaking in the crypt."

Wayne winked at me as he passed me, but when I turned around, Deborah was already resting on one of the two twin beds. As roommates go, Wayne and I got along great. He rarely if ever went out drinking, but he was always willing to take a break to shoot baskets or grab some food. The only time I ever saw Wayne drunk was when a group of us freshmen decided to go out for beers after a late night study session. Wayne was not accustomed to drinking to excess, and that night, well, he almost drank himself to death. We were doing shots, and Wayne did a couple just to go along with the crowd. I didn't do anything to discourage him even though I could see in his eyes that he had clearly consumed too much.

When we finally reached the sidewalk leading to the dorm, Wayne was throwing up in every direction. In fact, he hurled just about every twenty feet as we made our way inside. He got to the bathroom, and I could hear him throwing up in there. At one point, I asked him if he would be okay, and he answered, "Fuck no." After about an hour of losing his guts, Wayne stumbled out and went straight into our room. I was drunk, too, but I was aware that Wayne was dangerously intoxicated. He reached out to hold my hand at one point and said, "Please don't let me die." I held his hand until his breathing became normal, and then I passed out on the bunk above him. From that day on, I knew that we had almost killed him, and I never pressured him to drink again.

As soon as Wayne exited the room, Deborah started taking off her clothes. I stood in awe as she hadn't even bothered to turn out the lights. There she was, just a few feet away from me, and she looked fabulous. She wore all-white underwear, but it wasn't on her for long. She was completely naked before I was done untying my shoelaces.

"Fuck that," she said as she threw me onto the twin bed with my shoes still on my feet. "You either tear those rags off now or I am going to do it for you!"

At that point, I have to admit that I was terrified. Deborah knew what she was doing, and I did not have a clue. I got my clothes off as fast as I could, and she jumped on top of me. She was so aggressive that I didn't even have time to wonder where to put my hands. She put them on her hips for me, and before I knew it, I was inside of her. I tried to move, but she was in a position where the only one that could really move was her. That left me completely helpless, and then it happened. After only a few short minutes, it was over, and she knew it.

"No fucking way!" Deborah yelled out.

"I'm sorry, but you were grinding on me so fast that—"

"That was like less than two minutes. Haven't you ever done this before?" she asked incredulously.

"Yes. Of course I have, but in the other case, the girl let me do the...uh...moving around."

"Jesus, Sean. Do you mean to tell me that you have only done it once before?"

I hadn't realized until then that I had inadvertently given away the secret of my vast inexperience.

"I should have known," Deborah said.

"What? What did you expect? This was only our first time," I said, but she completely misunderstood me.

"Oh. You mean you were just getting started. Okay. So get over here and let's go another round."

And we did. And I did last much longer the next time. Probably ten minutes! And that seemed to be plenty of time to satisfy Deborah.

"Not too bad on the second shot, killer. Think you got a third in you?"

I didn't.

As I was walking her back to her dorm, I was simply beyond happy. It was one of the best days of my short life. This was better than any typical sexual fantasy as I knew this girl and I had liked her for so long. I had no earthly clue why she liked me, but I was bound and determined not to screw this up. I knew my next day would be spent studying intensely at the library. I had to learn everything I could about satisfying a woman sexually. So for the first time in my two years at SOU, I showed up at the library early and went to work.

CHAPTER 13

Shazam!

There was an absolutely ridiculous show on television back in the late sixties called *Gomer Pyle, U.S.M.C.* It was about a country bumpkin from the quaint southern town of Mayberry who, for some reason, joins the United States Marine Corps. The main character, played by Jim Nabors, had been an auto mechanic at the only gas station (Wally's) in town on *The Andy Griffith Show*. He was funny on the Andy Griffith show, but the stupidity of the plots on the *Gomer Pyle* show seemed juvenile and ridiculous even to an immature idiot like me. Of course, Danny loved it. Plus, it was patently obvious that Jim Nabors was about as gay as a guy could be. Not that there is anything wrong with that (there isn't!) as I am sure there are plenty of very muscular and masculine Marines who prefer the same sex. But Gomer was not one of these types. He was goofy, weak, and clumsy, and it made a show about Marine life seem absurd. Nevertheless, Gomer did have a popular saying that he made famous during the show's run, and it seemed to get people laughing whenever he said it. The expression was "Shazam, Shazam!"

Deborah and I were studying at the main campus library early that May, which meant she was reading, and I was sleeping on one of the cushioned love seats near the upstairs balcony. I always wondered if I snored when I would fall asleep in such a public place. I would definitely wake with slobber on my chin and a pain in my neck from sleeping with my head on an armrest.

97

"Wake up, Sean. I need to talk to you," Deborah said while jerking forcefully on my arm.

"What? Huh? What's...up?" I mumbled back.

"Come downstairs in five minutes. I will be waiting for you outside."

"Why five minutes?" I asked.

"Go look in the mirror, dumb shit. You'll see."

When I did see my image, my long hair had become flattened on one side and I looked a lot like Bozo the Clown. I fixed my hair by pouring warm water from the sink into my cupped hands and then throwing it at my head like I had done before that cancer danced years before. I didn't have a comb, so I just used my fingers to try to make it look less stupid. I quickly rushed out the front doors of the building and saw Deborah smoking a cigarette and pacing on the sidewalk.

"Hey, sweetie. What's up?" I said as nicely as I could, but something was wrong, and I knew it immediately.

"What do you think is up? Can't you tell?"

The truth is, I couldn't tell despite having unprotected sex at virtually every possible opportunity.

"I'm pregnant, you moron!"

"You're...wait...What?" I asked.

"Read my lips. I'm pregnant. You knocked me up."

"Shazam!" I blurted out.

"What did you just say?" she asked in anger.

"I said Shazam, like Gomer Pyle," I said demurely.

"Never ever say that again," she returned.

"Okay."

I scratched my messy hair and took in a few deep breaths to prepare for this conversation.

"What are you going to do...about...it?" I asked cautiously.

"What are you going to do...about...it?" Deborah echoed back angrily while inhaling a drag from her cigarette.

"I think we should...I should...you could...we could..." I stammered.

"What? Try to pretend it didn't happen? Let the thing drop out of me in biology class? That would be quite a show."

"Debbie, I…"

Deborah paused and threw her cigarette to the ground. From as early as I could remember, I had a very annoying habit of stepping on and snuffing out any cigarettes I saw that were still lit on the ground. I couldn't help but look uneasily at the burning ash on the one she had just discarded.

"If you step on that now, I will beat the living shit out of you," she said as the first tear fell down her cheek.

"Seems like you aren't supposed to be—"

"Say one word about me smoking and you are dead. Fucking dead! You got that?" Deborah shouted.

I went to try to hug her, but she wanted none of that. Most married men learn quickly that when their wives are in a state like this, the best thing you can do is stand there and keep your mouth shut. As a relatively new boyfriend, I had not yet learned that lesson.

"Maybe…you can…you know…handle it?" I offered.

"Say what? You want me to kill it? Is that what you want, Sean? I tell you what. Why don't you just kill me instead? That will take care of everything. Or wait. No. Go get a coat hanger and reach up there and pull it out. How about that?"

"I wasn't… You…you want to… You are going to what…keep it?" I asked.

"No, Sean. I'm going to give it to the police and tell them that you raped me. How does that sound?"

After that, I knew better than to ask anything else or to offer any suggestions. I just stood there silently, hoping desperately that the dang cigarette butt would go out on its own. Man, those things can burn a long time.

"Well, now you know," Deborah said as she adjusted her book bag over her shoulder.

"Now I know what?" I asked clumsily. I really didn't know what I knew at that point. Like Deborah, I was in a state of shock. "How long have you… When…did you?"

"Girls have periods every month, Einstein. And when you don't get one, you start to wonder, could I be…am I…pregnant? So I went down to the clinic and took a test. It was about an hour ago. And sure enough, you knocked me up. Way to go, killer."

I was not very fond of this new nickname Deborah had conjured up for me. It was Jerry Lee Lewis's nickname, too, and he wasn't the best example of proper behavior with women. Still, I couldn't help noticing how she wanted this to be all my fault somehow. It was true that I had never used any type of birth control, but I figured she did. Since she never asked me about me, I assumed she had one of those rubber cups in there or she was on the pill or something. But she wasn't. If I had known that, I could have worn a condom for sure. Looking back now, of course she got pregnant. We were two healthy twenty-year-old kids who were having unprotected sex several times a week. What did she, we, I expect?

"I'm not having an abortion, Sean. You need to know that. It is completely against my religion."

"You have a religion? What religion are you?" I asked sincerely. I wasn't sure that communism was a religion or just a type of government.

"I am Catholic. We don't kill babies, even if they are still in the womb. Got it?"

But having sex outside of marriage without protection is okay with your religion?

You will be happy to know that I only thought this. I didn't say it.

"Well, what do we do now?" I asked, but I quickly added, "How can I help? What do you want me to do?"

Deborah started to search in her bag, and she pulled out another cigarette. I couldn't help it, but my face must have become contorted as she lit it up.

"Say one word, just one. I dare you."

"I didn't even know you smoked."

Yep. I should have said nothing, but it was too late now. Deborah started to walk away from me, and I hurried to catch up to her (surreptitiously stepping on the first cigarette butt that was still burning red on the sidewalk). When I caught up to her, I placed my arm around her and pulled her close. This time, she let me, and the tears began to cascade down her sweet, beautiful face.

"I'm sorry, Deborah. But we will get through this together. I'm here for you. And I will do whatever we need to do. Okay?"

Remarkably, I was not crying or even close to it. I felt strange, but not bad. Not bad at all. And I had to admit that the thought of having my own child, even at such a young age, did not scare me. In fact, I didn't want to express it right then, but I was thinking I was almost happy about it. Deborah sucked in a very long drag of her cigarette, and this time, she threw the lit butt toward a pile of dead brush a few feet off the path. All I could think of was that the brush would soon catch fire and burn down the entire school, killing thousands. But given Deborah's state of mind, even if thousands would be dead, there was no way I was going to snuff that cigarette out. I simply pulled her closer, and then I said the worst thing I could have possibly said to her at that moment.

"I love you."

Deborah looked up, and for a couple of seconds, I thought she might just kill me right there on the spot.

"What is wrong with you?" she managed to spit out.

"A lot. Definitely a lot," I replied as she pushed herself away from me.

"Oh my god. I let the stupidest person alive put a baby inside of me. This has got to be the worst day of anyone's life ever."

It was hard not to be horrifically offended by that statement, but I wasn't. I loved this girl, and I would do whatever I could to help her through this. This was the girl of my dreams, and I was having a baby with her. She might not like me that much now, but I would show her that I would be the best father a person could ever be. I would support her unconditionally, and she would eventually grow to love me and recognize that I was her true soul mate.

"Don't call me for at least a week," she barked at me angrily before storming off down the sidewalk.

Okay, maybe not.

CHAPTER 14

How Not to Ask a Girl to Marry You

The summer break after sophomore year came quickly, and Deborah agreed to drive home with me in the Mustang. We had been seeing each other for meals at the dorm and even had what seemed like some relatively nonhostile dates, but the subject of the baby never came up. For the most part, we just went on with our lives as if there wasn't a growing fetus inside her body. In general, I could sense that she didn't want to discuss it, and I was able to keep my mouth shut until that car ride.

"How are you... How is...I mean...are you feeling okay?" I asked nervously.

"I feel fine. Why?"

"Well, it's just... Well, it's not really my business, or...well, it is in a way...and I just wanted to make sure—"

"For Christ's sake, Sean. What are you trying to say?"

The truth is, I wanted to know how the baby was doing. I was growing more and more excited about the idea that I would be a father soon, but she seemed to want to pretend that there was nothing any different about our lives.

"Look, Sean. We are heading home for the summer, and I really want to get a break from...everything. So please don't make things any more difficult than they already are."

Don't ask me why, but my basic survival instincts did not stop what came out of my mouth next.

"Um…Debbie?" I began.

"Deborah, please."

"Yeah, um…I know this may not be the best time to bring this up again, but would things be easier for you if we…got married?"

"Oh my god! You have got to be kidding me."

"What?" I asked.

"That's how you ask me? Would it be a help if we were married?"

"Okay. I'm sorry. I don't know how to do this," I stammered. "Umm…Will you marry me?"

"For Christ's sake!" Deborah said.

Deborah, at that moment, looked like she was going to be sick. She closed her eyes tightly and took in a long breath. I was terrified about what she might say next, so I quickly changed the subject.

"Are you all set for your summer job…and everything?" I asked.

Deborah had worked at the Christian Equestrian Academy for their summer camps almost every summer since she was old enough to jump on the back of a horse. She was still not showing that June, and neither of us had said anything to our parents about the baby. I was not sure how my parents would react, but Deborah was sure that hers would be irate with her. And me, too, of course. This was still a time when many girls often went off somewhere to have the child and then the parents raised it or the baby was put up for adoption. She and I hadn't decided much if anything of what would happen after the baby was born. But I figured the car ride home was as good a time as any to start that discussion.

"So you are going to be able to ride horses all summer?" I began.

"I don't know. I haven't really thought about it. I guess so," she answered.

"Those are some really rich kids that go to that camp. Right?" I asked.

"Yep. Fucking preppies. I hate all of them."

"I hate Homer," I said.

"Homer?"

"Yeah, my horse in the horse-riding class at school. He hated me."

"That's because you don't know how to act around horses."

"And you think riding a horse is okay for…you know…the thing?"

"The thing?" Deborah replied angrily.

"Yeah. You know. The thing," I said, pointing at her stomach.

"I'll be fine."

"But won't it get bounced around a lot?"

"The baby is still less than an inch long, Sean. Riding a horse or a roller coaster isn't going to matter at this point."

"Oh," I replied. "But you do need to be taking care of yourself…uh…with the…uh…the thing."

"You can call it a baby, Sean. Jesus!"

"Okay, with the baby," I said, trying to hide the gleeful smile appearing on my face. "It's just hard to believe that there is a real baby in there. Fingers and toes and everything. Just a bit small at this point."

"Jesus, Sean. You are a woman. You know that?" Deborah said in exasperation.

"You think you will get…you know?" I asked, demonstrating a growing stomach section on myself.

"No, Sean. You will get fat, not me."

"Come on, Deb. I'm just trying to talk about it some. It is going to happen."

"All right. Let's talk about it," she said while starting to light up a cigarette. "Yes. I will get really fat. Are you happy?"

I looked at the cigarette and then at Deborah as she tried to get the cigarette lighter to work. It had never worked in that car as far as I knew.

"I didn't mean fat. I just mean, will it get really big? Like a basketball in there when the kid is ready to come out?"

"Yeah. I guess I will get that basketball stomach eventually, but not for another few months," Deborah said as she threw her unlit cigarette out of the open window.

"And when do you think you will tell your parents? Before we go back to school?"

Deborah looked at me sternly as I drove, and I could feel that I had just crossed over a threshold into a place she was trying desperately not to go. Everything would start to change after what she said next.

"I'm not going back to school, Sean."

"What?" I asked.

"The baby is due in November. That's ten weeks into the next semester. I would miss finals and…everything."

"Oh," I uttered quietly.

"No. I will tell my parents at some point before the end of the summer, and I will stay home, have the baby, and then figure out things from there."

"And…what? You will live at home and…what…raise the kid there?"

"I hadn't thought about it, but that might be my only option."

I stared ahead as my mind raced and raced with considerations. I had learned with Deborah to think through my thoughts before talking, so I just sat there and really tried to formulate some intelligence on what to say next.

"You going to just stare ahead like a zombie, or are you going to say something?" Deborah said caustically.

"I'm thinking," I replied.

"Well, think faster. What are you going to do?"

"What do you want me to do?" I asked sincerely.

"I'm not going to tell you what to do. You have to figure that out."

"Oh," I said as I thought of what she would want me to say.

Honestly, I didn't have a clue what to say, and I certainly didn't know what the right or noble thing to do was. And that was when I said the worst thing I could have said at that moment.

"I guess I will go back to school. No need for both of us to drop out."

Yep. She didn't say another word for two hours until we pulled onto I-271, which meant we had thirty more minutes before we got to her house in Shaker.

"I'm sorry if I said the wrong thing back there, Deb. I just want to be…"

As the words were coming out, I got choked up, and Deborah could tell what was coming. I was a crier, and she simply hated that I could cry so easily. I tried to stop, but I couldn't. Tears were now streaming down my cheeks, and Deborah clenched her fists in frustration. I was embarrassed to be crying in front of her, but I hoped that my emotions would demonstrate how much I cared for her and our future child.

"I just want to do the right thing…for all of us. That's all."

Deborah reached over and took my hand and squeezed it about as hard as she could. In fact, she squeezed it so hard it really hurt, but I let her do it. If she broke a few fingers, so what? I didn't want to ruin one of the most profound and tender moments of our young relationship. And then, almost like magic, she smiled.

My tears had taken Deborah to a place that she rarely wanted to go. There was a sentimental side to her, but it was way down in there. Sadly, she was much more comfortable being mean and caustic to me, but I had reached that soft side. Thank God.

"You are okay. You know that?" she said as she relaxed her kung fu grip on my hand.

"I love you, Deb."

"What did I tell you about calling me that? Do you not listen to me at all?" she screamed, ignoring the fact that I had also said that I loved her again. She had never said it back to me.

When I pulled into her driveway, I got out and took her bags out and lugged them all up to the front door.

"Call me when you…whenever you want, I guess," she said as her father opened the front door.

"Of course," I replied.

I wanted to tell her that I loved her again, but I knew it wasn't the right time, especially there in front of her dad. And quite frankly, I wasn't actually sure that she loved me back. Deborah was such an independent person, and the idea of being tied to someone too tightly might have scared her a little. I mentioned the idea of marriage a few times over the next few weeks just to test the waters, and I could tell that those waters were shark infested. She would need to be fully mentally prepared before I could safely and sincerely ask her again, and I definitely planned to do that before the baby came.

In fact, I thought that Deborah and I were a little like those two mismatched taillights on my father's Buick. We weren't the same, and maybe we didn't belong together, but we were in the same car and headed in the same direction. Okay, maybe I'm not very good with metaphors.

CHAPTER 15

The River (Bruce Springsteen, 1980)

Bruce Springsteen's fifth studio album, *The River*, came out the same year Deborah got pregnant, and I played it constantly. It was a double album that had some really happy songs like "Hungry Heart" and "Out on the Street" and some very sad songs like "Wreck on the Highway" and the title song, "The River," which was, by far, my favorite song on the album. It was about a young couple, like me and Deborah, who got pregnant at a very young age. Bruce sang, "And for my nineteenth birthday, I got a union card and a wedding coat." The relationship in the song was doomed from the start, and the protagonist would go down to the river to deal with his sorrows. Man, I loved that song, but I didn't want that to be the same sad story for Deborah and me.

My job that summer was simple. I cut grass. I got up at seven and got home at seven, and in between, I cut more grass than I ever knew existed. It dawned on me how stupid it was that people spent so much time and money manicuring a little green plant, so it made their front yard look just like everyone else's.

"I want you to get rid of every dandelion and shred of crabgrass on my lawn. You got that young man?" one customer told me before we unloaded our equipment from the truck.

"Yes, sir. No crabgrass and no dandelions. Got it."

But what the heck was wrong with crabgrass and dandelions? Those little yellow flowers, in my opinion, were pretty, and if you pulled out all the lumps of crabgrass, most yards would look like they had been hit with napalm. But I did what they asked, and we poured poisonous weed killer and other chemicals all over their lawn to make it even more green than it should be. It's remarkable that all the neighborhood pets did not keel over from the toxic chemicals we sprayed—everywhere. And how did they cut all that grass before the lawn mower was invented? The entire thing seemed kind of crazy to me, and I vowed that my future house would have a dirt lawn and lots of concrete to park my numerous classic automobiles.

My job was exhausting, but I was actually getting into the best shape of my life. I had gotten the job through a friend of Danny's who needed someone to do the manual mowing (not the kind where you sat on a cutting machine that moved you). I was also the one on our crew who hauled the large bags of grass out to the truck as Shaker Heights ordinances would not allow us to put the bags out front or dump the grass in the woods behind the house. Hauling grass around and out to the street was the hardest part of my job, but it was putting some almost impressive muscles on my otherwise weakly frame.

"You are finally getting some good defmo, my brother," Danny said to me one night over dinner.

I was eating a hamburger, and Danny was eating something… well, I didn't know what it was, but he probably got it at his *nuts and more nuts* health-food store.

"What do you mean by defmo?" I asked.

"Definition, moron. You are getting buff. Toned."

"Yeah, so?"

"Yeah, well, now maybe you can get yourself out there and get some decent tang."

Danny had words that no one else used for things like *muscles* and *girls*, but strangely he expected everyone to know what he meant.

"Okay, I will bite. What is *tang*?" I asked him as he shoved a spoonful of what was probably spider and grub oatmeal into his mouth.

"Tang, brother. Tang. You know. Tang!"

"The orange drink that the astronauts drink in space?"

"No. Shit. Bitches. Fem-*al-eees*."

"Danny. Why don't you just say *girls* like a normal person?"

"What's the fun in that?" Danny asked.

"Well, I don't think Mom would appreciate you calling girls bitches."

"Fuck, man. You know what I mean?"

"Would you call Mom a bitch?" I asked sincerely. "Or a fem-*al-eeeeee*?"

"Fuck you, brother!" Danny shouted.

"I get all the girls I want, Danny Boy. I don't need def to get them."

"What bitches do you get, Sean? I only see you with that one, Deb-O-Nasty."

"Don't call her that, shithead."

"Why? Ain't she nasty? I heard she does the nasty."

I reached over angrily and pulled Danny by the collar of his two-sizes-too-small T-shirt.

"Call her that again and I will pound that disgusting swill you just ate right out of you."

"Easy there, Tarzana. Easy."

"See? Do you see what you do there? Why do you add the *a*? It's Tarzan. No *a*."

"What's the differ?"

"You are an idiot," I said, hoping to end the conversation.

This was typical of any exchange between Danny and me. We used a lot of words, but never really communicated anything of substance to each other. But this conversation didn't end there. Danny persisted, and it gave me the impression that he knew something was up with me and Deborah. But I had not told anyone anything—yet.

"You and this girl seem pretty tight. You dig draggin' on her?"

"Dig...wha...?"

"Licking her ass, shithead. Ain't you ever heard the term *dig draggin'*?"

"No. No one has. And no, I don't lick her ass. Who would do that? Disgusting!"

"Lots of people. Not me. But you are digging on her."

"I guess so. Why?"

"I don't know. There is plenty of girls in the pond. Are you really ready to settle down with just one fish?"

"Maybe," I replied.

"I'm not settling down until I got all the be-bop-a-doodle out of me."

"Yeah, well, that's you. And I am me," I said while swallowing a bite of my burger.

"I get that. I do. But you…what…you really like this bitch that much?"

"I do."

"That's cool. That's cool, brother. I feel what you are saying. You think she is the shits."

"The shits?"

We were quickly back to nonsense talk.

"Yeah. You know how good it feels to take a giant dump? This girl makes you feel that way," Danny said while putting another giant spoonful of garbage waste into his mouth.

"There is something seriously wrong with you, Danny. You know that. Right?"

"I'm happy for you, Sean-O. You know that. I'm your backstop."

"Again, *backstop*?"

"I got your back. I support your trail."

"I think we are done here," I said while standing and picking my plate up to go to the sink. "Please start eating normal food. I think your brain is turning to the shits."

"I'm taking stuff for my brain. You should too."

"What are you doing for your brain?"

"I told you this before. I take vitamins and supplements. And I do mental exercises. Like you said, we don't want to end up like Granddad did when he got demented."

Finally, a line of conversation that might benefit me in some way. But I must admit, I was scared to hear his answer.

"What is it you take?" I asked.

"I'll show you. I got an entire line of herbs and vitamins that increase your cognate ability."

"*Cognitive.* I think the word is *cognitive.* Father Dave told me that."

"Whatever. And when I am in bed at night, I also think of words to songs and poems. I memorize them, so I can use the muscles in my mind to keep mentally strong."

"You memorize poems?"

"Shit yeah, I do."

"What? Like limericks? There once was girl from Nantucket—"

"No. I do the good poems. Like Frost's 'Path Not Taken' or 'If' by Kipling. My favorite is 'Invictus.'"

I almost dropped my plate and silverware in total shock.

"You memorize real poems?"

"Yep. I even write some of my own sometimes."

This was like learning that Hercules did macramé and wore makeup. Suddenly, I saw my brother in an entirely new and quite impressive light.

"That's...that's awesome, Danny. I have written some poems myself, but Deborah asked me to stop reading them to her."

"That sucks, man."

"No, they are really bad, but I'd like to read some of your poems someday."

"Oh shit, no. Like you and your stupid notebooks, I don't share them. It's only for me. I don't want people to think I'm a candy drop."

And just like that, suddenly we were back to a normal Danny conversation.

"Okay, well, I gotta go to Deb's house. She should be home by now."

"All right, brother. Tell Debbie-O I said hey."

"You know if you ever call her that to her face, she will tear you to shreds?"

"You are scared as shit of her, aren't you?" he asked while he continued to stuff his face.

"Yes, I am," I replied.

CHAPTER 16

Meeting the Parents

After my virtual worthless conversation with Danny, I jumped into my Mustang to head over to Deborah's house. The summer was almost over, and she thought it would be a good idea for me to meet her parents before we sprang the big news on them. I was nervous and even combed my hair twice to make sure I didn't look too much like a felon. I put on a nice (clean) white shirt that I normally only wore to go to church. I did wear blue jeans, but I made sure there were no holes in them. I thought for a second about wearing something on my feet a little nicer than my Wallabees. Wallabees were a kind of cheap leather shoe that was something like a combination of a moccasin and a slipper. But they had shoelaces, and they were super comfortable. My only other option was some black penny loafers, but they had a hole in the bottom of both, so I opted for the Wallabees.

When I entered her house, Deborah simply opened the door and walked straight into the living room where her parents were sitting on two cushioned chairs across from a large colorfully patterned couch. Deborah was wearing a conservative and somewhat girly dress with pink flowers, which was nothing like what she would normally wear at school. The house also smelled a lot like Pine-Sol, but I assumed it was actually something nicer than floor cleaner that freshened the aroma of the place. The living area was a large well-lit room with really high-vaulted ceilings. I knew Deborah's family had money, and they clearly cared more about outward appearances than my folks. For example, they had what I assumed were original paintings (not prints) on the walls and two matching sculptures above the fireplace. I wasn't very knowledgeable on how homes should be decorated in those days, but I could tell this house was meticulously cared for in every respect.

Mr. Robbins was wearing a cardigan sweater, and it was buttoned up to the top button. Mrs. Robbins had a dress on that resembled the one that Deborah was wearing. I wondered if that was a coincidence or on purpose on Deborah's part.

"Hello, Mr. and Mrs. Robbins," I began politely. "Nice to see you, and thanks again for having me over here. This house is super nice and I'm really nervous in case you couldn't tell."

"Have a seat, Sean. Relax a bit. We are glad you could join us for dinner," Mrs. Robbins said sweetly as we moved into the living room and sat on the patterned sofa that looked like a jungle full of flowers, vines and giant green leaves.

I looked curiously at Deborah as she had not mentioned eating a meal as part of the evening's agenda. And I knew immediately that this was also way more than just a simple introduction to a new boyfriend. I was being evaluated for the suitability of dating their daughter. Deborah had not properly prepared me for this, and it made me even more nervous. At this new level of nervousness, I would no longer be thinking rationally, and that could be very dangerous.

"Sean, we understand you are studying business at SOU," Mr. Robbins said.

I looked at Debbie and then over at the Robbins's before wiping my sweaty hands off on my blue jeans.

"Well, it's sort of like business. I am thinking of going into the car business after school, like my dad."

"Oh, that is interesting. Your father works...where?" Mrs. Robbins asked.

"He works at the Ford dealership here in Shaker, Bud Larson Ford."

"Oh really? I know Bud Larson. Nice guy," Mr. Robbins said.

"I've never met him. My father thinks he is kind of a jerk sometimes."

Uh-oh. Not good. I had to retract that statement.

"But I'm sure he is just a tough boss. Ha ha," I said nervously in retreat.

Deborah gave me a panicked calm-down look, and I wiped my now-sweating forehead with my already-sweating hand.

"Deborah tells us that you two knew each other in high school," her mother said.

"Oh yeah, but not really. I went to Shaker, but I saw her at a dance once, and I thought she was amazing. She didn't like me much back then, but I can be very persistent. She thought my name was Steve, but I stalked her for a solid year at college, and then she finally agreed to go out with me."

I thought this had sounded fairly humorous, but it didn't get the desired reaction from anyone, especially Deborah.

"I knew him. I called him Steve because he called me Debbie, which I hate. Plus, he hung out with idiots, so I mostly ignored them."

"My friends were idiots?" I asked in surprise.

"I see," Mrs. Robbins said.

"So something smells really good in there," I said, looking toward what I thought was the kitchen. "What's cookin'?"

"What's the difference?" Deborah shot back curtly.

"I don't know. I was just asking. I'm sorry, but I'm…well, I'm hungry or at least my stomach is. But anything is fine with me," I said while nervously shifting my position on the couch. I couldn't tell for sure, but I think Deborah had subtly moved farther away from me over the past few minutes.

"No need to be nervous, son. It's not like you are here to ask us for permission to marry our Little Debbie," Mr. Robbins said with a smile.

"Oh, that's great. I get it," I said, chuckling.

"You get what?" Mr. Robbins asked.

"Like the Little Debbie snack cakes! I get it! No wonder she doesn't like to be called Debbie," I said, referring to the Little Debbie line of sugary baked treats that looked exactly like the twinkies and Ho-Hos from Hostess.

"What is he talking about?" Mr. Robbins asked harshly.

"Dad!" Deborah shouted.

"I'm just trying to ascertain his intentions," Mr. Robbins said.

"Don't worry about that," I said, feeling a small sense of relief. "I won't be marrying your daughter anytime soon. She already said no to me a couple of times, actually."

Okay, there it was. It had come out so effortlessly, but I knew immediately it was a very, very wrong thing to say.

"Are you serious? Why on earth would you two be talking about marriage?" Mrs. Robbins asked.

Her father knew instantly why it was, and a few seconds later, her mother knew it too.

"We're not, Mom. Sean is just trying to be funny. Right, Sean?"

"She never thinks I am funny," I said while wiping my sweaty hands off on my shirt this time.

No one said anything meaningful after that, but this might have gone down as one of the most stressful evenings of my life. The gaps in conversation were torturous, and I didn't think I could taste the food at all. I tried to hold Deborah's hand under the table, but she jerked it away angrily both times. After a quick dessert, Mrs. Robbins started clearing the dishes, and I stood up thinking that the torment of the evening from hell was finally over.

"Do either of you drink coffee?" Mrs. Robbins asked.

"No!" Debbie shot out a little too quickly. "No thanks, Mom. It's just that Sean and I have to...well, we have to go to a friend's house."

"Oh really. Whose house?" Mr. Robbin's asked.

"One of my idiot friends," I said.

Debbie didn't react quickly enough, so I offered up a lie that could not have been more obvious.

"We are meeting my...friend...Barry. He has a new girlfriend... and we are going to...meet her...wait...them. We are going to go meet them at Barry's house. He was my freshman roommate, but he flunked out. I live with a guy named Wayne now, and he smokes a pipe. Just regular tobacco, though. Not any of that funny stuff."

There! That was enough to get us out of there for sure, but for some inexplicable reason, I kept talking.

"Don't get me wrong. I'm not a pot smoker. I've only ever tried it a few times, but I didn't like it much. I ate an entire pizza that night by myself."

Great. Completely unnecessary and damaging information that probably brought my suitability rating down near zero. It was abundantly clear from this evening. I was not the type of man that Deborah's parents wanted for their daughter. From what I had just said, I don't blame them, but they really hadn't gotten to know the real me. They certainly didn't think I was funny, smart, or witty. I hadn't told them anything about my passions for drawing, designing, and cars or that I still wrote everything I did down in little notebooks so I could remember things better. They didn't know that I was madly in love with their daughter either, which I would think would be the most important thing in evaluating a potential suitor.

No, I had flunked this test or personnel evaluation in the worst way, and I knew it. Worst of all, Deborah knew it. This combined with the fact that I had inadvertently told Debbie's parents that she was pregnant meant that the worst part of the evening was still to come.

"What kind of moron says things like that?" Deborah said while angrily swiping her hand across my shoulder on the way to the car.

I held the door of the Mustang open, but Deborah slammed it shut before I could close it for her. As I walked around to the other side of the car, I actually thought about taking off on foot and simply running away right then and there. It wasn't a bad idea and might have been better than what happened next. I got in the car, and the windshield was already steamed up from Deborah's intense red-hot anger. It didn't take much to get a car windshield steamy in those days, but this was the quickest I had ever witnessed it. She was furious and about to blow her top.

"For one thing, you don't ask the hostess what they are serving you for dinner. You eat what they make for you. Don't you know anything?"

"Uh…I just thought it smelled good."

"And what? You think my father wants to know how many forks a Pontiac Ventura has?"

"It's called torque. And you do know that torque is different than horsepower. Right?"

"Is there a gun anywhere in this car?"

"Seriously, Deb. My father explained this to me. Horsepower is how a car achieves its speed, but torque is how it feels. You know that feeling when the speed of the car pushes you back in your seat? That is torque."

"Nobody cares."

"Well, he should. He said he was thinking about buying a Cadillac Seville for Mrs. Robbins and I advised him against it. Sevilles are basically the same as a Chevy Nova and you might as well get one of those with a V-8 and save the extra bucks."

"Sean, I don't know what to say. You know what you did back there? Do you know what I am in for when I get home?"

"I'm sorry. I really am. I was so nervous. I will do better next time, Deb."

"And what did I tell you about calling me Deb or Debbie or Debs? I hate it. Call me Deborah or nothing at all. Got it?"

"Can I call you babe? I like babe."

"I already want to murder you. Don't make it worse."

I pulled out into the street and started driving down Shelbourne Road, but I had no idea where I was going. Deborah just sat there wringing her hands together, and I noticed that she wasn't wearing her seat belt.

"Uh, Deborah, if you don't mind," I said, looking down at her lap, "your seat belt."

"Are you kidding me?" she responded.

When Deborah turned toward me, I honestly feared for my life. I loved this girl, but she sure didn't have much of a soft side. First, I was the one way more likely to cry at a sad or romantic movie. She claimed that she hated my soft side, too, but she seemed to like that I that sent cards and funny drawings to her. She never did any of that kind of stuff in return. She had never even said that she liked me.

As we drove along one of the winding streets in Shaker Heights, I started to wonder why she even went out with me. We didn't like the same music or movies, and she certainly had no interest in car design, football uniforms or horsepower. Why did she like me? I wanted to know. I needed to know, but now was not the time to bring it up or pursue it. The fact was, this girl and I were going to have a baby together. And I knew it would be up to me to keep us together until that day came.

CHAPTER 17

Potty Humor

My mother was making my favorite meal one night, and I was scarfing down taco after taco. She made them with the best ground beef and something called Ro-Tel Tomatoes. We used warm and crisp hard-shell corn tortillas and tons and tons of sharp shredded cheddar cheese. Add a spoonful of sour cream on top, and you had what was a masterpiece of south of the border flavors. I love tacos! In later years, my mother started using ground turkey meat instead of ground beef to give my father a healthier option. I didn't like them nearly as much with turkey meat, but I could still eat six of them at a sitting. And I salted the crap out of them. My guess is that each taco was at least 250 calories, so this was not a low-calorie meal. Danny, of course, opted instead to have one of his GNC protein concoctions, which smelled like a combination of sweat socks and cat barf. But he did stuff it all into a taco shell.

"You need to slow down, Sean. It's not good for your digestion to eat so fast," my mother said.

"That's true, Sean-O," Danny said through a mouthful of his swill.

"What?" I mumbled.

"She said not to eat like a pig, shithead," Danny added.

"Shut up!" I shouted, which caused half of the taco shell in my mouth to fly out and onto the table.

"Gross!" Danny shouted. "No wonder Debbie-O's parents hated you."

"Sean! If your father was sitting here, he would have smacked you for that!" my mother scolded.

"Dennis!" my mother shouted toward the ceiling. "Get down here. The food is getting cold, and the boys are being pills again."

I am not sure why my mother referred to us as *pills*, but that was the term she used, and I think it is a synonym for *idiot*. And we were, and it was my father that was tasked with disciplining us. The truth was my father was a hitter. And I don't mean that in a child abuse kind of way. He only smacked us with the back of his right hand, and we always deserved it. We were also spanked a lot as younger boys, and I do believe that if Danny hadn't been corporally punished, he would be dead today.

"This is going to hurt you more than it is going to hurt me," my father once said erroneously before giving me a swat with the wooden paddle he kept under the bed. I knew he meant his statement to be exactly the opposite, but there was no way on God's green earth that I would have corrected him right before being spanked.

"Seriously, Sean. I hope you didn't stuff yourself like that when you ate at the Robbinses' house the other night," my mother said as my father walked in and sat at the table.

As my father put his napkin in his lap, he gave Danny and me the look he usually gave us before he hit us.

"I didn't eat like a pig if that is what you mean," I replied to my mom. "I was super nervous, and truthfully, I didn't like the food that much. I mostly just pushed it around on my plate."

"Oh really?" my mother said excitedly. "You didn't like her cooking?"

My mother was a good cook and put a lot of effort into her dinners, but the dinners were always planned and prepared with my father in mind. He liked all of them, but for me, it was a hit-or-miss proposition. There were simply some dishes I couldn't stand. But my father was an enthusiastic supporter of my mother's cooking even though he often made some small suggestions.

"This could use a little more chili powder," my father said when tasting his meat loaf one night.

"I think you may be right," my mother responded, and from that point on, her meat loaf was seasoned so heavily with chili powder that I could hardly stand the smell of it. Both Danny and I would scrape the seasoning off the surface of the meat dish the best we could. Danny would also remove the onions one by one before even taking a bite. Danny didn't like onions in anything, and he told my mother that constantly. But as long as my father liked them, there were going to be onions in our food.

"What did you talk about with the Robbinses?" my mother asked before gently scooping a small spoonful of buttered corn up from her plate. I think there were like only three kernels of corn on the spoon. For me, that would almost not be worth the effort. Both my father and I would use our knife or fork to help load up the spoon with the appropriate amount of corn before shoveling it into our mouths. Danny would use his fingers, of course.

"They mostly asked me about school and stuff. Her dad seemed to want to know a lot about what I wanted to do with my life…with my job and everything."

"Hmm," my father said quietly.

"What? What else were they going to talk about with me?"

"Sounds like they were sizing you up," my mother said. "They must think this thing with Deborah is getting serious. Is it?"

"I don't know," I said. "It's only been a year or so with her and…I don't know."

"He's in loooove," Danny said.

"Shut up, doofus!"

"Boys!" my father said. "Do we have to do this every night?"

"Yes. I think we do," I responded although I know my father meant that question as rhetorical.

"Well, is it?" my mother asked.

"Is it what?" I asked.

"Is it getting serious?"

"Jesus, Mom. I just told you. I guess so. I'm not seeing anyone else, if that is what you mean."

"That means he is only doing it with her," Danny said while snickering.

"Danny, that's enough from you," my father said.

"Let's talk about something else," I pleaded.

"Maybe we should have her come over here for dinner. Seems like we should. Don't you think so?" my mother asked.

"Does Danny have to be here?" I asked.

"No, he does not," my father said abruptly.

"Then I will see what she says," I responded.

"She has a younger sister named Caroline, right? Bring her along," Danny said again through a mouthful of food.

"Stay away from her sister, Danny. I mean it!"

"You can't make me do that. I see her at Hawken games all the time. She is a cheerleader and has great pipes."

"Oh my god. What planet did you come from?" I asked.

"That's it. I'm done," my father said as he threw his napkin down on the table.

This was pretty much a typical dinner session at our house. Looking back now, I feel a little sorry for my mother. She would read cookbooks, plan out the meal, shop for the perfect ingredients, coordinate the timing of the main dish and all the side courses, and within five minutes, it would all be gone. All that would remain was the nightly arguing and banter between me and Danny. Yet night after night, my mother must have hoped that the next meal might go better and that someone might sincerely thank her appropriately for the effort.

"Good grub, Ma," Danny said as he took his plate and glass to the sink. I watched him as he walked out, and he looked back at me and did that thing with his finger going through the *o* made on the other hand. This was the *doing intercourse* symbol, of course, and I resisted getting up and going after him. Instead, I looked at my mother as she continued eating. Her plate was still almost full of food.

"Can I ask you something, Mom?"

"Sure, honey. What is it?"

"Well, I am just having some issues with Deborah right now. And..."

"What? What is it, dear?" my mother said eagerly while politely chewing.

"It's just that...well, she's just not that nice to me. I mean, there are times when I think she doesn't even like me. And yet here we are, still together. I guess I...I don't get it."

My mother carefully wiped her mouth with her napkin and leaned back in her chair as if what she was about to tell me was the secret to success in all relationships. Maybe it was, actually.

"Women are a mystery wrapped in a riddle, son."

"That's the dang truth," my father said as he also took his plates and utensils to the sink.

Okay, that wasn't going to be much help, so I persisted in questioning her.

"What does that mean?"

"It means you have to read the signs," she said confidently.

"I know when a girl hits you playfully on the arm, that is a sign that they like you. Right?"

"Yes. It sure is."

"Yeah, well when Deborah does it, it really hurts."

"Hmm," my mother muttered.

"And she never—and I mean, she never—laughs at anything I say. At least not anymore."

"Well, that's not good. Are you being appropriate, or is it silly potty humor?"

"Potty humor?" I asked.

"You know. Poo poo. Pee pee. Potty humor."

"Mom, I'm twenty years old. You know that, right?"

"I heard you two boys arguing the other day. You were angry at Danny for smelling up the bathroom, and he was just laughing and laughing."

"Mom, I think that crap he eats is slowly killing him. It is not a normal smell."

"I would suggest with Deborah that you just listen to her. It sounds like she is going through something difficult in her life and… well, she is taking it out on you."

Wow! That made total sense.

"So I just listen?" I asked.

"Yes. And don't try to solve her problems. Just let her tell you what is going on in her life and say supportive things in response."

"Like what?"

"You could say…um…'That must be really tough' or 'What do you think you can do about it' or…"

"Or what can I do to help her?" I added.

"No. No, Sean. That is the opposite of what you should say."

"But what if she asks me directly? What I am going to do to help?"

"Don't answer that. It is a trick question," my mother said. "You have to be very careful how you respond here."

"Like how? This is tough, Mom. What? I don't answer her at all?"

"You do, but in a subtle way, you don't. When she asks you what she should do, you nod supportively and…I don't know…rub her hand, but you don't give her a suggestion or offer to do anything."

"Man, women are—"

"Complicated," my mother interrupted.

"I was going to say nuts."

"And don't ever say anything like that to her."

"I know, I know," I said as I got up to leave.

"Thanks, Mom."

"Sean, you know you can talk to me about it if you want. This problem you and she are having, maybe we can just sit down and talk it through."

"Didn't we just do that?" I said as I carefully placed my dishes in the sink. Sadly, none of us ever thought to stay and help my mother clean up. I regret that now.

"Oh, and thanks for dinner. It was really good."

There! That wasn't so hard.

125

CHAPTER 18

Astroturf

For some reason, Deborah did not want me to come to her first prenatal doctor's appointment, and I saw that as a very bad sign. Her mother accompanied her on that visit, and I only heard about it later over the phone. When Deborah called, I had my notebook ready to write down all the pertinent information. I was getting more and more excited and really wanted to know what was actually happening there in Deborah's tummy. I was also making a list of girls' and boys' baby names so I would be ready for that conversation when the time was right.

Maybe it was a way to deal with my nerves, but I had also been doing a lot of drawing in my notebooks. And my latest objects of interest were stadiums. I loved arenas and spectator structures and drew all kinds of different versions for various sports. My interest probably started with an article I read in *National Geographic* on what was once the largest and most well-known sports stadium in the world—the Roman Colosseum. The fact that most of this building is still standing today is simply incredible. It has to be the most famous building ever, and I just loved the way it looked. It is a large oval shape and was even used to recreate battles at sea by flooding the place. I couldn't wait to go see it someday.

Coincidentally, in the 1970s, a large number of US cities were constructing what they now call concrete doughnuts that actually resembled the Colosseum. These were multipurpose stadiums that could be used for both the city's professional football and baseball teams. Like the arena in Rome, these new stadiums were also used for concerts and other sporting events. (No gladiator battles anymore, unfortunately.) The most notable of the sparkling modern concrete stadiums were

- Riverfront Stadium (Cincinnati)
- Three Rivers Stadium (Pittsburgh)
- Veterans Stadium (Philadelphia)

One very interesting thing about these three stadiums was that they all had artificial turf or, essentially, plastic grass. In those days, this turf was basically a gigantic plastic floor mat placed over a hard cement surface. The turf had seams where the mats would come together, so the fields were literally rolled out before events. I suppose this made it easier to convert the playing field from one sport to another, but it was an absolutely terrible surface to play sports on. In baseball, the hit balls could literally bounce over the wall. That rarely, if ever, happens on grass. Football players hated the hard surface, which, I am sure, contributed greatly to the large number of concussions each year. And the stadium that started the fake playing field phenomenon was my second all-time favorite building—the Harris County Domed Stadium, better known as the Astrodome.

My father's family was from Houston, and we visited there a lot when I was a kid. On one occasion, my father's brother had an engineering role in the building of the new domed stadium, and he asked if we wanted to come see the building while it was still under construction.

"Heck yes!" was my response.

I don't think Danny cared, but we all went, and what I saw is one of my favorite memories of my entire childhood. The place was just amazing. It was as modern as any building I had ever seen, and it was just enormous. At that point of construction, they had not yet laid the field, so the floor of the dome was just a large expanse of light brown dirt. The original plan was to lay a grass baseball field that the newly named Astros professional team would play on. The fabled

New York Yankees, with Micky Mantle, would be the first visiting team (preseason) to play in this majestic edifice.

The initial plan was to have real growing grass inside the dome by having over 4,500 translucent panels in the domed roof. That way the grass could get the sunlight it needed through the windows, but the temperature inside would always to be a comfortable seventy-two degrees. One of the first things my uncle showed us were the enormous cooling tanks or air conditioners on the outside of the stadium. They were like man-made waterfalls, and you could actually see the water cascading down inside the structures. Another highlight was the giant computer-controlled scoreboard, which had lights that could produce (for the time) remarkable animation. If a home team player hit a home run, the scoreboard would light up with fireworks that would progress up and down the walls beyond the outfield. For a kid like me, this tour was like being on board the *Titanic* before its maiden voyage. They even called the stadium the Eighth Wonder of the World, and to me, it truly was.

But trouble very soon followed for those teams playing inside the dome. Tragically, for day games, the glare off the large glass panels made it nearly impossible to follow the high fly balls once they got up into the air. The solution, they thought, for this problem was to paint the windows with some kind of tint. Essentially, they attempted to make the 4,500 glass panels act like giant sunglasses. Well, that did work for eliminating the glare, but it also eliminated the process of photosynthesis needed to keep the grass growing. The grass was already dying when they played the first exhibition game against the Yankees. This was just not going to work, and they needed another surface solution quickly.

Monsanto, at the time, was working with a synthetic grass that could be used on playgrounds in large cities like New York. Without a lot of time to spare, the stadium executives ordered up a large amount of this fake grass and put it where the real grass would have grown. It looked great but, again, more problems. The seams that held the fake grass in place on the dirt were problematic in the areas that transitioned from the outfield grass to the dirt of the infield. Grounders would be rolling along nicely but would jump in the air and shoot right or left once the ball hit the seam. Errors would be far too numerous, so they tried to just paint the outfield dirt green, but that looked horrible, and green paint got on everything and everyone. Without enough time to figure out a better solution, they went with the best option they had, and Astroturf was born.

I still remember the first game I saw there, and it was nothing like any sporting event I had ever been to in my life. There were large speakers hanging down from the roof that loudly played music like "The Yellow Rose of Texas" to the appreciative home fans. The roof did leak when it rained at times, but they were able to play a full home baseball season that year indoors for the first time in history. The temperature outside could be as high as one hundred degrees, but it was comfortably cool inside. Another exciting thing they did there was to dress all the groundskeepers in astronaut uniforms with space helmets. They would all come running out during the seventh-inning stretch to rake the dirt and replace the bases like they do in most outdoor stadiums. Just an amazing sight for a young boy. I don't think I even watched the game.

"Maybe that is what I will do with my life," I said to Danny. "I'll design sports stadiums."

"Yeah, sure, Sean-O. Like you could build a building. Dream on."

"I could do it. Look here," I said, showing Danny some of my crude drawings of stadiums and the associated team uniforms, too, of course.

"All these drawings look exactly the same," Danny said while flipping through page after page of domed stadium concepts. "They all look like igloos. Are your teams all going to play in igloos? Won't it be a bit cold?"

Danny laughed heartily, tossed my notebook in the air, and walked away. He was partially right. They all did pretty much look like igloos, but I enjoyed drawing them and even naming them things like the Monster Dome or Futura Dome and my favorite name of all, the World Dome. Cleveland desperately needed a new stadium for its professional teams, and of all places that needed a dome to eliminate harsh weather conditions, it was Cleveland. We really do have about nine months of winter up here followed by a week of spring and six weeks of summer and a fall season that seemed an awfully lot like winter. No, Cleveland would need a domed stadium, and the name I had for that one was the Snow Dome.

I was eager to share my stadium ideas with Deborah the next time I saw her, but my next discussion with her would not be in person. And it was a call that would potentially change my life forever.

"Hello, Sean. Do you have a few minutes to talk now?" Deborah asked as I prepared myself for what I figured would be an intense conversation.

"Sure. I got all the time in the world for you, babe."

"For Christ's sake, Sean," Deborah shot back. "You know I hate that babe crap."

"Sorry. What's up?"

"I went to the doctor today."

"You did? Without me again? Why?"

"Because I am pregnant, and that is what pregnant women do," she added curtly.

I was starting to tire a bit of Deborah's acerbic reactions to my innocent and well-intentioned questions.

"Huh? Well, okay. I wish I had come along, but what did the doctor say?"

"Everything is okay in there. I just need to take it easy now. Sixth-month mark, you know?"

"No. I don't know. What does that mean? Exactly?" I asked as I prepared to jot down notes on what the doctor had to say.

"Well, for one, he doesn't want me riding horses anymore. Not this summer anyway."

I had a gigantic "I told you so" all locked and loaded, but I kept it in the holster. Thank God.

"He said I was fine but that I should not get worked up or too stressed about anything," she said.

"Okay. What does that mean?" I asked.

"Well, I spoke with my mother and father, and we have decided that I am going to keep all this under wraps until the baby is born," Deborah said. "I hope that is okay with you."

I was immediately struck by the fact that by *we*, she meant her and her parents, not me.

"So I can't tell anyone?"

"Not a soul, Sean. Do you think you can do that?"

"Sure, but why? You will have to go out sometime, and people will see you. They will see the…uh…bump. And then there will be a baby. They are going to know. Right?"

"We just don't want people in town talking about this until after the baby is born. My father is nervous that it will hurt his business."

"Yeah, well, your dad is a d—"

"I'll have the baby on my own, and I will raise it," Debbie interjected just in time. "You don't have to do a thing, except keep your mouth shut."

As she said this, I had to sit down as it felt as if I had just been shot with a bazooka. The best I could grasp from this conversation so far was that I, the father, was not needed anymore. I was stunned.

"Aren't you going to say anything?" Deborah asked after a long and very awkward pause.

"Umm…I don't know what to say."

"Good. Don't say anything," she said. "That's probably smart."

"Wait. I do have some questions."

"Uh-oh. Like what?"

"Well, first, what is my role once the kid is born? I'm still the baby's father. Right? I will have a role in raising him. It is my kid too."

"Sean, I don't think that is such a good idea. I mean, I can handle it on my own. My parents will help me, and I will eventually get someone to watch the kid when I go back to work. But for now, my parents and I are going to handle everything."

The words stung and hurt so badly that I wanted to burst into tears. Mostly, I knew her words meant something else. It meant that Deborah and I were, for all intents and purposes, over.

"Don't I have a say in any of this?" I asked.

"Sure, but I have pretty much decided that this will be the best for everyone. For you too, Sean."

"How can you know that without even talking to me about it? Are you still mad at me that I accidently told your parents about the baby when I was there at dinner?"

"No, Sean. I have had time to go over all the options, and this one is the best."

"So my role with this baby is…what…nothing?"

After another long pause, Deborah finally spoke, and I didn't think there was anything that could have properly prepared me for what she said.

"Look, Sean. I really like you. You are a great guy. But this all happened accidently…you know, this baby…and everything. We are both too young to get married or anything like that. This will be good for you. You can go back to school like you wanted and get that…I don't know…sport uniform drawing degree."

"I'm drawing stadiums now."

"Whatever," Deborah responded.

"I don't care about college. You know that. I was just thinking out loud when I said that. I just want to be with you and the…you know…the…"

"I'm sorry, Sean."

Of all the scenarios I had imagined, the only one I never considered was that I would not be involved at all with this baby. I didn't know how to respond, and I could feel tears welling up in my eyes.

"Deb, please. Let's talk about this. Please."

"I can't talk anymore about this now. Sorry. I have to go," she said and then hung up without even a goodbye. This time, hanging up without saying goodbye didn't seem cool to me at all. It was downright mean.

I hung up the phone slowly and decided for some reason that I would take a bike ride to try to clear my head. It was just a few minutes past seven o'clock, and there would plenty of light for a nice long ride. I had showered after I got home from work, so I was wearing some red sweatpants and a blue T-shirt with a Dallas Cowboys logo on the front. It was probably my favorite shirt and was at least two sizes too large, so it was super comfortable. I slipped on some tennis shoes and took my slightly rusted Schwinn five speed out of the garage and started pedaling. I had so many thoughts and questions competing for attention in my brain that I was almost comatose. After ten minutes or so of peddling aimlessly, I was a little unsure of where I was and soon found myself riding down one of the main arteries in the city instead of the safer roads by my house. Shaker Heights is famous for streets that go in one direction and then curve around to go another. I think it was designed like that on purpose to keep outsiders from speeding through our community to get somewhere else.

There is also an intersection in our city that used to be considered one of the most dangerous in the entire country. It is where the major streets of Warrensville Center Road met up with two other major streets, Chagrin Boulevard and Van Aken Parkway. Northfield Road also intersected here at a forty-five-degree angle, but it only went in one direction. Before they shut off access to Northfield and Van Aken (many years later), even local residents could become confused as to who got to proceed through the intersection and when. There were lights and signals everywhere, but they were not properly staged, and the number of accidents here was legendary. And there was about to be another one.

I stopped my bike on Warrensville, with the intention of turning left onto Chagrin, when the light facing me turned green. I stood up on my bike where I was supposed to stop, I think, and then I pointed my arm left to indicate I would be turning onto Chagrin Boulevard. There was a turning lane and a turning light that signaled to me that it was my turn to proceed. But as I did, I saw a large car coming toward me, and I could tell that it was not going to yield to my turn. I got hit squarely by the oncoming vehicle and was thrown at least fifty feet, landing headfirst on the astroturf-hard pavement. I was knocked out immediately, but I do remember the last thought I had before being struck by that car. It was a Ford.

CHAPTER 19

Getting Toothpaste Back in the Tube

When I tell people my favorite season of the year, it almost always surprises them. My family is originally from Texas, so you would think that a cold weather city in winter would be a nightmare for me. But strangely, cold and snowy winter days are always my favorite. It's like God's way of putting makeup on the earth. The snow hides blemishes like dead patches in the yard and trees that are either dead or partially dead. The snow on the roofs of houses makes them seem friendlier, especially if you can see a plume of white smoke rising up from the chimney. That means that someone inside is warming themselves in front of a roaring fire and probably enjoying a mug of hot cocoa. I know I am describing a Norman Rockwell painting to be sure, but I would never want to live anywhere without a winter season.

When I awoke in the hospital, it was sunny outside and seemed to be a typical summer day. I could see from my bed the scaffolding for the hospital extension that was going up right next door. I reached up and felt that my head was bandaged, and I could see that I had a cast on one leg and a bandaged arm in a sling. There was a large man in an orange vest pounding on something outside on the roof, and with each *kabang* of his jackhammer, my head felt like it was about to split apart. I looked around the hospital room, which was large but otherwise unremarkable. There was a plastic pitcher of what was probably water on the table next to me. I was hooked up at a monitor that seemed like it was indicating that my vitals were normal. I assumed that, since there were no bells or buzzers going off, I was going to live.

"Are you awake, Mr. Stevens?" a voice gently asked while slowly opening the door.

"I am," I responded.

An attractive young Latino woman in a white hospital nursing uniform entered and approached me.

"We were wondering when you might rejoin the land of the living," she said with a smile.

"Uh...yeah. Here I am! I'm alive, I guess. What happened to me?"

"You were struck by an automobile, Mr. Stevens. You have been here with us for three days now."

"Oh shit! I mean shoot! And I am going to be all right? Up here, I mean?" I said while pointing at my head.

"It appears that you are," the nurse said while tapping on a plastic tube that led to a bottle of liquid hanging on a mobile IV pole. There was an IV connection going into my right hand, and she secured the tape around it. I don't know why, but it felt really good to be touched.

"Is there anything I can get for you? Are you hungry?"

"I don't feel hungry. But I will eat something if you think I should."

"Okay. Let me check what the doctor has approved for you. I will be right back," she said as she turned to leave.

"Excuse me," I said, loud enough to stop the nurse as she approached the door.

"Yes?"

"I am a little confused here, Nurse," I said.

"About what?" she asked as she took a step toward me.

"I don't...uh...I don't exactly know what is going on. I mean, where the heck am I?"

"Oh, Mr. Stevens, I am sorry. I should have told you. You are at University Hospital. You have a few broken bones as you can see and have what looks like some fairly serious head trauma."

"Oh. Oh, okay. Thanks."

"The doctor will give you more detail. My name is Viviana. I am your day nurse."

"Yeah, you see. That's the thing. Who am I? What's my name, I mean?"

The nurse came a step closer to me and looked me over carefully.

"You aren't sure who you are?"

"Not really. I mean, I can see that I am a boy and most of me is a real mess."

"And you don't know your name?"

"You called me Mr. Stevens. I assume that is my last name. That's about all I know."

"I'm so sorry."

"But this is temporary. Right? Maybe after I get something to eat, it will all come back to me."

"I'm not a doctor, but I do know that you have a contusion. And the impact has apparently impacted your cerebral function. I will go get your doctor. He will want to know about this right away. This could be a sign that there is excessive bleeding, and that…well, that is not good."

The kindly young nurse rushed out of the room, and I reached up again to feel the bandage that was covering most of my head. It was only a few minutes later when the doctor arrived. He walked in and came straight over to my bed and picked up my chart. I found it odd that he didn't say anything or introduce himself until he read through the entire contents of the file.

"I'm Dr. Moore, and I am one of the physicians overseeing your case."

"Nice to meet you, Doctor. Am I a going to be all right?" I asked.

"Nurse, let's get a MRI and EEG scheduled right away. I want to be sure we aren't dealing with something much more serious here."

"Uh, Doctor, what is going on? What is wrong with me?" I asked.

"We don't know yet. Obviously, we are dealing with some level of amnesia."

"Oh, I see. No, wait. No, I don't. Amnesia is when you forget who you are. Right? And I have that?"

"Well, we don't know yet. Sometimes, a contusion can cause hemorrhaging…and that is bad. We can't have that."

"What is hemorrhaging?"

"It's bleeding on the brain, except the blood has nowhere to go within the skull. So it can cause things like amnesia or memory loss. Sometimes it is temporary and sometimes is isn't."

"That sucks!" I said while adjusting the sheets on my bed to cover my chest.

The doctor came closer and put his hand on my good arm. It was a gesture of comfort, but it also meant "Relax, you are going to be here awhile."

"You seem to be talking fine. Do you have any numbness? Is there anything you can't move?"

"Other than my leg and arm and the majority of my body?"

"I see what you mean," the doctor said while picking back up my chart and making some notes.

"Do you know what month it is?" he asked as he continued to flip pages in the chart.

"I have no idea except that it looks like warm weather outside. And I wish that one guy would put his shirt back on," I said, looking out the window at a large hairy man holding a welding gun.

"How about the year? Do you know what year it is?" the doctor asked while placing the chart back in the bed pocket.

"Don't you know?" I asked, joking, but he just looked at me with a stern look that meant I needed to take this seriously.

I looked around the room, hoping that some spark would help tell me what year it was. But I had no idea.

"Come back after I eat something. Maybe I will know by then."

"I will do that. But you are about to have a very busy day. Lots of tests! We need to know right away what is going on up there," he said while adjusting the bandage on my head.

"Okay. Thanks, Doc."

"No problem," he said as he walked off.

The nurse approached me, and she had a very nice smile on her face, which gave me great comfort for the moment.

"You are going to be just fine, Mr. Stevens. We will take good care of you. Until five o'clock, that is. The night shift is pretty awful," Viviana said with a smile.

"Ha! Thanks," I said. I appreciated the sarcastic humor. It reminded me of someone, but I couldn't think who.

"You are very welcome," she said as she patted me gently on the arm. "Get some rest, and I will let you know as soon as they are ready for you in imaging."

"Okay, Vivian."

"My name is Viviana. Just add an *a* and you got it."

"It's good that I almost remembered your name. Right? Can you tell me my first name and the year so I can mess with the doctor when he comes back?"

"Your first name is Sean. And I wouldn't do that. Dr. Woodson literally has no sense of humor, and he won't like it."

"Oh, okay. Thanks for the warning."

"You can mess around with me, though, if you want," the nurse said and then immediately blushed at her unintentionally flirty choice of words. "I am so embarrassed. You know what I meant."

"Don't worry," I said. "I will always be straight with you, Maria. We have a long history together now, and trust is the only thing that will keep us going."

"I couldn't agree more," Viviana said as she walked away giggling.

She sure was cute, and it felt good to flirt a little, but I was scared about what was really wrong with me. I tried playing little games in my head with numbers, and I seemed to be able to do simple arithmetic. But how could I remember the words to the song "American Pie" and not my own name and address? There was a car magazine on the bedside table, so I assumed I liked cars. I opened it and flipped right to an article on the next-generation Pontiac Grand Prix Sedan. It was boxier than the earlier generation and had the oddest thing about it. The back door windows did not roll down at all. Not even a few inches. That's right. GM decided to eliminate this thirty-dollar option from all the coupés and sedans to save money. I thought that might be one of the cheapest things a car company ever did, but sadly, that would be wrong. The Ford Motor Company knew about the propensity for the gas tanks in their Pintos to explode on impact but figured the legal liability costs would be less than the twenty-dollars each it would cost to fix the millions of Pinto gas tanks. So they knowingly left the tanks vulnerable to deadly explosions when the car was hit from behind. From that decision, we can surmise that Ford valued a human life at around twenty dollars.

I flipped through to the next article that seemed interesting on the brand-new GM X cars. These were really odd cars in just about every way imaginable. They weren't small economy cars, and they weren't big enough to be midsize either. I think they became one of the first of what we now call intermediate-sized cars, which basically means their proportions were not good for anyone or anything. The only semi-innovation of the X cars, if you could call it that, was that they were front-wheel drive. There had been a few American-made front-wheel-drive cars before that (Oldsmobile Toronado and the Tucker Torpedo), but they were made in small numbers. But the full array of X models (Chevrolet Citation, Buick Skylark, Oldsmobile Omega, and Pontiac Phoenix) were all fitted with transverse engines that pushed the front wheels.

Front-wheel drive gave the driver improved traction, and that was about it. But anything that improved traction in the snow was a good thing in Shaker Heights. While large rear-wheel-drive cars were very comfortable on dry roads (cars like the Buick Electra, Ford LTD, Chevrolet Impala), they were simply horrible on snow. I would add ice to that statement, but no car is good on ice. Just ask any seasoned skier, and they will tell you. Ice is not good for a ride down a steep rocky mountain and not good for cars speeding down the highway either.

One strange thing my father taught me about driving in the snow was to *steer into the skid*. You won't really know what this means until you are actually spinning out, but it is somewhat like being the guy steering the back of a fire engine. You have to do the opposite of what would come naturally to you. Thus, learning this "steer into the skid" maneuver required that you somehow survived the first time your car started twirling around in the snow. And it really does work, and eventually I became pretty proficient at knowing how to control my spinning automobile.

During my first semester in college, I was learning how to do many things for the first time. Things like studying, folding laundry, playing six hours of tennis, and drinking something called 3.2 (3.2 percent) beer. To this day, I don't know why they had a version of watered down beer designated as 3-2, but it in Ohio it was legal to sell to anyone over the age of 18. We all learned very quickly that you had to drink a *lot* of 3-2 beer to feel any effects of the miniscule amount of alcohol. I used to joke that it might make more sense to just pour the pitcher of beer directly into the toilet and save yourself the trouble. But the truth was, if you did drink enough of it, you would eventually feel…something.

It was one of those nights where a few of us had nothing urgent to do, so we chose to drink instead of read, do homework, or prepare for a test. Again, SOU was known more for pretty girls and partying than for preparing students for the real world. It was, however, a good bargain in terms of overall tuition and cost of living. (I did learn that Deborah had elected S.O.U. for tennis and because her uncle went there a generation before.) At one point during the evening, one of my friends suggested that we actually get in a car and drive into Kentucky where we could buy some *real* beer. And by that he meant beer made by a company with a recognizable name like Miller, Coors, or Anheuser Busch. The beers we usually drank had unfamiliar names like Goebel's or Iron City or, my favorite, POC. Someone told me once that this stood for the Pride of Cleveland, but we called it Piss in a Can.

Four of us got into my Mustang and headed down one of the country roads that led to a place on the state border called Bangs Liquor. The owner's real name was something spelled with a lot of consonants, so we all just called him Bang. He would sell you anything alcoholic, and it was legal in Kentucky to sell real beer that had a reasonable alcohol percentage to eighteen-year-olds. So we bought two cases of Pabst Blue Ribbon and set back toward the school. (We assumed the blue ribbon was for the chugging contest won by its hard-drinking founder, Mr. Pabst.) But as we drove along, the snow started to come down heavily, and eventually we were in an all-out blizzard. I could barely see two feet in front of me, and the wipers on the Mustang were so old that they did nothing to improve visibility.

We were drinking the beer while driving, of course, and I somehow managed to stay on the road the first few miles back into Ohio, but then we hit a patch of ice, and the car started to spin out. Beer was flying all over the inside of the car, and amazingly, the only thing I could hear was the laughter of my three idiotic travel companions. I did try to steer into the skid, but in this case, there was no use. We were spinning out of control, and the only thing I could do at that point was hope and pray that we didn't hit anything or anyone.

When the car finally came to a stop on the shoulder of the old country road, I looked around at my passengers to assess the damage.

"Everybody all right?" I asked.

One of my roommates, a guy named Russ Peters, hesitated before giving us his trembling interpretation of the near-death tragedy we just experienced.

"That was...fucking *unreal*," he said just before taking another sip of his now half-full bottle of beer.

We all laughed hysterically while looking at one another's hair that was now drenched from beer that had sprayed out in every direction.

"I'll drink to that!" I said just as I heard a tapping on the driver's side window.

I looked through the glass, but it was hard to tell who was knocking on the window because of the snow. So I slowly rolled down the window, which revealed the distinctive cap and uniform of an Ohio State trooper.

"You boys all okay in there?" he asked while shining his flashlight throughout the car.

"We are all okay, Officer. Thanks for asking," I answered nervously as he continued to closely examine our faces.

"Any of you been drinking tonight?" he asked.

For most people, the instinct would be to tell the truth. It was, after all, beyond obvious that we were all drunk. You could hear muffled giggling from the back seat, but I was able to keep a straight face and lie through my teeth.

"We maybe had a little, but no one is drunk," I said, thinking that this didn't even sound convincing to me.

"You want to show me your license, young man?" the officer asked as he stood up straight and turned off the flashlight.

"Sure. I definitely want to do that," I said.

I reached for my wallet and retrieved my driver's license and quickly gave it to him.

"I'll be right back," he said before returning to his squad car.

No one in the car said anything, except to giggle a little, as we waited for the trooper to return. I wasn't sure what the cost was for drinking in a vehicle back then, but I knew the penalty for driving while drunk was not a good thing. In the late seventies, they were really starting to crack down on drunk-driving offenses, and I feared that this might be the case for us that night. When the officer returned, he asked me to get out of the car.

"I need you to do a few sobriety tests, Sean, before we can assess what to do here. Are you willing to cooperate with me?"

"Of course, sir. Whatever you say, but I suck at tests."

I got out of the car and stood face-to-face with the trooper, and he asked me to touch the end of my nose with my index finger. Snow was still pouring down on us, and the brim of the trooper's hat was covered with it. I did that first test okay, and then he asked me to walk a straight line, heel to toe, for about ten feet. He demonstrated how to do that but almost lost his balance himself in the slippery snow. When he returned to stand in front of me, he handed me back my license and smiled.

"Fuck this! I'm getting back in my warm squad car. Just drive straight back to your school, and don't kill anyone."

"Yes, sir," I said to a chorus of cheers from my friends in the Mustang.

The truth is, he should have thrown the book at me. Drinking and driving is a stupid and very dangerous thing to do. We all know that now, but we didn't know it then. Sadly, none of us would learn our lesson that night as each of us would eventually be arrested for a

DUI later on in our lives. But we made it through that snowstorm and finished the two cases of Pabst beer before the end of the weekend.

Of course, these are all memories that I did not have in my damaged mental state at the hospital. I was struggling to remember anything concrete. I knew I was young enough to be a student somewhere, but I didn't know where I went to school. I worried that I didn't have any friends or family as I had still not had any visitors. I thought maybe I was so sick they wouldn't allow them to be in the room with me, but I didn't know that for sure.

"Okay, Mr. Stevens. They are ready for you now," the pretty olive-skinned nurse said as she propped open the door to my hospital room. I took one last look at the magazine cover before tossing it back down on the side table.

"*Awighty!* Let's go get see if I still have a brain," I joked as the nurse wheeled me and my bed toward the door.

"I'm sure your brain is still in there. We just need to make sure it is functioning properly."

"Vivica, I can tell you this for certain. My brain has never functioned properly."

"I'm sure, Mr. Stevens," she said while sweetly smiling down at me.

"You can call me Sean. Right? That's my name—Sean."

"Okay, Sean. You got it. And again, mine is Viviana."

"Isn't that what I said?" I asked, but she only smiled back in response.

As the nurse pushed me down the hallway, I watched as the myriad of hospital personnel rushed past me on either side. I was hoping to see a familiar face or something that would remind me of who I was, but nothing came to me until they wheeled me up to the MRI machine.

"What the heck is that?" I asked one of the technicians as they started to shove me into this very small tube.

"It's called magnetic resonance imaging. It is new. It allows us to look at your brain without cutting your head open."

"Oh," I responded, but then something else hit me. When the technician looked down at me, I knew I definitely recognized him from somewhere.

"Wait a second. I know you. What's your name?" I asked.

"I'm David Rockwell. Why? What is your name?"

"I'm Sean Stevens. At least, that is what they tell me."

"Oh yeah. Holy shit! I'm your cousin. Your mom is my aunt."

"Shit! How funny. Wait. My mother is your mother's sister?" I asked.

"That's what aunts are. Aunt Vicky. Your father is Uncle Dennis. I don't know him that well, but we were at your house a few Christmases ago. Your brother is—"

"He's a moron."

"No, he is really funny, but a little…off. Right?"

It was at that moment that I knew who I was and who my brother was.

"Remembering things is a really good sign, right?" I asked.

"Beats me. I just shove people in and out of this thing all day."

"But I don't get it. Where are my parents? Have they been here? Do you really have to put me in that contraption?"

"Sorry, Sean. Just doing my job."

And with those words, he shoved me into a tiny claustrophobic tube with only half of my mind functioning. The following thirty minutes were probably the worst of my life so far. Not only was the MRI machine hot and noisy but I also could hardly breathe in there. Yet something about the cramped conditions got my brain synapses firing again, and memories about my life were flooding back to me. I remembered that I was a college student at Southern Ohio University and I had a girlfriend. I had a serious girlfriend! Her name was Deborah, and she was…shit…she was pregnant. Holy cow!

While it was great to start remembering things again, the life I had briefly forgotten was full of uncertainty. And I knew that I was going to have to make some big decisions when I got out of this giant toothpaste tube. And somehow, I knew at that moment that I had to be stronger mentally, or those big decisions would be made for me. I had been strong enough to survive being hit by a car, and now I needed to be strong enough to fight my other battles. Either way, I knew that the now-stronger version of Sean Stevens, whoever he was, was about to begin.

CHAPTER 20

What the Hell Is a Honda Civic?

My parents and my brother did visit me that evening, but I wasn't much in the mood to socialize. The MRI had been miserable, and I still wasn't sure about my brain as there were a lot of things I was struggling to remember.

"You weren't wearing any underwear, moron. Did you know that?" Danny asked through a series of giggles.

"I had just showered, moron!" I returned.

"So?"

"Leave him alone, Daniel," my mother said. "He has been in a serious accident. At some point, he will explain why an appropriately raised person would go out for a bike ride at night and…not…wear underwear. I'm sure he has a good reason for that."

I didn't.

"They said it will be another few days, and then we will know the results of the brain scan," my father said.

"Know…know what?" I asked.

"Then they will know how brain damaged you are. Right, Mom?" Danny asked.

"No, dear," my mother began. "We will have all his test results back, and then we will know what to do next."

"Danny is right. I'm probably permanently brain damaged," I said angrily.

"You seem fine to me," my father said as he picked up the car magazine and began to flip through it.

"Thanks for that car mag, by the way," I said.

"Thanks for what, sweetie?" my mother asked.

"For the car thing there. The one Dad is reading," I replied.

"We didn't get that for you. Must have been Deborah," my mother continued.

"Deborah? Was she here?" I asked.

"We saw her coming out yesterday. She was in some kind of big hurry," my mother said.

"She just didn't want to talk to any of us. And I hate to tell you this, brother, but she looked kinda chubby," Danny added.

"No she didn't. I think you look kind of chubby, fatso."

"Take it back, moron. I may be heavy, but it is all muscle. Muscles weight more than fat. I bet you don't know that."

"Boys! Please!" my mother shouted. "You two drive me crazy."

"Stop driving your mother crazy!" my father said as he tore some advertisement out of my car magazine. It was probably a coupon to save fifteen cents on a can of motor oil.

"Danny has some major issues. You know that, right?" I said somberly to my mother.

"We know," my father said matter-of-factly as he stuffed whatever he tore out into his shirt pocket.

"I wish I had been up when Deborah came by. I need to talk to her," I said.

"I'm sure she will be back to see you tomorrow, son," my mother said. "She is such a sweet girl."

"No, she isn't," Danny said.

"You don't know her, Mom. Believe me, she is not what anyone would call sweet," I said as Danny nodded affirmatively.

"Well then. I guess I don't know her. But I will give her a chance. We all will. When you are better, we will have Deborah and her parents over for dinner, like they did with you. Won't that be nice?"

"Oh man!" Danny blurted out through a huge smile. "I gotta be there for that!"

"Please, Mom. No dinners and especially not with her parents or that moron," I said, pointing at Danny. "Jeez. They don't like me much and meeting our family might make it even worse."

"Are you trying to be funny, Sean?" my father butted in. "If so, I don't appreciate it."

"No, Dad. It's just...there...are things about her and...me and..."

I stopped in mid-sentence as I was feeling breathless.

"You just need to rest, dear. Don't you worry about Deborah or us or anyone. You just relax and sleep and get healthy again. Have you eaten anything since you got here?"

"I tried, but I don't even know what that shit is," I said just as Danny lifted the metal cover over the plate of food by the side of the bed.

"Is this it? They gave you this crap to eat? No wonder you aren't getting better," Danny said.

"Yeah," I replied.

"Fucking no way," he said while poking the meat with a fork. "I think it is supposed to be chicken. If you eat this crap, you will never get out of here."

"I'll bring you some decent food tomorrow, Sean. Just eat the Jell-O and crackers. That can't hurt you," my mother said.

"I'll bring you some of my organic energy mix. You will love it," Danny added.

"No thanks," I replied.

"They charge fifty cents an hour to park, people, and I'm not made of money. Let's get a move on!" my father demanded.

If Ford valued a human life at twenty dollars, it was now clear that my father valued mine at somewhere around fifty cents. Good to know.

"Sleep tight, dear," my mother said as she gently patted me on the arm. "I will bring you some fresh underwear tomorrow."

"Ha!" Danny blurted out as my father opened the door to the room.

"Get better, son. Now come on. We only have ten minutes before they charge me again."

Danny flipped his middle finger at me as he left the room, and then the door closed slowly behind them.

As I lay there, I wondered what if anything Deborah was thinking. It was nice that she left me the magazine. At least I hoped that it was Deborah who left it. It could have been that nice nurse, Viviana. She and I talked about cars one day, and she told me that she drove a Chevrolet Chevette.

"Sorry, Vicky, but that may be the cheapest car ever made."

"It is? I like it. I think it is cute. It is really good on gas."

"That's because it only weighs about forty pounds. If you get hit in that thing, you are toast."

And sadly, that was true of the Chevette. Here was this tiny underpowered car on the same roads and highways as large sedans weighing three times as much. It was like a fifth-grade girl playing running back in professional football. You can try to avoid the giant linebackers, but eventually you are going to run into one and *not good.*

While the pretty nurse and I seemed to be making some kind of connection, the only person I really cared about seeing was Deborah. I missed her, and I wanted to see her in the worst way. I wondered if she cared at all that I had almost been killed. I still didn't know any of the major details of the accident. All I knew was that I was catapulted a long way before introducing my forehead to the rock-hard pavement. The other details of the accident were all a mystery to me until the next day when I got a very soft knock at my door.

"I don't want any more soup. Please. No more soup!" I yelled as the door slowly opened, revealing a very slight black man with thinning gray hair. He was wearing a hat from like the 1950s, and he took it off as he entered the room.

"If I may, do you think you are well enough to spare a minute to converse with me?" the old man whispered just loud enough for me to hear it.

"Sure. What is it?"

The man ambled slowly up to the bed and rested his hat on the chair beside me. He was very kind looking, but he seemed to be very nervous too.

"I'm sorry, Mister. Are you sure you are in the right room?" I asked.

"I am sure. You see, well, son...you see, I...I am the one that hit you...with my car."

"You drive a Ford."

"I do. A Galaxie 500 coupé, but it is not much of a car anymore. It used to be."

"What? You totaled it running into me?"

"Oh no, son. It's just an old car. Like me, it has seen better days," he said.

"Does yours have the 390 or the 429?"

"I got the smaller engine. That was all I could afford back in '65. But it has been a great car. Hardly any problems and big enough to haul just about anything. But that's not good if you hit someone on a bicycle."

"I love it. The stacked headlights, the huge grille, the squared-off backlights. It's one of my favorite designs. I used to draw it all the time."

I could see the man's hands trembling, and I looked over toward the chair near the bathroom.

"You want to pull up that chair? We can talk cars. Do you like cars?"

The man pulled the chair over and slowly sat down. When he did, he was hesitant to lift his head and simply refused to look me in the eyes.

"I just can't tell you how sorry I am, son. I didn't see you. I was just driving along that intersection in Shaker, and then...there you were. I promise you, I wasn't doing anything except driving and... then..."

"That intersection is nuts. There is no way it is anyone's fault. I wasn't paying good attention. I was having kind of a bad day."

"Well, I am sorry. Getting hit didn't help things, I'm sure. I feel just awful."

"No need to apologize. I am going to be all right. At least that's what they are telling me."

"That's good. I'm glad. But the Shaker police were plenty rough on me. I still got to go to court."

"Why? What did they do?"

"The pulled me out of my car and threw me to the ground. I was scared half to death."

"No friggin' way. Well, that is just wrong, and I will let them know that it was my fault."

"I'm seventy-five years old, and I live on a small pension. I can't afford to go to jail."

"Are you kidding me?" I asked in amazement. "If anyone goes to jail, it ought to be the city planners that designed that fucking intersection."

"I never know what to do there. It's so confusing," he said.

"Look, Mr...uh?

"Brooks. My name is Brooks. Samuel Brooks."

"Look, Mr. Brooks. Bring your lawyer. Bring a tape recorder. Bring in all the witnesses you want. That accident was either my fault or nobody's. You got that?"

"I'll pay whatever you need for the medical costs. I promise you."

"Forget it. My father's work plan has all that covered, or he would have been yelling at me about it already."

"That's mighty kind of you, son."

"You can call me Sean. My name is Sean Stevens."

"Nice to meet you, Sean Stevens. And I am so happy you are going to be all right. You are going to be all right. Aren't you?"

"These friggin' people speak a different language with all their medical gibberish. But I think so. They aren't coming in near as often lately. That has to be a good sign."

"Should be. I have never been in a hospital before."

"No way. Never."

"No, sir. Never. I wasn't even born in one. My mother had me in her own bed at home. We couldn't afford a hospital. But I turned out okay. So far anyway."

"Shit. Where were you born? Here in Cleveland?"

"Yep. West side. My parents worked downtown, but I worked at the Ford Engine Plant in Brookpark back in the fifties."

"No way!" I said. "And you just retired?"

"I did. Spent twenty-five years there attaching carburetors. It was a good job."

"Like I told you, I love cars."

"So do I," the old man said with a crooked smile. "I never had two nickels to rub together, but as soon as I got one nickel, I used it to buy me a good car."

"I own a 1966 Mustang. Got the 289 in there. It was a four speed, but now it is an automatic."

"Dang, son. We built that engine right there in Cleveland. That 289 is one of the best Ford power plants ever made. I don't know why anyone would want a six cylinder in a Mustang when they could have a 289. Just a great engine."

"I say that all the time. Six cylinders in a pony car. Are they crazy?"

"They have even been putting a four in them new Mustang Twos. Imagine that. It got eighty-five horsepower. And they call it a Mustang! I could run a grocery cart up a hill faster than that thing."

"Ford is losing it. My father works at Ford, too, but at a dealership."

"Oh yeah, which one?"

"Bud Larson over on Warrensville. That's where Mr. Larson's Ford place is, but he has a Lincoln Mercury store in Solon and a Jeep place in Brecksville. I heard he just opened a Honda store there too. But who the heck is going to buy a Honda?" I said with a laugh.

"Honda makes a good motorbike. And I've seen that new car of theirs, the Civic. Not so bad. But not fast. It's not supposed to be, I guess."

"It's so small. I bet they rust out in a few years."

"Don't count out the Japanese, Sean. We had been buying more and more parts from Japan to put in our engines over here. They make good stuff."

"Well, I would never buy a Japanese car if my life depended on it, that's for sure."

That turned out to be absurdly untrue, but what did I know? I was head injured. The fact was, in 1980, Hondas and Datsuns and Toyotas were just starting to become popular. I knew a girl with a Datsun B-210. It was okay looking, but the motor sounded like a blender set on *puree*. I had another friend that owned a Celica GT. It seemed funny to me that you would put a GT moniker after any car made in Japan, but this car had some power and wasn't bad looking at all. But for me, in those days, I liked the way American cars looked and drove. Most of them anyway. Certainly not the Ford Fairmont. They lost their minds designing that ugly hunk of junk.

"I'm sorry to be taking up so much of your time. I just wanted to say that I was sorry and…if there is anything I can do."

"Look, Mr. Brooks. It was an accident, and the police shouldn't be harassing you. I will make them understand. I promise you."

"You sure are a good young man. Thank you, Sean."

Mr. Brooks picked his hat up off the bed and stood slowly.

"If it is okay with you, do you mind if I stop back in a few days…to see how you are doing?"

"Of course. We can talk cars till the cows come home."

After saying that, I hoped desperately that there wasn't anything insensitive about that stupid expression. As far as I knew, it just meant that cows are slow and they take their time.

"I'd like that. I'd like that a lot."

"Bring pictures if you have them. I'd love to see some of the cars you have owned."

"Did you like the magazine I left you?"

Aha! That was how that magazine got there. It was nice thinking that maybe Deborah had left it. Oh well.

"I did. Thanks for that. I read every word of it. Twice."

"I'll get you another one. *Car and Driver* is all I read. *Motor Trend* is good, but too many ads. I don't think they rate cars right in there anymore. Can't trust 'em, but they have good pictures, and I like to look at the pictures."

"Me too," I said as the man turned and slowly walked toward the door. "Thanks for coming by to see me."

"You just get better, son. I will be back."

"Sounds good."

When the door shut behind him, I started to feel a pressure in my ear and then a ringing sound. It got louder and louder, and then my entire face started to sweat. I reached for the red buzzer and pushed it as hard as I could. And that was the last thing I remember from that day. I was really scared that it might be the last thing I remembered—ever.

CHAPTER 21

Well, That's the End of That

The next time I opened my eyes, I was in a room that looked like a used car-parts storage closet. There were pipes and tubes and lights and gadgets everywhere, and I was hooked up to most of them. I had what looked like a hydraulic lift over my head and wires coming in and out of me. The worst part was that my head felt like I had been bowled over by a wrecking ball. It hurt to blink, but when I did, I saw what I thought just might be Deborah.

"Hey there," I mumbled, but I wasn't sure it was audible. There was, after all, a large metal tube inserted in my mouth and down my esophagus.

"Don't try to talk. I just wanted to stop by to see you."

I opened my eyes wide, and Deborah must have gotten nervous, so she just started rambling.

"They said you had some kind of hemorrhage. I don't know what that means, but it must be serious. You are in intensive care, and I don't know how much longer you will be here. They had to cut your skull open to relieve some pressure. Oh my god. The scar you are going to have is not going to be pretty. I don't know. I hope it works, though, but they aren't saying much. Like I said, I had to beg them to let me see you. I told them I was your fiancée. Funny, right? Fiancée?"

I shook my head and then blinked several times and moved my eyes toward Deborah's stomach. She knew exactly what I was trying to ask.

"Oh that. The baby is fine. I've got another seven weeks and then...well, then I disappear for a few months and...you know the rest. I don't want you to worry about that, though. I have it all taken care of."

I pointed down at my midsection and then at her midsection, and she looked back at me like I was a complete crazy person. I did it again, and then it hit her. Somehow she knew what it was I wanted to know.

"Oh. Oh yeah. I don't know yet for sure whether it is a boy or girl. I have a feeling it is a boy. The doctor thinks it's a boy too. So it's probably...you know...a boy."

I nodded my head aggressively, and she smiled.

"Sean, I am going to name him Elijah. It was my grandfather's name, and we will call him Eli. I hope that is okay with you."

It would have been nice to have a say in that decision, but I instantly liked the name, so I nodded in agreement.

"So, uh...I will let you know when things are settled, and if you want...you can see the baby. But no pressure. You just focus on getting better. Okay?"

I could hardly believe the words I was hearing. How could she even question if I wanted to see my own child? Of course I did. I wanted to be a huge part of this child's life, but that clearly wasn't the role Deborah had in mind for me. She had never once asked about me providing money for my child, but perhaps that was simply a given, or maybe they didn't need it. Deborah never talked about money. She had it, and she probably had whatever she needed to get through all this baby stuff without any help from me. Plus, depending on me for financial support would only give me a better rationale for having a say in the upbringing of this child. So she probably didn't want to push it.

"I will check in with your parents from time to time, and they will keep me informed of your progress. I'm sorry...you...well, that you got hit by that car. I hope you are going after the asshole who did this to you."

I shook my head vigorously at this and even stared sternly at her to make sure she got the message.

"What? You are just going to let the guy get away with it?"

I nodded.

"Typical. That's just like you, Sean. You will probably tell the guy that it was your fault."

I nodded again even more aggressively.

"That's your call, I guess. If it were me, I would have the asshole thrown in jail for life."

For the first time in my entire relationship with Deborah, I actually wanted her to leave. As pretty as she was, and she sure was pretty, she was not always a beautiful person on the inside. She could be so self-centered and mean. In fact, she rarely, if ever, said anything nice about anyone. I knew I also tended to talk about people negatively at times, but I vowed that I would try not to do that anymore. Most people were decent on the inside. If they weren't, it was likely their environment and upbringing that screwed them up (except for people like that Son of Sam guy). I was lucky. My parents were kind people, and even my brother had a pretty good heart deep down under all those muscles. Way, way, way, way down, of course. Danny was just one of those people that was not comfortable unless he was joking around with you. It would take a lot to get Danny to share anything he was really thinking. And for the most part, I was okay with that.

"Okay then. I guess I am going to leave now. You take care, Sean."

I nodded, and Deborah took her hand and gently brushed the hair out of my eyes. It was a rare and tender moment from her, and I gazed at her lovingly as she smiled down at me. But then her smile turned into a giggle and then a laugh.

"I still can't believe you weren't wearing any underwear," she said as she pulled the strap of her purse onto her shoulder. "Danny is telling everyone!"

When she left the room, I wanted to pick up something and throw it at her. But I could hardly move, so I just sat there and started to do some of my mind exercises. One of my favorite songs from that period was Aerosmith's "Dream On," and I tried singing that one in my head. But of course, Steven Tyler's singing made the words almost impossible to discern, so I mostly just guessed at them. Then I would take a shot at the Rolling Stones' "Angie" and the Beatles' "Let It Be." I never had trouble learning Beatles lyrics. They sang them clearly and just so well. John's voice on "In My Life" is amazing and Paul's on "Hey Jude" might be the best-sounding vocal in history.

I would sing the words in my head, and it seemed to me as if my brain was functioning well. But then I started to think about things I had once memorized like the state capitals and the Pledge of Allegiance. As I tried to say those in my mind, the words just wouldn't come. In fact, the only part of the Pledge of Allegiance I could get was the first part—"I pledge allegiance to the flag"—and then I was stuck.

It was probably a few days later that they moved me from intensive care back into a normal hospital room. But this time, it was a double room, and I had a roommate separated only by a thin curtain. I listened in as his family talked to him about his upcoming procedure. From what I could surmise, he was a man in his early fifties, and this wasn't the first time he had had serious heart and brain issues. He had suffered a severe stroke this time, and they were going to have to go in and clear out the blockages that led to his attack. I could not understand him when he spoke as the stroke had left him partially paralyzed. He almost always had three of four people in the room with him, and I was envious of how much attention he got from his family and friends.

"They gonna make you all better, Paw Paw?" a young child asked. I couldn't see the person, but I assumed this was a grandson or granddaughter. Probably around five years old.

"Uh…Hmmm," the man responded with difficulty.

"They are going to make him all better, sweetie," an older woman in the room said gently. "Just like the last time. He will be able to talk just like before."

"Don't worry," another family member said to the young child. "Paw Paw isn't going anywhere."

They wheeled the man out the next morning, but he never came back. He didn't make it. It was his time, but I felt horrible for the little child who would not understand that this is how it goes in this world. We cannot predict the time, age, or circumstance in which God calls us home. As I thought about my own destiny, though, I knew I was supposed to be alive. It was not my time. But that day could be just around the corner, and I wanted to be ready. My mind was still a bit of a mess, but I wasn't going to just sit still and let those memories fade or disappear. I was going to do something about it, and I did.

CHAPTER 22

The Incredible Power of Prayer

The sun was shining brightly through my hospital room window, and I was feeling surprisingly energetic. I was sad about my roommate passing away, but they had another man in with me now, and he was only there for tests. I assumed he would be in and out, so I wasn't making a huge effort to get to know him. Plus, I had visitors the day the guy was wheeled in. It was actually a record for me in terms of people that stopped by. First, my parents and then Father Dave popped in and for some strange reason, he brought Danny with him. I hadn't seen much of Danny in recent days, and I was guessing that my parents had encouraged Father Dave to bring him along. It was always interesting to see Danny and Father Dave interact as Danny was an avowed atheist. The truth was, I didn't think Danny really knew exactly what that term meant, but he claimed that he did not believe in God. I think he did it just to piss off my parents.

Danny was sitting on the windowsill, and Father Dave was sitting in the red leather chair next to the bed as we talked about the news of the day. It looked like Ronald Reagan, the actor, would be the republican nominee to run against then president Jimmy Carter that fall. I wasn't sure which of those I liked more, but Jimmy Carter seemed like he was a nice guy. Yet Reagan could say things in a way that seemed to make a lot of sense. I figured it would be a very tight race in November. It wasn't. Reagan won in a landslide.

I was sitting up on the bed, and we had drawn the curtain fully between me and my new hospital mate. He was not having visitors at that time, so I assumed he would be listening in on the ridiculousness of what was my brother, Danny.

"Are you getting any be-bang while you are here from them nurse-a-ronees? Gotta love them sexy uniforms. Right, Father D?" Danny said, which provoked an immediate look of consternation on the face of Father Dave.

"Jesus, Danny. We got a minister right here. And he is wearing a collar for Christ's sake."

"You can cool it with the language, too, Sean," Father Dave said with a sly smile. "I think that taking the Lord's name may be worse than what Danny said about the sexy nurses, actually."

"Really?" I said. "But I meant it more like…uh…Jesus rocks! You know?"

"Anyway," Father Dave said while trying to shake off the immature banter coming from both of the Stevens boys. "Let's talk about you, Sean. What's going on? How do you feel?"

"I think I am getting way better physically. My arm is okay, but I will be on crutches for a few months. But the thing that really worries me is my brain."

"He's worried that he won't be able to remember how much stronger I am than him."

"Yeah, Danny. That's what I am worried about. My perception of my quality of life is based on whether I can beat you in arm wrestling."

"Ha!" Danny shouted. "You could never beat me with those flappy wings of yours."

"What kind of memory issues do you mean?" Father Dave asked while inching his chair closer to the bed.

"Like I was telling you at my grandfather's funeral, but it seems to be getting worse. I can't seem to remember basic stuff sometimes, things like where I am from or where I went to school when I was little. It takes me longer to remember names, and sometimes I don't ever get them. I mean, I know my family and shit like that, but if you asked me the name of my football teammates from ninth grade... well, they just aren't there."

"I see. That is concerning."

"Yeah, and I forget things like when I got here or what the doctor said when he stopped by this morning. Things like that."

"But the tests all show that you should recover fully. Right? So that is good," Father Dave said.

"Do you remember your super-stanky babe Debbie-O? She was here again yesterday. I hope you ain't forgetting that piece of tang."

"What? Danny, those words don't even make any sense. *Stanky* means smelly, right? Why would I like a smelly girl?"

"Some parts can be smelly, if you know what I mean."

"All right, idiots. That's enough of that," Father Dave said in disgust as he adjusted his minister's collar.

"I think he got dropped on his head a few too many times when he was a baby," I added before Father Dave slapped his hands together in an attempt to get us both to shut up.

"Sorry, Father," I said, and Danny nodded along eagerly.

"Okay, let's get to what I found out on this memory thing. I called my friend, and there are some avenues we can take that go beyond the medical field. Science is one thing, and medical science is vital, but God can also do miracles beyond anything man can do."

"Like the immaculate conception. Right, Father?" I asked. "Jesus got born without a man. Right?"

"That is actually not what the immaculate conception is, Sean. That term is for the conception of Mary in the womb of her mother—in Saint Anne's womb. The arrival of Jesus is referred to as the virgin birth, not the immaculate conception."

"No friggin' way!" Danny said. "I bet even Catholics get that wrong."

"Most people do," Father Dave added.

"Did you see Franco Harris's catch against Oakland? It hit off another guy's helmet and went right into his arms. He ran it all the way in to win the game. They call that the immaculate reception," I said with a smile. "I like the Raiders uniforms way better than Pittsburg's."

"Let's do this, boys," Father Dave said as he opened up a small red book. "Let's talk about what God can do here. You do believe in the power of prayer. Right?"

"Not me, Father," Danny blurted out. "I believe in the power of my pecs."

"Anyway! Let me read you a few verses on how God answers all prayers. You may not be aware of some of the—"

"Do we have to, Father? I'd rather you just tell us what we should do. I will pray all day long if I have to," I said.

"Is there an exorcist in that book?" Danny asked.

"The ritual is called an exorcism. I would be the exorcist," Father Dave said as he flipped to another page.

"Get out!" Danny said energetically. "So you can make us like float around the room and shit like that?"

"No, Danny. I would attempt to stop something like that if it was happening. But I don't see either of you floating around or breathing out fire."

There was a soft knock on the door, and a young nurse poked her head in.

"Excuse me, gentlemen. But there is another gentleman here that wants to see you. Is it okay if he comes in, or would you rather him come back after your guests leave?"

"Who is it?" I asked while attempting to sit up straighter on the bed.

"Just a second," the nurse said before letting the door close. A moment later, she opened the door again. "It is Mr. Brooks. But he says that he can come back if that is better for you."

"No, not at all. Please tell him to come in."

The nurse stepped aside, and Mr. Brooks entered the room wearing a light brown suit and a gold tie. He was a very thin man and just a bit over five feet tall. He was again wearing an old-fashioned hat called a fedora, which he took off and held at his side.

"I'm sorry to interrupt. I just wanted to see how the patient was doing, and then I will be on my way."

Father Dave stood up and approached the older man with his hand held out.

"Nice to meet you, sir. Please come in. You can have my seat."

"Oh no. No thanks, Father. I can see you boys are busy."

"Don't be silly. Have a seat here in my chair," Father Dave said while moving out of the way for Mr. Brooks.

"I'll just stay a minute. How are you feeling, young man?" he asked as he sat slowly down on the red chair.

"Wait. Is this the guy that hit you?" Danny asked.

"It was me that hit him. Moron! And don't even go there!" I said sharply.

"Did you hear that he wasn't wearing underwear?" Danny said while laughing heartily.

"Here's an idea. Let's take out an ad in the paper so everyone can know that I didn't put on clean underwear after my shower that day."

"What do you mean clean? Yours are never clean," Danny said.

"Boys, please. Let's get back to what we were saying about God and what he can do to help in the healing process," Father Dave said before turning toward Mr. Brooks. "Are you a man of faith, Mr. Brooks?"

"Me? Oh yes, sir. I wouldn't be here today without my faith in God and his son Jesus. He has gotten me through some really rough times. Sometimes, I don't know how he got me through, but God has saved me time and time again."

"Sounds like you can be a good part of what we are planning to do with Sean here. We are going to pray for him and for his mind to come back to where it was. Would you be willing to participate in this service with us?"

"It's not an exorcism," Danny blurted out.

"If y'all want me to. Sure."

"So I have been learning more about this with the help of a friend, and we are going to follow a service from the 1960s that was meant to heal people that have suffered some type of extreme trauma. It is written here in this book of special rites and observances."

"You mean rituals?" Mr. Brooks asked.

"Sort of. It was written by some zealots during the period of the Vietnam War. It was meant to help returning soldiers with their war injuries and other psychological issues. I thought it might do us some good with Sean and his healing process," Father Dave explained.

"I see," Mr. Brooks said while leaning forward on his chair.

"Count me out, fellas," Danny said as he jumped off the windowsill and started toward the door. "You go ahead with your voodoo. I am going to see if I can get that cute nurse's phone number."

"Okay. Not for everyone. I understand," Father Dave said as Danny swung open the door and left.

"Well, now that Satan has left the room, let's get started," I said. "I'm ready if you are. Let's go."

Father Dave opened his little red book again and flipped to a page about halfway into the tome. He reached over and took my hand and then reached over and held Mr. Brook's hand.

"Heavenly Father and Creator of all things, we ask that you join us in Spirit as we request your help in healing our friend, Sean, here. You have shown us that you have the power not only to forgive sins but to heal all kinds of infirmities as well. You, our Father and Creator, are all powerful and all knowing and have the ability to bring darkness to light and death to life. We ask today that you heal Sean's mind and memory and provide him with the tools he needs to do your work and to love others as you have loved us. We will, in exchange, offer ourselves to you as a sacrifice. We give to you ourselves and our sprits in exchange. To help others. To do your will. To spread your love and the message of your eternal forgiveness. On this day, Father, Mr. Brooks, me, and Sean ask that we become instruments of your will and purpose. We only ask that you heal us so we are fully capable of completing the tasks at hand. We ask that you give us the seeds and tools needed to spread your heavenly love to those most in need. We ask this today and in your eternal, holy, and powerful name. Amen."

CHAPTER 23

What Just Happened?

I'm not sure how to describe what happened after Father Dave finished his prayer. It was almost like a scene out of a horror movie. The lights flickered and then went out. Then they came back on, but they were now at a level of brightness that caused us all to shield our eyes. The red numerical figures on my monitor flashed on and off. I pushed the red emergency button on my bedside, and the noise was not the alarm that had sounded before. It was the sound of trumpets and hundreds of them. I could see through the small window on my door that hospital staff were trying to get inside, but the door wouldn't open. The pitcher of water on the side table had spilled all over the bed and onto the floor. I looked over at Father Dave, who appeared terrified as he flipped through the pages of the little red book, but Mr. Brooks continued to sit calmly in his chair. Remarkably, he seemed relaxed.

"Father, if we have angered you in some way, please forgive us," Father Dave said from his knees. "We ask only that you allow us to do your will. Please, Heavenly Father, do not be angry. We meant nothing but good here. We pray for your will to be done, Father. In your holy name, we pray that your will be done. Thank you, heavenly God."

With that, the lights above flickered and then returned to normal. The door burst open, and the hospital personnel came pouring in.

"What the hell is going on in here?" an orderly screamed out as he entered the room and rushed to my bedside. Two female nurses in their all-white uniforms and cute little white hats rushed in after him. The orderly pulled the curtain back on the other gentleman in the room who was curled up in the fetal position on his bed, apparently scared out of his mind. One of the other female nurses went to his bedside and placed her hand on his shoulder.

"Are you all right, Mr. Hawkins?" she asked.

"Either get me or get them people outta here!" Mr. Hawkins said as he pulled his legs farther up toward his chest.

"I'm sorry, Mr. Hawkins. Just sit tight, and we will get you into another room right away. I'm so sorry this happened," the young nurse said.

"Were you fooling around with the equipment in here?" the male orderly said sternly in my direction while checking the lines going out of the machines and into me.

"We never touched any of that stuff," I answered defensively.

"Perhaps it was my fault," Father Dave said. "I was doing a prayer service, and maybe we should have…I don't know…checked with the hospital first."

"They was doing a séance!" Mr. Hawkins yelled out.

"It was not a séance," I said. "What the pastor was doing here was a nontraditional healing service. He was invoking God to come and heal us and to put us in communication with him. It was to help us make straight our paths so that purity and forgiveness coincide and help synergize the process of healing. No one was hurt. I assure you."

As those words were exiting my mouth, I was literally listening to them as if they had come from someone else. Prior to that moment, I did not know a séance from a snowball, and I had certainly never experienced a synergistic healing service before. I had no idea what was going on. I looked over at Mr. Brooks, who was staring down at his hands curiously. He looked up at me and smiled and then back down at his hands.

"I ain't sure what just happened here, but I sure do feel different," Mr. Brooks said.

"Me too," I added.

"Well, it looks like the machines are all back to normal. Nurse, help me get everything cleaned up here," the orderly said.

"Of course," the nurse said while picking up the water pitcher off the floor.

"Yes, well, please don't do…whatever you just did…again," the orderly said.

"If you are ready, sir, we will wheel you out of here now, Mr. Hawkins," the other female nurse said to my terrified roommate.

As they moved his bed through the doorway, Danny came back in the room drinking some fruity thing in a plastic cup that he must have purchased at the hospital cafeteria. He looked curiously at Mr. Hawkins and then back at me as he made his way toward the bed.

"What's with that guy?" Danny asked. "He looked like he just saw a ghost or something."

"Not a ghost but a spirit," I said, and once again, the words seem to leak out of my mouth unintentionally.

"I think I better be going home now," Mr. Brooks said while standing. "I feel kinda hungry, like I haven't eaten in a long time. For some reason, I am wanting to get me some pizza with extra anchovies."

"I love pizza with extra anchovies," I blurted out. "Let's all get some."

"I ain't never had an anchovy in my life. I ain't even sure I know what they are, but all of a sudden, I like them," Mr. Brooks said as he reached for his hat, which had fallen on the floor. He was fixing a part of the hat that had been dented when he looked at me and then back at the hat.

"You had a fedora on the other day, but that's a Stetson hat, isn't it?" I said.

"I believe it is," Mr. Brooks replied.

"I have never used that word before in my life. I thought a Stetson was a type of cow until just now. What's going on here, Father Dave?" I asked while sitting up in bed and looking at the front and back of my hands.

Father Dave came over and looked into my eyes and then over at Mr. Brooks.

"Let me ask you something, Mr. Brooks. Where did you go to high school? Answer me quickly," Father Dave said as he approached him.

"I went to Shaker Heights High School. Class of 1978. Wait. That ain't right. It's 1979."

"No, he went to John Hay High School. Class of 1946. Isn't that right, Mr. Brooks?" I asked.

"Yeah. That sounds right. How could I have…"

"Quick, Sean. What is your wife's name?" Father Dave asked as he turned quickly toward me.

"My wife has long passed back in 1961. Her name was Agnes, Agnes Singletary. That was her maiden name," I said while looking around the room at the three stunned faces. "Wait! What the fuck did I just say?"

"I think I know what happened here," Father Dave began. "We were all holding hands. I prayed for a healing of your memory, but I think… I think maybe the wires got crossed."

"My great-grandparents were slaves in Georgia," I blurted out.

"I drive a green Mustang, and my girlfriend, Debbie, is very mean to me," Mr. Brooks said.

"What the fuck?" Danny said. "You guys are fucking creeping the shit out of me."

"What do we do?" I asked Father Dave.

"I don't know. I truly don't know."

"You lost a son in the Vietnam War. Didn't you, Mr. Brooks?" I asked.

"I did. His name was Harold. He was a good boy. Got shot in the back by one of his own men."

"You thought it might have been on purpose, didn't you?" I asked.

"Well, the soldier never apologized or said anything to me. Harold was my only boy. You think an accident like that…even if you didn't mean it…you would still apologize to the father. Don't you think?"

"Like you did for hitting me," I replied.

"I told you he did it on purpose!" Danny shouted out gleefully.

"No, you idiot. Mr. Brooks did apologize, and it was an accident. I told you that."

"I know. I'm just messing with you, Brooksy," Danny said with a smile. "I hope Sean's head didn't do too much damage to your bumper."

"You say things that really, really worry me, Danny," I said.

"I ain't the one that just said I used to be a slave, big brother. That's you."

"It was my grandparents...I mean...his grandparents. Shit. I got all these memories floating into my mind, Mr. Brooks. But they are your memories. Are you getting ones from me...from my life?"

"Are you...well...I have to ask you something. Are you going to be a father?"

"Say what?" Danny shouted out.

"I uh...uh-oh."

"You knocked up that bitch, Debbie-O, didn't you, brother? That's why you and her are having so many problems. Mom and Dad are going to murder you."

"Is it true, Sean? You are going to be a parent?" Father Dave asked.

"Only her parents know about the baby at this point. It's a boy. I'm not really going to be involved. You can't tell anyone, Danny. You either, Father Dave. Okay?"

"Children are God's blessing to us," Mr. Brooks said while starting to pace. "I would do anything to bring back my boy. He would probably be a father himself now, and I would be a grandpa. No, you need to be involved in your child's life. You have to make that happen, Sean. Trust me. You don't want to find out later on that you had that chance and didn't take it."

Again, I knew instantly that Mr. Brooks and his son had not had the best relationship. Harold had been a lot of trouble in his school, and Mr. Brooks was struggling to raise him on his own. Not knowing what to do, Mr. Brooks sent Harold down South to live with his wife's relatives. He hadn't seen or heard from him in years until he got the telegram about his son being shot in Vietnam. That terrible telegram that let him know that Harold was no longer alive.

"I'm so sorry for your loss, Mr. Brooks," I offered softly. "But you will see him soon when God calls you home. And you can be father and son together again. At least that is what I hope."

Or was that what Mr. Brooks hoped?

"Father Dave, can you switch us back? I think Mr. Brooks needs his memories back and...so do I."

"I will see what I can do," Father Dave said while looking toward the door. "Danny, do you mind?"

"What? I don't want to be involved in this," Danny responded.

"No, son. Just go to the door and make sure no one comes in. Okay?"

"I can't believe you got that girl pregnant, you sly dog. I didn't think you had it in you."

"What's that supposed to mean? You think because my body isn't 90 percent muscle, I can't have sex with a girl and make a baby? Please tell me you don't believe that, Danny."

"Boys, please. Sean, come closer to me. And, Mr. Brooks, please take my hand. Let's see if...God can fix this."

"Maybe God meant it this way," Mr. Brooks said with a smile. "But just temporary so we could know what it feels like to be in somebody else's shoes for a minute or two."

Father Dave held our hands and knelt down next to the bed.

"Dearest God, Father of all creation, we ask that you switch back the memories of my two friends here, my two faithful servants who plan to use your gifts to demonstrate your love and devotion to us. I ask this humbly as your servant priest. Please put the memories back where they belong. And thank you, Lord, for your love and kindness. In God's name we pray."

This time, there were no blinking of lights or sounding of trumpets. The room was eerily quiet, and then Danny turned his head back toward us.

"Somebody's coming!" Danny whispered excitedly.

"Right. Look...casual," Father Dave said as he leaned against the wall. Mr. Brooks smiled and put his hat back on his head.

171

The doctor entered the room and looked curiously at each of us as he walked toward me.

"Something going on in here that I should know about?" he asked suspiciously.

"No. Nothing. Why?" Father Dave replied.

"Yeah. We are just sitting here talking. Nothing more than that," I said.

"Everything is fine, Doctor. I was just leaving," Mr. Brooks said as he walked around the doctor and toward the door. "I feel just fine now, Sean. How about you?"

"Me? Oh yeah. It feels like I'm back to normal again. My grandparents were not slaves, and I have never even been to Georgia."

"All is right again in the world," Father Dave said with a wink.

"I think they all need doctors," Danny said to the physician who turned to walk out behind Mr. Brooks.

"Better get some rest, Mr. Stevens. We'll run some more tests in the morning," he said as he closed the door.

"I have to go too, Sean. I'll take Danny home."

"Please do."

"You got Debbie-O pregnant. Dang. I'm bursting. I gotta tell somebody."

"Her name is Debbie, I mean Deborah Robbins, idiot, not Debbie O-anything."

"The O is for…you know."

"Come on, Danny. There are some things we really need to discuss," Father Dave said sternly.

"Hey, Father, for some reason I am having memories of making out with a nun. What's up with that?"

"Funny," Father Dave said as he pushed Danny toward the door.

"You are still single, right? Is it a sin to kiss a nun?" Danny said while giggling.

"Not a word to anyone, Danny," I said loudly. "Not until I say so."

"All right."

Father Dave put his arm around Danny, and the two left the room. I knew right then that no further tests were necessary. My mind and memory were fine. What happened in that prayer service had worked, at least for now. And for some reason, that made me incredibly happy and even a bit bold. I wasn't a person that would ever be described as being bold, but I was feeling it now, and it felt good. I closed my eyes slowly, and as I did, I knew I would be asleep for quite a while. I was tired, but I also felt about as good as I had felt in a very long time.

CHAPTER 24

You Can't Tell Danny Anything!

Contrary to everything I had previously believed about him, Danny was starting to prove that he could be a fairly supportive brother. I know he wasn't in the room when our memories all seemed to switch, but he was there for the second prayer, and well, there seemed to be a change in him—a really good change.

"Hey, Sean. I got your bedroom all set up for rehab on that leg. You are going to need to do a lot of strength exercises to get it back to where it used to be. But I can help you," Danny said as he assisted me through the front door of our house.

"Thanks, Danny, but I am not lifting weights. Sorry."

"No, man. This is all about stretching and strengthening. No weights except...well, for some really little ones. I know you don't want the monster machine pipes that I got on me. I don't think you could handle the looks I get at the pool either."

"Oh please," I said with disgust.

"It's true, Sean-O. Girls just can't keep their eyes off my tree trunks. You know?"

Okay. He hadn't changed that much, but he was being nicer.

"Hey, Danny, I got something to ask you."

"Shoot, brother."

"You never talk about college, but this is your senior year. Are you planning on going?"

Danny looked in both side rooms and down the hall before sitting down on one of the stairs off the hallway. I stood and kept my balance by leaning on my crutches.

"I ain't going to college."

"Say what?" I exclaimed.

"Shhh. Don't say nothing, but I did just horrible on those fuckin' nine-hour tests. I didn't even show the scores to Mom and Dad. College ain't for me. I don't like school anyway, so why would I go?"

"I don't know. Sports, girls, drinking, fun, and girls."

"I get you, bro, but I don't need college for that."

"But Mom and Dad always said we had to go. You know what Dad always says."

I put a contorted frown on my face and pretended to be my father.

"You know, boys, that success in life and higher education go hand in hand. You can't get ahead unless you have been instructed in something that makes practical sense, like business, accounting, finance, engineering, you know. Those things where you have to wear a tie and suck up to people."

Danny laughed and started to move into the living room.

"You got Dad down perfect. That's for sure."

"What have you been doing for money, Danny? You had enough to buy that Olds 442. That's a good car. It couldn't have been cheap."

"Ha! You don't know the half of it. I spent a part of my college savings on that thing."

"Oh shit, Danny. Dad is going to kill you. You know that, right? Didn't he ask you where you got the money?"

"I lied. I told him that the car was a no-title rebuild and the only thing authentic about it was the 442 emblem. I even told him it had a six cylinder in it and jokingly called it a 221 since it was so slow."

"I heard the engine in that thing. That's a four barrel with eight bangers if I ever heard one."

"It can do zero to sixty in like 1.2 seconds," Danny said with a smile.

"Danny, you do know that's not right. Don't tell people that. Even Apollo rockets don't go that fast."

"Mine does," Danny said happily as we settled down into the two soft-cushioned chairs in front of the living-room picture window.

"Shit, man. How did you get the money out of the bank? Didn't Dad have to go with you?"

"Nah. I got a buddy who is a teller at Third Federal. We had to make up a new title and everything just to get the car registered. I told him that I would have Dad sign the loan docs when I got home, and he believed me. So I just signed Dad's name on them."

"I'm pretty sure all that is illegal, Danny."

"So what? What's going to happen? Like Dad will have me arrested? Me?"

"He might. You need to tell him what you did in case it ever gets investigated," I added cautiously.

"I'll tell him eventually. But I plan on paying him back first with the money I am making at my job."

"You got a job now? What about high school?"

"I still go once in a while when I can. I'm flunking everything, so the teachers don't bug me much about it."

"Haven't they contacted Mom and Dad?"

"Not yet. Gotta love that public school system. I am eighteen now, and they gotta go through me. I get the mail before Dad gets home and just throw the letters away."

"What is this job you have?"

"I work at Queen's River Steel over in Solon. You know. Johnny Schottky's father owns it. He gave me just regular shit to do, but now he has me moving parts and working on the lathe press. We make parts for airplanes and shit. Can you believe that?"

"And you like this job?"

"I love it, man. Greatest thing I ever done. The day goes by in a flash. Plus, I am lifting heavy shit all day, so I am getting all kinds of new def, brother."

"You don't need any more definition, Danny. But I am happy for you."

"Just don't say nothing to Mom and Dad till I am ready. Okay?"

"Sure. Just like the thing…you know…the big thing that I told you about in the hospital. We keep our secrets to each other. Right, Danny?"

"Oh shit, man. I meant to tell you."

"Tell me what?"

"I told them."

"What? Why? Why the heck would you do that?"

"I'm sorry, brother. I just…well, I was with them one night and…I just told them," Danny said emphatically.

"Shit, Danny. They know?"

"They have known for a while now. I'm guessing you will be hearing about it later today. They didn't want to kick your ass while you were still sick in the hospital."

I shook my head and considered screaming at Danny for being such a shit, but the more I thought about it, I realized that he had probably done me a favor. After all, I had done pretty much the same thing by accidentally telling Deborah's parents within minutes of meeting them. I was going to have to tell my parents anyway as Deborah would soon being having that baby, and then everyone would know.

"Jesus, Danny," I said in exasperation. "I get how it can happen, but how did they get it out of you?"

"We were riding home from going to dinner, and Dad asked me what was new. So I told him about you and the baby."

"That's it. They didn't…you didn't…they didn't trick it out of you or pressure you?"

"Here's the deal with me, brother. Don't tell me anything you don't want other people to know."

"Got it. I will try to remember that."

My mother entered the living room and looked over at me with a loving smile. Then she looked over at Danny, and her expression soured.

"Danny, don't you have something you need to do? Some homework, for example?"

"Sure, Mom. I'll go do homework," Danny said as he winked at me.

My mother sat down in the chair Danny just vacated and leaned forward.

"How are you feeling, son? Is now a good time to talk?"

Danny laughed from a distance as he entered the kitchen.

"Sure, Mom. What do you want to talk about? How about we discuss what the heck is wrong with your idiot youngest son who can't keep his stupid mouth shut?"

"Oh, Danny. He meant well."

"No, he didn't!" I shouted.

"It's just...that...I...how...I mean...how...how did this happen?" my mother began.

"Seriously, Mom? You are asking me how it happened?"

"You know what I mean. You are just twenty years old. Didn't you think about the consequences? Why weren't you more careful? Being a parent is a huge responsibility. It changes everything!"

"I'm not sure I want to have this conversation. What did Dad say about it?"

"Your father, well, he isn't happy, but he is so uncomfortable talking about things like that...he probably won't say anything, except—"

"Except what?"

"Well, he isn't going to give you money for...the...well, the—"

"We aren't going to kill it, Mom. The baby is almost due. Like in only three weeks."

"Danny didn't tell us that," my mother said while looking toward the kitchen. We both knew that Danny was in there listening to every word we said.

"It's a boy, Mom!" Danny yelled in from behind the kitchen door.

"It's a boy?" my mother asked excitedly.

"It is. The name is going to be Elijah."

"You didn't tell me that!" Danny screamed. "Good name though. Hercules would have been better"

"So glad you are pleased, idiot!" I screamed back.

"Three weeks, huh? Wow! That's fast. What are you going to do? I mean, you will be there for the birth. Right?"

"We are working all that out," I said just as Danny strolled back into the living room, chewing on an incredibly huge piece of something that resembled a sandwich.

"Remember what Brooksy said? You should be there, brother. It's your kid too," Danny said while chewing.

"I need to work all that out with Deborah. So far, she isn't much for having me involved in anything."

"Did you two…break up?" my mother asked while reaching out and placing her hand on my knee.

"She kinda broke up with me, but I'm not giving up. It seemed like after I met her parents and they found out, then she was pretty much done with me."

"Oh my," my mother said as she leaned back in her seat.

"Sean told them accidentally when he went over there for dinner. They were serving some kind of casserole with fish in it. Right, Sean?"

"Why on earth does that matter?!"

"I'm just saying. If the mother can't cook, then the daughter probably won't either. And you want a wife that cooks good healthy food and has it ready as soon as you get home. Right, Mom?"

"Danny, could you please go upstairs and get your father? I think we need to discuss some things with Sean here, and I would appreciate it if you would go to the gym or something. We need privacy."

"Thanks a lot, Mom. Here I am trying to help my big brother, and you kick me out of the house."

"Just go get your father, Danny. Thanks!"

Danny turned to go upstairs and gave me the "zipper across the lips" gesture to remind me not to tell my parents any of the stuff he had told me earlier. As much as he deserved it, I did not inform my parents that he had practically dropped out of high school, illegally purchased what might be a stolen car, and forged my father's signature on official loan documents. I was perfectly content keeping all that a secret from my parents.

CHAPTER 25

Living in a Crackerbox

My father, Dennis Stevens, was the prototypical middle-aged suburban husband. He had a good job, but not superhigh paying. He was thrifty on things like going out to dinner and fancy cars, but my father would spend money if he had to on things like college for his kids or a nice vacation for his wife. He chose to live in Shaker Heights primarily because it had good public schools, but the other exceptional allure of Shaker was that the majority of the houses were attractive, fashionable, and well-built. This wasn't a neighborhood of homes that all looked pretty much the same as in so many new developments today. Shaker has some of the largest, most beautiful and expensive houses you have ever seen. But even the other less-affluent areas where the homes were smaller had character, and each was distinctive. There are sidewalks on every street with overlapping trees lining both sides of the road. The best word I could use to describe Shaker Heights was charm. That was true of just about every house in Shaker, except one.

Danny and I called our house the "Crackerbox" as it was rectangular and had nothing distinctive about it except that it had windows that cranked open from the side. That's it. The house did not even have air-conditioning, and this meant that the two hottest months of summer (July and August) were simply miserable for us in the Stevens home. And with the side-cranking windows, we couldn't even install single room air-conditioning units to help cool off at least a part of the house. There was a giant fan in the attic that was supposed to circulate the air to help make us comfortable, but all it seemed to do was push hot air around. And it made so much noise that my mother insisted that it be turned off all the time unless someone was about to die of heat exposure.

The one good thing about the house, however, was that my brother and I had our own rooms, and they were a decent size. Danny's room faced the backyard, and my room faced the front and had a nice view of the street where you could *see* much nicer homes right across from us. Danny and I had to share a bathroom with pink tile and an almost orange bathtub. I think the bathtub started out pink but had faded because of all the toxic chemicals used to clean up after two disgusting teenage boys. My mother didn't like the house either, but she never complained. After we moved in, my father promised my mom that he would do a full kitchen renovation. But sadly, he did most of the work himself which actually made the kitchen look even worse. Danny and I were tasked to paint the cabinets, and because of getting paint all over the glass panels, we had to replace them completely with a cheaper, non-windowed variety.

The only improvement in the kitchen was a new oven, but even that was just a basic no-frills unit from Sears. As bad as all this sounds, my father bought the house because it was solid, practical and good enough for his family. Oh, and it had to be a great deal too, of course and my father liked it most for that reason. He meticulously cared for the grass, gardens, and trees like they were works of art, and for my dad, they were. He offered once to pay me ten dollars to cut the lawn but warned me that it had to be done to perfection with diagonal tracks in front and horizontal tracks in back. He would take money off for any scald marks or missed patches. After mowing, we still had to rake and bag the grass, and there could not be any remnants of cut grass on the driveway or sidewalk, not even one blade. I told him that there was no amount of money he could pay me to do this job. So my dad pretty much always cut the grass himself.

When my father came downstairs to talk to me about Debbie's pregnancy, he was dressed in an awful summer shirt (a Hawaiian print) and green shorts that were at least four inches too short revealing pale legs that were hairy except (inexplicably) his ankles. He had a white belt on, brown socks, and you guessed it, sandals. How my mother allowed him to sleep in the same bed with her at night was a mystery, but that was my father. He solemnly entered the room and sat on the couch across from me. My mother looked nervously at me and then nervously back at him. Surely, his outfit must have been just as concerning to her as me being a prospective parent.

"I think I will go get dinner started," my mother said as she wiped her hands off on the sides of her dress.

"I want salmon crockets, Mom," Danny shouted down from upstairs.

He meant to say *croquettes*, of course.

Salmon croquettes were like little salmon burgers that were a mix of salmon and vegetables and some other stuff. They were shaped like burgers, and my father loved them. Danny did, too, but I would rather eat garden mulch. I hated them, and Danny knew it. As a result, he would get my serving since my mother always allowed me to eat a bowl of cereal rather that send a growing boy upstairs hungry.

"Your mother has informed me of your…situation," my father began stoically. "I can't even start to tell you how disappointed I am in you, Sean. I mean, how could you do this to your mother and me?"

"He didn't do it to you guys, Dad. He did it to Debbie-O. Ha!" Danny shouted out.

"Danny! Please go somewhere," my mother shouted back. "Take that noisy car of yours and leave your father and Sean some peace so they can talk. I'm begging you!"

"Okay, okay. Let me get dressed for the gym, and I will get out of here. Give me two minutes, Dad, and I will let you go ahead and beat Sean to death."

My father rolled his eyes and shook his head. He had even less patience for Danny's moronic sense of humor than I did.

"Please, God, tell me what I did to deserve these two?" my father prayed aloud as he looked up at the ceiling.

"Be nice to him, Dennis. He just got out of the hospital," my mother said as she held open the swinging kitchen door.

"Does Dad know that he wasn't wearing any underwear?" Danny said as he jumped down the steps.

Danny was wearing a red T-shirt that said, "Don't FUCK with me" on the front and "I warned you not to FUCK with me" on the back. My father looked at him with disgust as he passed us on his way out.

"Good luck, Sean. I will see you when I get home, I hope."

Danny smiled and waved playfully as he shut the door behind him. My father adjusted his position on the couch to be more upright, almost like a psychiatrist would before addressing his patient.

"Look, son. What is done is done, and I see no reason to belabor the issue. But I do think we need to cover some ground rules."

"Ground rules?" I asked. I had no idea where he was going with this.

"I will help you out with the finances, but you and that Deborah person need to work too. Yet I don't want your mother having to watch the baby every day of the week. You will have to take evenings, weekends, and you…know. This isn't your mother's child. It is yours, and you will need to do the majority of the work."

"Uh, Dad…you don't seem to—"

"And, Sean, I can't have this being spread all over town either. I want to keep your…situation…as private as possible. Do you understand me? I have a job and a reputation here in Shaker Heights. We just can't have people…talking."

"Dad!" I said loudly enough to make him stop. "You and Mom don't have to do anything. Deborah is handling the entire thing. She doesn't even want me involved. In fact, she really isn't even…talking to me."

My father looked desperately over toward the kitchen where my mother was still standing in the doorway.

"I didn't know about this either until today," my mother said to my father.

"So…you aren't going to…you aren't going to get married?"

"Dad, no. I asked her a couple of times. I told her I loved her and wanted to be the best husband and father a man can be. But she turned me down flat. She is having the kid in some other town and

SCOTT JAMESON SANDERS

then…I don't know what happens after that. I think her parents have that all figured out for her. But they aren't telling me anything… Other than that, I am not needed. When I call there, they just keep telling me that she is visiting relatives."

"You see, dear, Things are different today. Couples either get rid of the baby or they go away to have it. But they don't get married. It's…all different now," my mother lamented. "Isn't that right, son?"

"So you will have no…you won't…I don't get it. Vicky, Help me here."

"He's going to have to work this out with Deborah and…then I guess we will know how it impacts us. It sure doesn't sound like we are going to be grandparents or anything like that."

"Well, you will be technically or in the genes. But other than that, I just don't know yet," I said.

"Sean, I have to say. I expected this of Danny…but not you. I thought we had a good thing going. You were in college, and you were going to get a good job and make something of yourself."

"I can still do that, Dad."

For one of the only times in my life, my father looked completely lost and overwhelmed.

"Vicky, help me understand. So we don't have to do anything? It just all happens and we…do nothing?"

"Looks that way, honey. Sean is a good boy. He will figure all this out."

My father got up slowly from the couch and walked toward the kitchen like he was in a trance. Times certainly had changed since his day when this would have been handled very differently. The big question for me, however, was how I would handle it now.

CHAPTER 26

Shaker's Not So Finest

A few weeks after returning home from the hospital, I was walking again with only minimum use of my crutches. (Mostly, I used them to hold doors open, but I was walking fairly well.) The cast had been so badly scraped up and damaged from me scratching inside it that it was literally no longer anything more than a pile of rags wrapped loosely around my foot. The orthopedic doctor called me his worst patient ever as I did very little of what he told me to do to help my arm and leg heal. I just wanted to live life like a normal person again. Strangely, the one thing that had healed and seemed better than before the accident was my mind. I could remember almost anything and my brother witnessed it one night when he and I were watching a television show called *Jeopardy*, hosted by Art Fleming.

"Who is Sam Spade?" I blurted out toward the television screen as Danny stuffed his mouth with popcorn. He had popped it with an air popper, so it had no taste whatsoever unless you put salt and butter on it, and Danny would never do that.

"What is Tanzania?" I shouted out again, and this caused Danny to throw some of his popcorn at me.

"What the fuck, Sean. Just watch the show, man. Jesus!"

"It's crazy, Danny," I said as I went over to turn down the volume. There are things I am remembering that I have never learned in my life, and yet somehow now I know them."

"It was you and that fucking exor…existor…cistism. You better hope you aren't part of the devil's army-league or something like that."

"Why would knowing more things make me an instrument of evil? And it is legion. Not army league. They word you are looking for is legion."

"You see?! Right there. Why do you say shit like that? You are starting to sound like Father Dave."

"Do I?" I asked.

As we sat there, I reflected back on that day in the hospital. Father Dave had held hands with us, too, and he was a smart guy. His sermons were always full of history, facts, big words, and lots of sayings like that. Had some of his memory or intelligence somehow gone into my mind? Uh-oh. Was he now making sermons with the mind or memory of someone with minimal intelligence like me?

"If I were you, I would go back to that priest and do that… thing again."

"Why? What's wrong with being a little smarter?"

"I don't know. It just isn't you? You aren't a smart guy, that's all I'm saying."

"Thanks. Thanks a lot, Danny. You aren't a genius either, you know."

"You think I don't know that? I know like two things for sure, and one of them is that I ain't a smart guy. But I also know that I got a bod for love, and that makes up for it. What do you got?"

"I got stuff," I responded.

"Like what? You know that the tallest mountain is in France?"

"It's in Tibet, stupid. Mount Everest is in Tibet, wherever that is," I said just as the doorbell rang.

Of course, Danny sat there motionless as I scrambled to get my crutches, so I could get up and go get the dang door. My dad was at work, and my mother was probably upstairs ironing or cleaning up our filthy rooms. She was coming down the stairs as I was approached the front door.

"Sean, please, I can get the door. You go sit down. Why didn't Danny get up?"

"I think it is for me, Mom," I said as I had seen a 1965 Galaxie 500 pull into the driveway from the den window.

We had a circular driveway, and the car came to rest right in front of our front door, but the motor didn't stop when the car did. It was doing that thing a lot of old cars do. They keep running and knocking even after you take the key out. Fortunately, in a few minutes, the gas in the cylinder would drain out, and the car would make a popping sound and then go quiet.

"Mr. Brooks, what are you doing here?" I asked as I swiftly opened the door to allow him to come in.

My mother came the rest of the way down the stairs and went right over to shake his hand.

"Hello, Mr. Brooks. My son has told me so much about you. Please do come in. Can I get you some coffee?"

Mr. Brooks took off his hat and slowly entered the hallway, but he looked nervous. Very nervous.

"What's wrong? Are you okay?" I asked as he handed his hat to my mother. By then, Danny was standing in the doorway with a big smile on his face.

"Hey, Brooksy!" Danny said. "Looking good for a man over a hundred."

"I am only seventy-five years old, Daniel. I told you that."

"I'm just messing with you," Danny asked with a big smile.

"Wait a minute, Danny. Why are you here? Shouldn't you be at school?" my mother asked while looking sternly at Danny. "Shouldn't you be at the high school working on your senior project?"

"It's Friday, Mom…and uh…no school today."

"On Friday? There is no school on Friday now? That just doesn't sound right."

I knew there might be trouble brewing between my mother and Danny, so I pointed toward the living room. Mr. Brooks followed me in and sat in one of the two large cushioned chairs. When he sat down, however, the overstuffed chair seemed to engulf him completely. He couldn't have been much more than a hundred pounds, and he looked so small and uncomfortable sitting there. My mother noticed it and quickly pulled up a wooden ladder-back chair and offered it to him.

"Here you are, Mr. Brooks. Those old chairs need new cushions so badly. Please sit here, and I will get you some coffee. Do you take anything in it?"

"No, ma'am. Just plain old coffee is what I like."

"Excellent. I will be right back."

My mother went off, and Danny left the hallway to go upstairs. I sat in one of the other comfortable chairs and positioned my crutches so they would lean up against the adjacent wall.

"So what brings you all the way here from Warrensville, Mr. Brooks? I hope you aren't still feeling bad about the accident. I am doing fantastic now. Better than ever."

"I'm glad, Sean. I'm really glad. But I had to come see you. My mind...It's still not right since that day. Do you ever have days where you have things come into your mind, but they aren't yours?"

"No, but I...Now I know things that I just couldn't know. You know? I was just watching a game show with Danny, and I knew almost all the answers. And I am a dumb shit."

"Let me ask you something, Sean," Mr. Brooks began. "Did you ever...uh...did you ever run away from home as a kid?"

"I don't think so," I replied.

"I had this memory come to me. Your father was...Well, he wasn't treating you like a good father should...so you got your stuff and followed some train tracks as far as you could. You were gone for two or three days before the police found you and brought you home."

"No. I never ran away, and my father never did anything bad to me other than a few whacks to my behind. But I deserved them. He is a really good dad."

"That's what I thought," Mr. Brooks said as my mother handed him a full cup of coffee with a saucer beneath it.

"Are you sure you don't want some cream or sugar, Mr. Brooks? It is no trouble."

"Well, I do like a little cream, if you got some. But don't go to any trouble."

"It's no trouble. I will be right back," my mother said before turning and rushing back toward the kitchen

Mr. Brooks leaned in closer to me and cleared his throat.

"You think maybe them memories happened to Father Dave?"

I leaned back in my chair to think. It made sense. Father Dave was well educated, but he never—and I mean never—talked about his childhood. He was good-looking and single, but he never went on dates. His sermons, as good as they were, never mentioned his family or where he lived or anything like that. I was about to respond to Mr. Brooks when there was a loud knock on the front door. And then the doorbell rang, and the knocking continued like there was something urgent going on outside.

My mother handed Mr. Brooks the small ceramic pitcher with the cream and went slowly to the front door. When she opened it, there were two police officers standing there in their dark blue uniforms. They were positioned with their legs slightly spread apart, and they had their hands on their gun holsters. They looked very serious, and my mother was instantly very nervous.

"Danny! You better get down here!" she said, never taking her eyes off the two Caucasian officers.

Danny came bounding down the steps but stopped in his tracks halfway when he saw the policemen.

"Oh shit. Mom, I can explain."

"Excuse me, Mrs. Stevens. And you are Mrs. Dennis Stevens. Correct?"

"Yes, I am Victoria Stevens," my mother said.

I was stunned as I had never heard my mother use her full first name before. It was always Vicky. She was scared, and Danny was petrified.

"You see, Mrs. Stevens," the taller of the two officers began, "a neighbor of yours called us a few minutes ago, and well, we are just here to make sure everything is okay. And that you and everyone here is okay."

My mother blinked her eyes several times, and Danny breathed a huge sigh of relief. But then I saw something in my mother's eyes that I had never seen before. It started out as relief, but transitioned to a look of pure rage. She had figured it out way faster than me. But Mr. Brooks knew what was going on, and he stood and placed his coffee cup gently on the side table.

"I guess I will just be going now. I apologize for the trouble, Mrs. Stevens."

"You aren't going anywhere! Please sit down, Mr. Brooks," my mother said sternly. She looked up at Danny, and he retreated back up a few steps.

"Danny. I want you to go call your father and tell him that he needs to come home right away. Can you do that, son?"

"Sure, Mom. I will call him from up here," Danny said as he turned to rush back up the stairs.

"If there isn't any trouble, Mrs. Stevens, we can be leaving. We just wanted to be sure you and your family were okay."

"No. You aren't leaving until my husband gets here. I want him to see in person the kind of police we have in this town."

"Ma'am, we were just doing our job," the officer said.

Strangely, they both still had their hands on their holsters, and I'm sure this only further infuriated my mother.

"I want to know who called you," my mother said sternly. "I want to know who it was, and I want to know now."

"We can't divulge that information, ma'am. It was just a cautionary call, and we are checking it out. I don't think you need to make anything more of it than that."

My mother backed up a step and rubbed her forehead. I knew my mother had some powerful beliefs about race and equality, but I never knew they were this powerful. Mr. Brooks again tried to stand up from his chair, but his legs were shaking, and he had to sit back down.

"If you can't tell me who called, I need to have your badge numbers and the name of your superior officer."

"Mrs. Stevens, we have the right to check on our residents if there is reason to believe there might be…a problem. We aren't doing anything wrong here."

"Well, let me assure you two idiots that there is plenty wrong with what you are doing."

"Like what, ma'am?" the taller of the two officers asked while adjusting his hand on the black leather gun holster on his left side.

"Like intruding upon my family and our guest without cause."

"I wouldn't say that is what we are doing," the shorter officer said. "The automobile, the one out there, isn't the kind of car you normally see driving around Shaker Heights. We are just trying to be cautious."

"That kind of car is the practically the same as the one my husband drives, and yet you never came to our door to check on him. Let's see. I wonder why that is."

"Ma'am, it is our job to protect the residents of this community. That is what you pay us to do."

"I don't pay you to do this. Not this!" my mother replied.

Both officers adjusted their stances as if they were preparing for some kind of escalation. Danny returned to the top of the steps.

"He's coming, Mom. Dad is coming home. Soon. Right away, actually."

"Thank you, Danny. You just stay right where you are. Help me keep an eye on these two to make sure nothing stupid happens. Understand?"

"Yes, Mom. I do. I understand completely," Danny said nervously.

"Good. Now, Sean, you and Mr. Brooks go ahead and continue your conversation. Mr. Brooks, please enjoy your coffee. My husband will be home any minute."

My mother was handling this so skillfully I could hardly believe it. I thought she sounded like a lawyer on the *Owen Marshall, Counselor at Law* television show. She was not going to be satisfied until she saw this through to a proper conclusion. I was impressed beyond my imagination. My father's dealership was only a few miles away, and it wasn't even five minutes before he came rushing in through the back door.

"What is it? I came home as fast as I could," he said as he charged into the living room. "What's going on here?" my father said breathlessly.

"Well, Dennis, let's see. First, we were fortunate enough to be visited by Sean's friend, Mr. Brooks."

My father looked at Mr. Brooks and pretended to tip a hat toward him. Mr. Brooks made the same gesture back.

"And just as we are about to enjoy our coffee, these two show up with their hands on their guns, asking us if there is any trouble here."

"Why would there be any trouble? Wait. Did Danny do something?" my father asked.

"No…well, maybe, but…no. One of our wonderful neighbors alerted the police to the presence of our visitor, and apparently, there is some kind of ordinance in Shaker Heights where your car has to cost a certain amount or you will be investigated."

"We are following proper police protocol for instances like this, Mr. Stevens," the taller officer said. "We are just being cautious."

My father walked into the hallway and placed his hand gently on his wife's shoulder.

"Let me see if I got this right," my father began.

Now my father, on the other hand, reminded me of Perry Mason when he would begin his defense.

"With no provocation, except maybe the presence of a fine Ford automobile, you come into my home with your insanely overreactive police protocol and proceed to scare the crap out of my wife, my sons, and our guest. Is that about right?"

"Well, someone in the neighborhood called first," the taller officer said.

"I know who it is," my mother said angrily. "She will be hearing from me."

"Mr. Stevens, it appears everything is okay, so we can be going now. You and your family have a nice day."

"Yes, but let me assure you that you haven't heard the last of this. I know the chief of police down at the station. I know him well, and this type of treatment is not going to be tolerated. Do you hear me?" my father shouted as the officers walked slowly to their car.

I am happy to report that the officers did finally take their hands off their gun holsters. Maybe some of what my parents said sunk into their stupid brains.

"Vicky, get your purse. We are going down there right now to see Hank."

"Yes, dear," my mother replied as she turned toward our guest. "Mr. Brooks, please enjoy your coffee. I am so sorry about all this."

Mr. Brooks lifted his cup with a shaking hand and took one sip of what was now a lukewarm cup of coffee. He looked stunned and maybe even embarrassed. Mr. Brooks had probably been through something like this a hundred times before, but I don't think he ever ran into anyone like my mother in those situations. I know parents tell their children how proud they are of them when they do good things, but at that moment, I was about as proud of my parents as a person could be. It was a lesson for me in standing up for what is right, and I have never forgotten it. And this mindset was going to be essential for me over the next few months. My parents did go down to the station and made their case to the police chief. The two officers were admonished for their actions, but mostly for having their hands on their sidearms throughout the ordeal. I never saw either one of them again.

I hobbled over to the door and handed Mr. Brooks his hat. He was still feeling a bit woozy, but he smiled at me and patted me on the arm.

"You make sure you thank them good folks of yours for doing what they done. I didn't ever think I would live to see anything like it."

"I will, Mr. Brooks. Thanks for coming to see me. Let's talk again soon. Okay?" I said as he walked slowly to his car.

"Sounds good, Sean. You just keep getting better. We can talk about all that other stuff the next time we meet."

Sadly, there would be no next time.

CHAPTER 27

Hats Off to Mr. Brooks

It was only three days later when Father Dave called me on the phone to give me the sad news. Mr. Brooks had passed away in his sleep. He hadn't been sick or anything, but it seems that his body had just worn out. As Father Dave reminded me of his position on the end of life, it was just his time. I was sad in a way that I had never been sad before. I wanted to cry, but for some reason, I couldn't. And that was not usual for me. I was beyond what normal sad felt like. I could only stand there in stunned silence as Father Dave gave me the details.

"He and I had just talked the day before. You know, about our memory thing. He told me about something in my life that went down a long, long time ago. I was just heading over to his place this morning to discuss it, but he didn't answer the doorbell. The police came and broke the door down, and there he was. He was lying there in his bed, just as peaceful as a dove. I swear, Sean, it seemed like he even had a smile on his face. He looked so happy. I couldn't think anything, except that he was back with his wife and his son. And they were in paradise."

"Well, I am happy for him, I guess. But I really liked the old guy. So did Danny."

"So did I, Sean. He was a very special friend. A very special person."

"Wait until you hear what my parents did when he visited me at my house. Oh man!"

"I heard, Sean. I heard all about it. It meant a lot to him what you and your parents did. I'm proud that you stood up to what is still so wrong with our society. People act like they are all liberated and understanding, but they aren't inside. They are afraid and ignorant, and they harbor their prejudice just below the surface. That makes them even more dangerous in some ways."

"Sounds like you got a sermon brewing."

"I do. It will be a doozy," Father Dave replied. "The church may fire me for it, but so what? Communities like Shaker Heights have their good and bad apples, just like anywhere else. But we have a lot of very wealthy people, and many of them think that they have some God-given right to push their influence on the rest of us. They want the trash cans to be hidden behind the house in Shaker, but we all know that they have trash just like any other town that puts their cans on the street."

"Is that a metaphor, Father Dave?"

"Why, yes, it is. Good for you, Sean."

"Yeah, you see, I didn't even know what that word meant a few weeks ago. And now I do. Do you think it had anything to do with—"

"With our little service at the hospital? Maybe. For a while, I couldn't recall even some of the very basic things I learned in seminary. Strange."

"No, that part sounds like me. I have been a lot smarter than usual, and I assume that came from you."

"Hmm, I have noticed that in my sermons, I have been a bit less—"

"Loquacious," I blurted out, hardly believing that word had even passed over my lips.

"I was going to say *wordy*. But I think people are enjoying my homilies more. And now that Mr. Brooks has passed away, it seems like my mind has pretty much gone back to normal."

My mother walked into the kitchen and winked at me as I sat at the table with the phone to my ear.

"Is everything okay, sweetie?" my mother asked.

"Mr. Brooks died," I replied.

"Oh no. I'm so sorry. Poor Mr. Brooks," my mother said while grabbing some plates out of the cabinet. "That is just so sad."

"Actually, it's not, Mom. Father Dave is telling me that he had a smile on his face. He was happy. And now he is even happier."

"I hope so. He was such a sweet man," my mother said as she began setting the table.

"Look, Sean," Father Dave continued, "Mr. Brooks was a member of the First Baptist Church down on Prospect. They are having a small service for him there tomorrow. I assume you want to come."

"Of course. Danny too. Mom, do you and Dad want to go to the funeral service tomorrow?"

"Let me ask your father, but I think we can make that. Yes, tell Father Dave we will be there."

"They will be there, Father Dave."

"I heard. That's great. I don't suspect there will be a lot of people there as he was—"

"Pretty old. I know," I said.

"Okay, Sean. I will see you there."

"One last thing, Father Dave. There was something I wanted to ask you about."

"Shoot!"

"When he was over here, he told me about some memories that...well, they weren't his. Memories of a mean father and running away."

"Those memories are mine. Or I should say they are memories I have tried to forget."

"Your father was...is he?"

"My father died six years ago, Sean. I hadn't spoken to him in ten years. My mother is still alive, but she is in Florida. I don't talk to her much either. Let's just say my childhood was less than ideal."

"I'm sorry. Is that why you are still single and no kids? You don't want to be a father like your dad was?"

"Perhaps you could say that. But listen, Sean. Those are my issues, and they are private. I would appreciate it if you didn't—"

"Then don't tell Danny. I won't say anything, but you should talk to someone about these things, Father Dave, with no due respect," I offered.

"It's with *all* due respect, Sean."

"It is?" I asked.

"It is."

"Yeah. That makes more sense. Back to the old stupid me, but you should deal with those issues. That's all I am saying.

"No, I know. You are right. I will. Just not now."

"You are a great preacher, but you can't bottle things up. Just like me and anyone else. Take Danny, for instance."

"Now he needs to get into some serious therapy. I agree," Father Dave said. "I wonder what it is that is driving his need for…muscles and all that macho stuff."

"I think my mother really wanted a girl the second time around," I offered. "Or maybe it was when he saw our puppy get run over. He was not able to process that very well."

"Huh? Maybe," Father Dave replied.

"We all need to get these issues out there and resolve them. You need to do that, with all due respect."

"Wow. You really did get a lot smarter, didn't you, Sean?"

"I think I got a little bit of your smartness, Father Dave. I hope you don't mind, but I want to keep it."

"Ha ha. I get it. Thanks, Sean. So I will see you at the church?"

"Yes, Father."

"Listen. You and Danny need to call me Dave. Not Father Dave. All right?"

"That is not going to happen. It's Father Dave or nothing!"

"Okay, okay. See you soon, and take care."

"You too. Goodbye, Father Dave."

I realized that I had said goodbye and didn't just hang up. It wasn't the right time to try to be cool. But that time was coming and coming very soon.

CHAPTER 28

Congratulations! It's *Not* a Boy!

The next time I heard anything from Deborah, she had just returned home from wherever it was she went to have the baby. She had left a message with my mother that all was well and the child was healthy. I already knew she had returned home, though, as I had been driving past per parent's house almost every day hoping to see her Karmann Ghia outside. I never saw her cool VW sports car, but I did notice a lot of people coming in and out of the house one day. It was a party of some sort, and I was obviously not invited. I pulled over to the curb and grabbed my cane to walk to the front door. I was walking fairly well by then, but still needed help getting up and over things like curbs. I saw someone through the front window as I walked up the drive, and obviously, he saw me.

"Oh no. Not today. We have company over. Please. Just give us a call, and we will talk later," Mr. Robbins said from inside the front door. He had barely opened it, but I could see that it was him.

"That's not going to work for me, Mr. Robbins. We need to talk and talk now. That is my baby, too, and I have every right to see him."

"Wait here," he said.

Mr. Robbins shut the door, but I could hear him saying something to someone inside. A few minutes later, he opened the door again, came outside and slammed it behind him, probably to scare me. It worked.

"Come with me," he said as we walked around the side of the house and into the backyard. They had a nice patio in back with one of those canvas awnings that you could crank on to block the sun. It was cranked on at the time. When we got there, two of the guests quickly got up to leave and shut the sliding patio doors behind them.

"Look, Sean," Mr. Robbins said as he kicked a chair toward me. "We have relatives over here now, so this is going to have to be very brief."

I sat down slowly in the chair, but I made sure to keep my focus and gaze directly on Mr. Robbins. I was feeling that bold feeling again, and I wasn't going to let him bully me.

"Let me just say for the record, we have been very nice about this, but we also made it very clear that you are not going to be a part of this child's life. That's the way I want it. That's the way Deborah wants it, and that is the way it is going to be. You got it?"

"With no due—I mean, with all due respect, Mr. Robbins, that's not at all how it is going to be."

"Look, young man. We can get the authorities involved if you insist, but if I were you—"

"No need to do that, Mr. Robbins. I already got the authorities involved, and they are on my side here. You have no legal right to keep me from seeing my child. That is a fact! My dad got a lawyer, and we will get the police over here to force this issue, if that's the way you want it."

"What is going on out here? Why is he here?" Mrs. Robbins said as she walked out of the kitchen and onto the patio.

"Mr. Tough Guy is intending to make a scene. Today of all days."

"Sean, can you just come back tomorrow? Today is not a good day. We have relatives and people over and—"

"Why is today no good? What makes today any different?" I asked.

"We had the baby baptized today. If you must know," Mr. Robbins said.

"Yes, I must know. And that was not appropriate to do without the father's consent or especially my presence. Your lawyers should have told you that."

"John, can you please just ask him to leave? Nicely," Mrs. Robbins pleaded.

"You need to get out of here, Sean. And you and I guess your father will be hearing from my lawyers. That's right. I said *lawyers*. Plural! We will fight you on this this and spend whatever we have to in order to keep our granddaughter safe and away from the likes of you."

"Wait…what did you say?" I asked.

I was suddenly in a state of shock.

"I said if you even think that you are going to be able to—"

"No, not that. The other thing."

"What other thing?" Mr. Robbins asked.

"You said…Did you say it's a baby girl?" I asked.

And suddenly, a tear leaked out of my left eye and then another from the right eye.

"It was a bit of surprise to all of us," Mrs. Robbins said as she approached me.

I wiped my face with both hands, but the tears kept coming. So much for being bold.

"It's a girl?" I asked. "Does she have a name?"

"It's Mary. Mary Elisabeth," Mrs. Robbins said with an emerging smile.

"Wait. Which one is it? Mary or Elisabeth?"

"Are you really that stupid?" Mr. Robbins said tersely.

"John, please. He is the father after all. Give him a bit of a break."

"No. And neither will my legal team. You will be hearing from them. Good luck and good day, Mr. Stevens," Mr. Robbins said as he got up to leave.

He leered angrily at me as he closed the patio door behind him.

"Deborah is still debating whether to call her Marybeth or just Mary or just Beth," Mrs. Robbins said.

"I like Marybeth," I said through another cascade of tears.

Mrs. Robbins pulled out a deck chair and sat down across from me.

"Hits you like a ton of bricks, doesn't it?" she said kindly.

"It's a baby girl. Wow! I mean, I like boys too. If it had been a boy I mean. Wait. I'm not saying this right."

"She is so pretty. Wait until you see her. And healthy too. She was seven pounds."

"Is seven pounds...is that...good for a girl?" I asked.

"It is, Sean. It is very good. Look, why don't you come back in a few hours after our guests leave? I will get my curmudgeon of a husband to understand, and we can all have a civil conversation. No one wants lawyers to be involved. Right?"

"Right, Mom!" Deborah said as she stepped out through the sliding doors. "Can me and Sean have a few minutes? I will be right back in, Mom. I promise."

"Sure, dear. You two talk. Sean, I'm sorry about...Well, we will work things out. Congratulations! She really is the most beautiful thing."

Mrs. Robbins walked inside but looked back at me with a sweet smile as Deborah (without a sweet smile) sat in the chair opposite me. She looked so good, and you could barely tell from her midsection that she had just had a baby.

"You look really, good, Deb," I said while wiping the tears out of my eyes.

"What? Have you been...crying?"

"Sort of."

"Jesus, Sean. Get some testicles. It's just a baby."

"You are kidding, right?"

"Of course, I am kidding," Deborah said, and then the biggest—and I mean biggest—smile came over her face. "Believe it or not, I can't stop crying either. And all she does is cry too. It's a crying fest! She eats and shits and cries some more, but I just...love her."

"You did it, Deborah. Great job...uh...getting it out of there," I said, looking down at her stomach.

"You wouldn't believe the pain. My god. It was coming out feet-first, so they had to reach in there and turn her around. Imagine that?"

"Ouch!"

"Don't you want to see her?"

"Of course I do!" I said. "But I think your father is ready to have me shot by the Shaker Heights police. And believe me, you don't want them to get involved."

"Who cares about him? Or the police! Come on. Come and see!" Deborah said as she jumped up from her seat. "There are lots of people in the house, so my father won't go too crazy. Plus, I will hold your hand as we go up the stairs. He won't make a fuss if he sees that. Come on."

I got up and grabbed Deborah's hand, and she pulled me in through the sliding doors and into the hallway where her father was standing.

"Hey, what the heck!" Mr. Robbins shouted out. "What is he—"

"Let them go, John," Mrs. Robbins said sternly as she pulled him into an adjacent room.

"Come on!" Deborah said as we rushed upstairs. "She may be asleep, so you want to be a little quiet, but I don't care if you wake her up. She has been out for at least an hour already. Just don't startle her. Okay?"

"Okay," I replied sheepishly.

"Are you ready?" Deborah said as she stood in front of the bedroom door with her hand on the doorknob.

"I think so," I replied while taking in a huge breath like I was about to dive into the cold ocean water.

"You are going to freak out," she said as she slowly pushed the door open, revealing a small white crib with a mobile of blue bears spinning above it. Debbie went over and looked in the crib and smiled back at me.

"She's up. Come on. Don't be shy."

I walked slowly over to the crib and looked down at what had to be the most beautiful sight I had ever seen. I know everyone thinks their baby is the most beautiful, but I think this one truly was. She had light brown hair and a very pale, but healthy complexion. She was lying on her back, and her eyes seemed to light up when I looked down on her.

"She is…just…amazing," I said while praying that I wouldn't start crying again.

Deborah moved over next to me, and we both stared down at her for what must have been five minutes. She didn't do much, but she didn't have to. She was a real person, and she was breathing and healthy. It was a miracle even bigger than the USA winning the Olympic hockey gold medal that winter. Much bigger.

"I have to feed her now. Want to watch me?"

"I…uh…Are you sure?"

"Come on, you nerd. You've seen them before. She seems to really prefer the left one for some reason."

"So do I," I said before thinking about the wisdom of introducing my immature humor at a time like this.

Fortunately, Deborah ignored me (or didn't hear it) and lifted our child out of the crib and went over to sit on a wicker rocking chair in front of the window. Everything in the room was blue, of course, since they expected her to be a boy, but it didn't matter. Deborah pulled her blouse up and loosened her bra, and that baby went to town.

"She's really hungry," I said, trying not to say anything else stupid, especially about her breasts. "What does it feel like?"

"It's weird. At first, I thought I wouldn't like it and I would bottle-feed her. I mean, this seems a little crazy, right?" Debbie said, looking down at Marybeth. "But then I tried it, and it is…I don't know, really. It is like this amazing connection that only a mother and child can have."

"I get it. Unfortunately, men can't do that."

"You, of all people, would do it if you could. Right?"

Deborah smiled back at me as the baby continued to feed.

"Yeah, I probably would. Men do have nipples, you know?"

"I know, right? Worthless appendages," she said, laughing.

"Well, I guess I should let you…finish up here. I think your father may have already called in a SWAT team."

"Don't worry about him, Sean. My mother and I will work on his attitude. He will calm down. I've been thinking through all of this, and you can see her as much or as little as you want. We can work all that out."

SCOTT JAMESON SANDERS

"We can work it out. Yeah, we can work it out," I sang to the tune of the Beatles song with that title. "And I won't be a pain in the ass to your dad, I promise."

"Sean, there are a lot of things for you and me to discuss. And we should do that soon, but for today, I just want us to enjoy her. We can do that, right?"

"Yessiree," I said while looking lovingly at my child. "Yes, I was award that that sounded a lot like Danny."

"And please don't cry again. I don't want her to think her father is a total wuss. Okay?" Deborah pleaded.

"I'll try," I answered.

I didn't cry anymore, but I was simply mesmerized.

"You are just the most beautiful thing! Yes, you are!" I said lovingly to the small child.

"Oh, please. And no baby talk. I have to absolutely insist on that. Please, Sean."

"You go your way, I'll go mine, sister."

"You see? Right there!" Deborah said while sitting up in her chair.

"Right there, what?"

"What you just said."

"What?"

"What has happened to you? You seem different to me."

"I do?" I asked sincerely.

"It's something. I don't know. You seem more together or something. I can't explain it."

"Well, you know. A few things have happened," I began. "There was getting hit by a car and almost dying. There was my amnesia, the hemorrhaging, the ICU, and quitting college and getting a real job. Oh, and me preparing to be a first-time father. Just a few things that might make a person seem a little different."

"I know. But I still get the sense that there is something else going on here."

"There was the prayer thing, but that seems to have faded away. We are all back to normal. Well, except for Mr. Brooks because he is dead now."

"Mr...who? Wait. Who?"

"He was a great guy, but he died. He was the one who hit me with his car."

"That guy?"

"Yeah. And then Father Dave came in and we did this prayer thing and…I think it changed all of us. Danny too."

"Well, let me just say that I like what I see."

"Wait! Did you just say you like something about me?"

"I have always liked you, Sean. You know that. Jesus!"

"No. I don't think I do."

"I like you plenty! Okay, I said it."

"Oh my gosh, Deborah. Then…why…what? I mean…"

"My parents are so concerned about what people are going to say. I was too. You know, not being married and all, I guess, but I don't care anymore. Fuck 'em if they can't handle it! You are the father of this child, and they need to deal with it. So does my father."

My eyes might have almost popped out of my head right there.

"Uh-oh. I don't want to get you crying again. No more tears, okay? Not in front of our baby. Okay?"

"Okay," I said while trying my best to suck up any tears that might have been on the verge of appearing.

"Good!" she said as she pulled the baby closer to her chest.

"I still can't believe you got that head all the way out of there. It must be like the way a snake can stretch his mouth over an animal about three times its size."

"Oh my god. Did you just compare childbirth and my vagina to the way a snake eats?"

"Sorry."

"Don't be. That's pretty much what it is like. You should be happy you missed that."

"I wouldn't have watched. I wouldn't have been able to handle it."

"Smart."

"Okay then," I said as I looked around the room. "Do you think I can just jump out this window and make my getaway?"

"No," Deborah said with a smile. "You can just walk out the front door, but I wouldn't mingle down there. Just go down the stairs and straight out."

"Got it! Don't mingle."

"Goodbye, Sean."

"So, Deborah, do you think it would be safe...I mean...can I call you...in a few days?"

"Call me tomorrow, you dope. I'll get my mother to take the baby, and you and I can take a walk...or something and talk about all this. There is a lot to discuss, you know?"

"Okay. By the way, I didn't see your Karmann Ghia? Do you still have it?"

"No. Sorry. I know you liked that car, but my father bought me something called a minivan. It's a Dodge, I think."

"I saw it out back. It's a Dodge Caravan. Those are great vehicles. Lots of room, and the door on the side slides instead of opens out. Perfect for a baby. That was a smart move by Chrysler."

"Jesus! You and your cars."

"I love them. I can't wait to buy her one, but in a few years, I guess."

"Just a few," Deborah said as I backed my way slowly toward the door. "Don't forget. Call me tomorrow."

"I won't forget, and...uh...thanks for...being so cool."

"Thanks for what? I should be thanking you!"

"For what?"

"For this!" Deborah said as she gently squeezed the baby who had already fallen back to sleep.

"Oh sure. Anytime."

"Funny. Now go, and don't tell anyone down there that you just saw my tits."

"Sorry. Danny is going to want to hear about that."

"You are both pathetic," Deborah said with a smile.

I closed the door as softly as I could, and just as I expected, the tears began to flow. Crying or not, I did as Deborah had suggested and literally bounced down the steps and ran right out the front door.

I can honestly say that, to this point, this was, by far, the best day of my entire life. I couldn't wait to get home and write all about it in my notebook.

CHAPTER 29

Taking It Seriously

As much as I liked to kid and joke around, and I still do, I knew that I had to think through a plan for my life that would be smart and prudent. A part of that plan would not include going back to college. My parents were not happy to hear that, but I was pragmatic with my father, and it seemed to work.

"You see, Dad, I want to be in the same town as the baby, but I will get a job. I have been talking to Mr. Davidson, one of the salesmen at your dealership, and he said that their new Honda store was looking for salespeople. So I—"

"Honda! You want to sell Hondas? What's wrong with Fords?"

"Fords are fine, Dad, but Hondas are for a younger generation like mine. New parents, you know? They are front-wheel drive, and they get supergood gas mileage. I have checked them out, and they are decent cars and selling pretty fast."

"A Ford Escort is better than any Honda Civic. Any day! I can promise you that!"

While this was patently untrue, even back then, I didn't want to argue with my father, so I let it go.

"Anyway, you know I love cars, and I will work really, really hard, Dad. You will see. And I will take classes at night if that makes you happy."

"Not if you have a daughter to take care of, you won't. Classes can come later."

"Good thinking, Dad."

"But, Sean, you are going to have to pay rent here, you know? You can't just live in our house and eat our food for nothing?"

"Okay, Dad. No problem."

"Well, I guess I could cut you a break on rent and food for a little while until you get your sales going."

"I won't live here too much longer, Dad. I promise," I said. "I know you and Mom want to have your love nest back after all these years."

"Wait, you think Danny is ever going to leave?"

"Oh yeah. Sorry."

"Do me a favor, son, and help me keep Daniel on the straight and narrow. I am not so sure about your brother sometimes."

"He's got a huge heart, Dad. I know that," I said with a smile. "But I will do what I can to help."

And I did do that. I made sure Danny got that GTO properly licensed, and he started paying my father back for taking his college money out without his permission. My father was pissed at him for a month for forging his signature, but that eventually wore off. Danny and I did hang out a lot together when I wasn't working or taking care of the baby. As it turned out, Deborah wanted me to come get the baby most evenings for at least an hour. Evidently, she needed the break and so did her parents. Danny almost always came along, and we would just take her for rides in the minivan or for walks in the Shaker parks. They both seemed to enjoy every minute of it.

I did finally have the expected confrontation with Mr. Robbins, and it went about as well as I could have expected.

"So you aren't going to be any more trouble? You two will have joint custody and share in all the parenting responsibilities. That means expenses too."

"Yes, sir. Not a problem."

"And you will always be very careful with her. No risky shenanigans like when you lost your car?"

"Of course not. Wait, you heard about that?"

"Just assure me that you will be responsible with her at all times."

"I won't ever take any chances with Marybeth. I promise you."

"We are calling her, Mary, Sean. I thought you knew that."

"Oh. Okay. Mary it is."

"So tell me one last thing," he said, with his eyes seemingly closed in deep thought. "Didn't you even once think to just…you know…get married like most people do when they have a baby?"

"I thought for sure you knew. She didn't tell you?"

"Tell me what?" he asked.

"I asked her twice when it first happened. And then I asked her about once a week before you guys found out. I asked her again after you guys learned about it and even a couple of times after that. I even asked her last week."

"Are you being serious?"

"Of course, I am. I love Deborah. I always have."

"And she—"

"She likes me okay, but I am sorry to say, I think that's about it."

"Are you sure?"

"Mr. Robbins, no person would put themselves through rejection as many times as I have and not be in love."

"No, I mean, are you sure she doesn't love you back? That one is a difficult female, you know. Not like my other girls."

"I'm pretty sure she isn't like any other girl alive, but I'm not giving up. I've got a good job now, and I stopped saying 'what's up?' all the time. And she seems to be happy with how I handle things with Marybeth, I mean Mary."

"I had no idea you had been turned down so many times."

"For all my faults, I can be pretty persistent."

"Tell me about it. I…uh…well…I better let you work things out with her on your own. But, Sean, let me say one thing to you. And I hope you don't take it the wrong way."

Uh-oh. I wanted so badly for this conversation to end well, so I took in a deep breath and hoped for the best. And then it hit me. He was going to ask me why I hadn't done more to prevent Deborah from getting pregnant. And I had no good answer for that, but I wasn't going to lie to him. I resolved to tell him the truth. I was a different person back then and I wasn't being responsible, but I would be now. I had to be. There were three lives involved now.

"It's just this. And I guess I will just have to ask you," Mr. Robbins began.

"Please, sir, you can ask me anything."

"That day you came over, the day of the baptism?"

"What about it?" I asked.

"You came over here all tough and insisting to be involved with the baby. You remember?"

"Of course. Yes."

"You were really assertive, Sean. Really assertive."

"I'm sorry, Mr. Robbins. But I was right, you know. She is my child too."

"No, it's not that. It's…well, people don't usually talk to me that way."

"Well, sorry, but she is—"

"No, Sean. I was impressed."

"You were?"

"You said that you had consulted a lawyer and that you knew the law and that you were going to make sure you were not going to be denied your legal rights."

"Yes."

"Was any of that true?"

"No, sir."

"That's what I thought," Mr. Robbins said while playfully slapping his knee. "You had me on the ropes, son. I have to admit it."

"Okay, then. Was any of what you said true? About what you would do to make sure I didn't see the baby?" I asked.

"Every word of it. Until Mrs. Robbins talked some sense into me."

"That's what I thought."

"Come on, Sean. Let's you and me go have a beer. You do drink beer, don't you?"

"No, sir. Sorry."

"Is that true?"

"No, sir."

"Come on. Maybe we can have two before the ladies get home."

Second best day of my life. Right there.

CHAPTER 30

A Walk in the Park

After only a year or so of selling Hondas, I was starting to be ranked either first or second for new car sales every month. My friend Ben even bought one from me, but he also insisted that I split my commission with him. That was Ben. Barry said he wouldn't be caught dead driving a teenage girl's car and that is what he thought of Hondas. I told him that I would sell him one someday, but it would be years before Honda made anything fast enough to please Barry. I loved the job, and I especially loved meeting and talking to the young couples that came in. Most of them were in the same situation as me and Deborah, except they were married, of course. I even used my first big commission check to put a down payment on a brand-new 1981 Honda Civic station wagon. It was one of the best-rated small cars of that era, and I loved it. It was silver on the outside and black cloth on the inside. I had an infant seat installed in the back that I never took out. The car only had 60 horsepower, but it got around fine. My Mustang with the 289 engine was rated at 225 horses, but now that just seemed excessively fast to me. I had intended to trade it in on the Civic, but my father asked me to sell it to him. Remarkably, he gave me exactly what the car was worth even though I wasn't finished paying him back for it.

"Just take the money and use it…for…you know…baby stuff," my father said as I handed him the keys.

"Wow! Thanks, Dad. You are going to love it."

My father had always wanted a *play car*, and I was happy when I saw him peel out down the street when he and my mother went for a joyride. It was a Ford after all. My father had finally treated himself to something impractical. I think we should all do that from time to time. But now I was entering my practical period of life. With my Honda, I had to get used to watching other cars fly off the line at stoplights, but I didn't mind. If Marybeth (yes, I still called her that) was in the car with me, I would proceed only after looking in both directions—twice. And then, ever so slowly, I would proceed into the intersection, especially if it was that horrible one in Shaker Heights or one of the stupid roundabouts or if we were crossing rapid-transit tracks.

One of the most unique things about the community of Shaker Heights was that it was built in the early twentieth century principally as a suburb and mostly for lawyers and bankers that worked downtown. Because of that, they built train lines that led from the heart of Cleveland to various stops in Shaker Heights. No need to drive your car to work. You just could either walk or drive your car a few blocks to a station where you could leave your car for the day. A great convenience back then, and people used it. Not all the tracks still exist today, but the main lines on Shaker Boulevard and Van Aken are still in use.

The only problem with the trains back then was that no one was ever quite sure when it was safe to cross over the tracks because, again, streets came at you from all angles in some intersections. The confusion caused by the intersecting of trains and cars at Shaker Square was almost catastrophic. Putting train tracks in the middle of major thoroughfares might not have been the best idea of the hallowed city planners. Still, riding on the one of the rapid trains is kind of cool, and you can still take them all the way to the Terminal Tower in Downtown Cleveland. Marybeth loved to ride on them just for fun. So did Danny.

As the end of another summer approached, Deborah decided that she would go back to college but would continue living at her parents' house for the time being. She took evening courses at Cleveland State University, and this gave me even more time to be with my precious daughter. Deborah often needed me to watch her on the weekends, too, so she could study, and I even brought Marybeth to work with me once. I must have sold a record number of cars that day while showing her off to my clients. But my idiot manager told me, despite the successful sales, to keep the kid at home from that point on. He explained that he was afraid everyone would start bringing their kid into work with them.

"So what's wrong with that?" I asked him. "We could set up kind of a day-care thing here for working parents, and our productivity would go through the roof."

"Go sell some cars, Sean," he said tersely before walking away.

It was an idea ahead of its time, I guess.

My entire family loved it when the baby was with us. My mother especially doted on her. She didn't have a daughter to dress up and do girly stuff with, and Marybeth was more than happy to oblige when it came to an afternoon of shopping with my mother. Even at less than a year old, she and my mom would rush from store to store, and my mother always came out with bags of clothing that she would have to hide from my father when she got home. Deborah's parents spoiled Marybeth, too, so that kid had plenty of toys, books, games, and clothes, that's for sure. I'm not sure this is true, but I don't think you can over spoil a baby. Maybe you can, but you sure can't over love them. And that kid had love coming at her from every direction. I once gave her a little Cleveland Browns onesie, which had Brian Sipe's number seventeen on the back. Sipe was my favorite Browns player from that era, but this gesture did not go over well with Deborah.

"Not going to happen, sport," she began. "Leave the clothes to the females please."

I knew she didn't really mean it to sound so mean, but I kept the Sipe onesie at my house just to be sure she didn't throw it out. Marybeth wore it only when Deborah wasn't around.

"Sipe is okay," Danny said about the onesie. "But he needs to pump some iron. His throws are so weak, I don't know how he plays in the NFL. She should wear a linebacker's jersey. Clay Matthews is a monster."

My brother, Danny, was simply hysterical with Marybeth. He would hold her and rock her appropriately like a baby, but he talked to her like she was an adult. Perhaps, Danny had met his intellectual equivalent.

"So you see, you never want to mix your proteins. Just keep to one type at each meal, and make sure you have a plan to work it all off with a good cardio within a few hours. I used to go to the gym in the morning, but that is too early to work off the carbs, so you want to go in the early afternoon. That is the ideal time."

I am paraphrasing there as I didn't have the slightest idea of what Danny was talking about, but he sure loved to talk to her, and she loved him right back. I never had to ask if he wanted to come along for a ride or a walk. He always did, and most of the time, he just seemed to show up. We were walking in the park near one of the Shaker Lakes one day when a couple of young men approached us. Marybeth was in her stroller but was sitting up and very alert as the two men got closer.

"Do you mind if we take a quick peek at your baby?" one of the two men asked politely.

"No. Sure. Take a gander," Danny said with a huge smile. "She's fourteen pounds already. That kid is packing it on, but it's not fat. Look at her arms and legs. It is all lean there. No flab."

"She is gorgeous," the other man said. "It's a girl, right?"

"Yes. Her name is Mary, but we call her Marybeth. She will be a year next week," I said.

"Oh my. You two are so lucky. If you don't mind us asking, how did you...you know?"

"Oh. We did it the old-fashioned way," I said, but I could tell that this only confused the two men, so I clarified. "She has a mother, but we aren't...together, you know. We aren't married."

"We are considering adoption ourselves. But there is no way anyone is going to let two gay guys adopt a baby in Ohio."

Danny looked at me and then at the two men and then back at me.

"I don't get it."

"Just let it go, Danny. Nice to meet you two."

"No wait!" Danny shouted. "Are you telling me that they make it harder for gay people to adopt babies than they do...un-gay people?"

"Not harder. Impossible. They only want heterosexual married couples," one of the men said somberly.

I was terrified beyond comprehension of what might happen next. And what did happen was more shocking than I could have ever imagined.

"Well, that's bullshit! That's total bullshit!" Danny said angrily. "What does being gay have to do with being a good parent? Heck, it might even make you a better parent. That's what I think, anyway."

Oh my god. Danny was making perfect sense.

"You guys just need to keep fighting. Don't give up. Having a baby is your right, and you can't let a couple of government assholes tell you otherwise. Lie if you have to but be tough, and don't give in or give up!"

"Is that what you two did?" one of the men asked Danny.

Uh-oh.

"What? What do you mean?" he asked.

I wanted to run.

"What? Me and scraggly here? Shit, he's my brother. That's his kid, not mine."

I was somewhat relieved, but I still wanted to run.

"Wait. Let me ask you guys something. And I want an honest answer," Danny said in what was almost a whisper.

Uh-oh.

"Sure," the two men said, nodding at each other.

"You didn't think I was gay, did you? Just him. Right?"

"Okay, Danny. It's time to get back to the house," I said abruptly.

"I mean, look at me. I'm toned and buff and he...he..."

The two men started walking away from us immediately, and I prayed that they couldn't hear what he said next.

"I ain't no gay basher. But I am not gay either. Just cause a couple of cool guys are taking a nature walk in the park with their one-year-old child doesn't mean"

"They can't hear you, Danny."

"But they...they thought...you and me..."

"Let it go, big guy. Let it go."

"All right," Danny said while taking the handle of the stroller and pushing it himself. "But next time we run into anyone out here, you gotta tell them…that I'm not gay. You got it?"

"I got it," I said as Danny pushed the stroller back down the winding sidewalk.

The lakes could be remarkable this time of year, and I hoped that the rest of our walk would allow us all to take in the fresh air and beauty of what might be the best attribute of Shaker Heights.

"Maybe I gotta pump some more iron. I been hanging out with you too much."

"Oh boy. Here it comes."

"How could they think that I'm gay? I mean, come on! I lift. I wear super tight shirts to show off my biceps. Gay people don't do that. Do they, Sean? It's just…Well, I can't be putting out that kind of a vibe. I drive a fucking hot muscle car! Right, Sean? Sean?"

So much for taking in the beautiful Shaker Heights scenery.

EPILOGUE

The Golden Balloon

It was Marybeth's third birthday party, and we were having the cel-
ebration at Deborah's parents' house. My entire family, including an
even more muscular Danny, was there, and Marybeth had some of her
three-year-old friends over as well. We had cake and games and pop-
sicles and all the typical things you have at a three-year-old's birthday
party—all except for the clown, of course, since both Danny and I had
a tremendous fear of clowns. I'm not sure why, but neither of us as
kids could ever watch a clown show on television, and the aversion just
carried on into adulthood. I think it was from once watching that Bozo
the Clown show that we could get on cable. He talked like he had just
smoked a pack of Lucky Strikes, and he wasn't friendly looking at all. I
don't think Danny and I are alone in our mysterious aversion to Bozo.

Mr. Robbins and I were doing well, but I still wasn't completely
comfortable around him. He could be awkwardly quiet and that
intimidated the heck out of me. He came over and stood next to me
at the party but didn't say anything at first, so I stared blankly ahead
and began peeling the label off my empty beer bottle.

"You going to watch Ohio State this Saturday?" I blurted out
nervously.

It was a stupid question for Mr. Robbins as he wasn't an Ohio
State fan. He never even talked about sports, so he just chose to
ignore me for the moment. But eventually the awkward silence even
seemed to get to him.

"Sean, I have been meaning to ask you something," Mr. Robbins began.

"Oh, okay. What?"

"I was thinking that you shouldn't call me Mr. Robbins anymore."

"Oh really? What...would I call you then?"

"How about my first name, John?" he said as he now stared blankly ahead.

"Really? You want me to call you that?"

Mr. Robbins hesitated for a moment and then began shaking his head.

"No. Sorry. Bad idea," he said. "But Mr. Robbins doesn't sound right to me either."

"No, I agree," I said while trying to think of something else I could call him besides his real name. *Dad* was never going to work for me as I already had a dad. A really good one.

"How about I just call you Granpa? Like Marybeth does."

"You okay with that?" he asked.

"I'm okay with that," I said as we clinked our beer bottles together.

"You are going to have to call that kid Mary when you are around me, Sean. You know that, right?"

"Sure thing, John," I replied with a smile.

"You are ruining a rare good moment. You do know that? Right?" Mr. Robbins said, smiling back.

"Yes, sir."

"Have you thought at all about my offer to have you come work for me? I can get you onto my junior management team, and well, it is a good job and, I must say, a ridiculous salary."

"Thanks so much, Mr. Robbins, but I am super happy selling cars. I know you probably look down on my job, but I'm actually really good at it—"

"What are you talking about? I admire the heck out of you for it."

"You do?" I said in surprise.

"Sales is where it is at, son. If we don't have good salespeople hitting the road and bringing in orders, there isn't much for the rest of us to do. Me included."

"Wow!" I exclaimed.

"I get it, son. You stay in that job. But if you ever get sick of it, you know where to come. Right?"

"Yes, sir. I will. I promise. You just called me son, you know?"

"Funny. Have you seen Deborah? I haven't seen her in quite a while," Mr. Robbins asked while gazing around the backyard.

"No. Actually I haven't seen her, and it is getting close to time to cut the cake and do gifts."

"She went somewhere in the minivan," Mr. Robbins replied. "Said she would be back in ten minutes, but it has been way longer than that."

"Oh shit. I hope…No…I'm sure it is nothing," I said, but for some strange reason, I was instantly horrified that something bad had happened to her. "Dang Shaker Heights roads are way too dangerous!"

I was plenty worried, especially because it seemed like things had gotten really good with me and Deborah. She was doing well in school and was about to finish up her bachelor's degree in political science. I still didn't really know what that meant, but she intended to start teaching right after the Christmas break. Things were so good with us, in fact, that I was even considering making another marriage proposal to her. I knew it was a risk, but I told her that I had purchased a ring and that she needed to let me know when she was ready. She rolled her eyes sarcastically and said, "Oh, okay." I was happy with that as it wasn't an outright rejection like all the others.

Over the previous year, I had moved out of my parents' house and into a small Tudor-style home on the northern border of Shaker and University Heights. Debbie helped me pick it out, but I knew the second I saw it that it was the right place for us. It was over by the high school, and it had an enormous oak tree in the front yard. I had tied a rope swing to it for Marybeth, and she just loved it. The house was small, but it had great potential, and Danny loved helping me fix it up. Unlike me, he was really handy with tools, and he had even installed a garage door opener for a building that had barn-style sliding doors. He installed the electric motor and chain on the side wall of the old, detached garage and rigged it so both doors would slide open when I pushed the button on the remote. I considered this one of the smartest things I had ever seen in my life.

With Debbie going back to work soon, I knew we would need help with Marybeth and all her activities. Play groups, music classes, and all the other things three-year-old kids did would be too much for a working couple, so I suggested that we get a part-time nanny to help us. I even suggested that Danny do it, but that was not well received. I think he would have been great at it, actually. Our daughter would stay at my house most of the time now, and I silently hoped that Deborah would soon come to stay too. I knew she was struggling with the idea, but I assured her that we would make it work. Deborah even fell asleep one night on my new sofa. I was afraid to wake her up, so I called her parents and told them she was staying with me. Amazingly, they didn't seem to mind.

It was becoming clear to most of us that Deborah was softening a bit too. She was tired a lot from doing school, a part-time job, and raising a daughter, and this seemed to make her nicer for some reason.

"You can't be a hard-ass all the time when you have a three-year-old," Father Dave told me after church one Sunday. "Kids mellow you out a bit, and well, things change. You change. You have changed too, Sean, and let me add, it is almost all for the better."

"What part isn't?" I asked him.

"Just the hair. You comb it now, and it is so short," he replied with a smug smile.

"Yeah, I know. I do that for work, but I promise you, I mess it up as soon as I get home."

"Good," he said before shaking the hand of the next parishioner.

It was another agonizing five minutes before the red minivan pulled into the Robbinses' driveway. I came rushing over as Deborah struggled to pull the helium-filled balloons out of the sliding van door. Strangely, on those early minivan models, the sliding back seat door was only on one side—the passenger side. They rectified that in future models, but that was all she could get on a Dodge Caravan.

"Fucking Bordenaro's Market," Debbie began. "I ordered the balloons a week ago, and they only got them done this morning. I almost said, 'Fuck it,' but I didn't want there to be a birthday party without balloons. You know what I mean?"

"Sure, I guess I do," I said while carefully trying to help her get the balloons out of the van without accidentally letting one go.

I was just so relieved she was home and safe. She must have purchased thirty balloons, and they were all different colors—red, blue, and pink, of course—but one of the balloons stood out as it was larger than the others and golden in hue. The girls at the party all came running over, and Debbie cautiously handed each girl a balloon.

"Now don't let go of it or it will—whoops! There goes one!" Debbie said as one of the blue ones got away from a small girl.

"Don't worry, honey. I got an extra one for you just in case," she said to a very grateful young child.

After Deborah had given out most of the balloons, she came over and stood next to me to watch the girls play. Many of them were running in and out of an inflatable contraption that her parents had rented for the event. It was called a Jupiter Jump, and Danny had been inside it almost the entire party. Yes, he was jumping in there, too, but mostly I think he was making sure the girls didn't get hurt bouncing into one another.

"And now, Sean, I have one very special balloon just for you," Deborah said as she reached into the van and pulled out the golden one.

"I have to tell you, Deb. For some reason, I was really worried about you today. You were gone longer than expected, and I was scared that—"

"Are you going to look at the balloon or not?"

"I see it. It is very pretty, but—"

"Look at it. Look at it closely, Sean."

I pulled the balloon closer and even considered tying it to my wrist to keep it from flying off. But as I turned the balloon around, there was the one word written on it, and I knew immediately why she had taken so long at the store. She must have waited for them to print up this one balloon especially for me. And the word printed on it was *yes*.

"So what do you think?" she said as she struggled to push the sliding door to her van closed.

Despite the great innovation of a sliding door, it just wasn't that easy to slide shut. Unfortunately, the doors didn't close electronically on those early models either or at least not on the this base version of the Dodge Caravan.

I held the balloon tightly with both hands and looked around to see who might be looking at us. And sure enough, there were her parents and my parents just a few steps away, waiting to witness my reaction.

"No wonder your father wasn't worried. He knew what you were doing. Didn't he?" I asked, hoping to keep the waterworks at bay for just a few more seconds.

"You aren't going to blabber like a big baby right here in front of everyone, are you?"

By then, Danny had seen us gathering on the driveway, and he quickly approached us.

"What the heck? Is it cake time yet?" he shouted in our direction.

"Danny, come closer. We need you here with us," Deborah replied.

Danny walked briskly up to us with a balloon tied to his wrist.

"Why? What's up?" he asked.

"I guess I have to do all the work here," Deborah said while looking around at all those gathered near the van. "You see this gold balloon?"

"Yeah I see it," Danny said. "It says yes on it. So what?"

"So I am saying yes to your brother."

"Yes, to what?" Danny asked while looking curiously around him for a clue to what was happening.

I lifted my head to the sky and then looked back down at the ground as I truly didn't know what to do or say. Suddenly, it was as if the screams of young girls and the noise from the inflatable jumping thing were silent. I could hardly move a muscle, but I knew I had to say something eventually.

"You really mean it?" I asked as I sniffed up what was the beginning to form in my nose and eyes.

"No, Sean. I had to think about it for four years, and I am still not sure. Yes, I mean it, you jerk."

Both sets of parents started to clap their hands as I pulled Deborah into my arms and kissed her passionately. And then the dam broke.

"I'm sorry, folks. I am about to lose it," I managed to squeeze out.

"Oh, I get it now," Danny said before looking over at me. "She is finally going to marry you, you lucky dog!"

I looked at Deborah, and she nodded gently and smiled back at me. I couldn't stop the tears even if I had wanted to. And I didn't.

"Dang it, Sean. Stop the blabbering!" Danny shouted. "She is going to change her mind if you keep doing that."

I tucked the golden balloon under my arm like a football and rushed around my parents and through the front door and straight into the downstairs bathroom. Yes, I cried and cried, but it felt so good.

And when I was finally ready to exit the bathroom, I took a long look in the mirror and closed my eyes in prayer. I was thankful for so many things, and I asked God to help me appreciate my life and those he chose to put around me. I thought of Mr. Brooks and Father Dave and especially how lucky I was to have Deborah and Marybeth and even her parents in my life. I thought of how lucky I was to have such good parents and even a unique and precious brother like Danny. I even loved where I lived. Shaker Heights was as good a place as any to raise a family, and I vowed I would always live there, and I have. I was a very fortunate man, and that was when I knew it conclusively.

When I opened the door to go out of the bathroom, there standing right in front of me was Marybeth. She had cake all over her face and was holding one of the red balloons. I took my golden balloon and knelt down to show her the *yes* printed on it.

"You see this?"

"Yeah, Dad. I see it. What does it mean?"

"It means that me and Mommy are going to be together with you forever."

"I don't get it. You guys are already with me, Dad."

"I know, but this means that me and Mommy are going to get married. And the three of us will live in my new house, and we will be together. You see?"

"I see! I'm glad you and Mommy are getting married."

"Me too, honey. Me too."

"How many times did you have to ask her, Dad?"

"About a million."

"That's good. Want to go get some more cake with me?"

"I sure do. Let's go."

New best day ever.

ABOUT THE AUTHOR

Scott Jameson Sanders is an independent businessperson and avid writer of songs, screenplays, and now books. This is Scott's fourth book to be published. The first book, called *The House of Remember When*, was released in 2017. His second book is called *The Box Salesman*, and it was released in 2020. The third book is called *Call Me Cecila* and it was released in 2021. Scott lives on the east side of Cleveland with his wife, two daughters, and two very sweet dogs. Scott and his family like to travel internationally, and he currently does business in Asia, Mexico, Europe, and Columbia, as well as the United States. He enjoys classic cars and owns a 1964 Mercury Park Lane convertible that the family enjoys during the short summers in Northeast Ohio.